P9-DHQ-796

FOLLOW ME AND DIE!

Preacher raced down the slope at a gallop and into the valley below. At the top of a rise he stopped and wheeled around.

"I am Man Who Kills Silently!" he shouted, his words clear in the cold air. "Hear my words!"

The Pardee gang stood on the opposite hillside and watched the mountain man as he rose in his saddle a thousand yards from them. They were powerless to do anything except watch and listen.

"Leave now and never return, or you'll all die in the mountains!" Preacher shouted. "From now on I show you no mercy. Get gone east and never 'crost the Missouri again. Them's my last words on the subject!"

Preacher wheeled his horse, broke into a trot and disappeared over the rise. When he knew he was safe from view, he cut west and then, after a mile, turned north and rode steadily toward the Entiat. He knew Malachi Pardee and his cutthroats would not heed his warning. He also knew a spot where he would make his stand and put an end to this war.

He looked back once and said, "Follow me and die, boys. Follow me and die."

THE FIRST MOUNTAIN MAN
BLOOD ON THE DIVIDE
WILLIAM W. JOHNSTONE

PINNACLE BOOKS
Kensington Publishing Corp.
www.kensingtonbooks.com

PINNACLE BOOKS are published by

Kensington Publishing Corp.
850 Third Avenue
New York, NY 10022

Copyright © 1992 William W. Johnstone

All rights reserved. No part of this book may be reproduced in any form or by any means without the prior written consent of the publisher, excepting brief quotes used in reviews.

If you purchased this book without a cover, you should be aware that this book is stolen property. It was reported as "unsold and destroyed" to the publisher, and neither the author nor the publisher has received any payment for this "stripped book."

All Kensington titles, imprints, and distributed lines are available at special quantity discounts for bulk purchases for sales promotions, premiums, fund-raising, educational, or institutional use. Special book excerpts or customized printings can be created to fit specific needs. For details, write or phone the office of the Kensington special sales manager: Kensington Publishing Corp., 850 Third Avenue, New York, NY 10022, attn: Special Sales Department; phone 1-800-221-2647.

This book is a work of fiction. Names, characters, businesses, organizations, places, events, and incidents either are the product of the author's imagination or are used fictitiously. Any resemblance to actual persons, living or dead, events, or locales is entirely coincidental.

PINNACLE BOOKS and the Pinnacle logo Reg. U.S. Pat. & TM Off.

ISBN: 0-7860-1879-8

First printing: May 1992

10 9 8 7

Printed in the United States of America

PROLOGUE

He was called Preacher. No one knew his real name. Sometimes even he had difficulty remembering it. He had left his home in the settled East as a boy and had never been back. He'd been to St. Louie several times, but that was as far east as he'd chosen to go. His preferred home was the mountain wilderness, the High Lonesome, the Big Empty.

He was called Preacher because he had, years back, been taken captive by a warring tribe, and when he saw they were about to torture him to death, he started preaching. He preached all day and all that night. The Indians finally concluded he was crazy and let him go. He'd been Preacher ever since and he was known from the far north of Canada down to the deserts of the Southwest, from the Mississippi to the Pacific. He was also known as one hell of a bad man to tangle with.

Preacher was not a big man, more of average height for his time. But he possessed great upper-body strength. He was lean-hipped and whang-leather tough. He was handsome in a rugged sort of way. He was of the breed called mountain man.

Those men roamed the western wilderness for a few decades, then vanished into history. When the fur trade played out, most drifted on into obscurity. A few did not. Preacher was one who did not. Preacher saw the writing on the wall about furring and gave it up long before many of his friends did.

He wasn't worried about making a living. If he never saw another gold coin again, he would survive. He could do everything there was to do in the wilderness, and had done most of it. He could pan for gold (Preacher always kept a small sack of gold for hard times), scout for the Army, or lead a wagon train through. He could catch wild horses and break them (he preferred to gentle-break them), and he even knew how to farm. But that was at the bottom of his list of things to do.

He thought he was about thirty-five years old. Give or take a year or two.

And he knew or had known most of the famous and infamous mountain men of his time. Jedediah Strong Smith. Joe Walker. Bridger. Beckwourth. The Cherokee-Negro Ed Rose, who became a Crow chief with a harem of four wives. Old Bill Williams, that sour and secretive man who was more than once accused of cannibalism. Kit Carson, who could write only his own name and read nothing at all but yet became a brigadier general in the U.S. Army. Hugh Glass, who was badly mauled by a grizzly but took so long to expire, his friends got tired of waiting around for him to croak and left him to die alone. But Hugh fooled them. He managed to crawl to a Sioux village and the Indians nursed him back to health. Mountain men were notoriously hard to kill. Preacher knew them all and they respected him.

While Preacher was by no means the very first mountain man, he certainly was there during the heyday, and lasted long after that chapter was closed and all but forgotten. Preacher was the first white man to see many areas of the West. He rode trails that before him had been ridden only by Indians. Preacher named creeks and rivers and the names stand today.

Indians still sing songs about Preacher. And some say Preacher still rides the ghost trails of the High Lonesome.

BOOK ONE

Put your faith in God, my boys, and keep your powder dry.

Valentine Blacker

ONE

Preacher had been smelling smoke for a couple of days, and when the plumes finally came into view, he had steeled his mind and stomach to the horrible sight of dead and mutilated and tortured bodies of men and women and children.

Too damn many people in their wagon trains trying to move west and getting themselves ambushed by hostiles. "This land ain't ready for settlers," Preacher muttered, as he rode up toward the crest of a ridge. "Why in the hell don't people see that?"

He topped the ridge and stared in utter disbelief. No burning wagons here. No tortured and savaged bodies. He couldn't believe his eyes. It was a damn settlement. A diddly-damned settlement right in the middle of nowhere. He counted the houses. Five houses and a big, long log building that was probably some sort of community meetin' house that also served as church and schoolhouse.

Disgustin'.

Preacher had seen some white folks just last week, and now he'd run up on some more. The wilderness was fillin' up faster than a city. Why in the hell didn't people stay to home?

Preacher stayed just inside the stand of timber on the ridge and thought that if this kept up, in two, three more years they'd be a damn road all the way from

New York State to the blue of the Pacific. Women a-flappin' their dress tails and shakin' their bustles and a-battin' their eyes and doin' all them other strange things that women is prone to do when a man is around, and they'd have hoards of squallin' kids a-runnin' around and farmers cuttin' up the land and growin' things. And the Injuns would get all riled up and go on the warpath and they'd be graveyards fillin' up faster than who'd a thunk it.

Pitiful. Made Preacher sick to his stomach just thinking about it.

"Horse," he said to Hammer, "do we want to go down yonder and listen to a whole passel of nonsense out of the mouths of them pilgrims?"

Hammer swung his head around and gave Preacher a very dirty look. Hammer didn't like people no more than Preacher did. Although neither man nor beast disliked humans as much as he let on.

Preacher swung down from the saddle and stretched, then squatted down on the ground, eyeballing the settlement from his position on the ridge. He had to admit, though, that somebody among the movers had them an eye for land and had picked them a right nice spot to light. There was a pretty little creek runnin' soft and sweet nearby, with stands of cottonwood and willow and oak and elm dotted all about. Preacher guessed that Fort William was about forty miles away. He'd been figurin' on meetin' up with some ol' boys there and gettin' drunk and tellin' lies and dancin' and shootin' and lots of other good stuff.

But this totally unexpected sight had shaken him right down to his moccasins. He couldn't figure just what the hell these folks was doin' out here. The summers were hotter than the fringes of hell and the winters were brutal. This wasn't crop land. Preacher figured those folks down yonder could raise kids, but that was about it.

"Just ride on around these crazy folks," Preacher

10

muttered. "Leave them be. 'Cause if you ride down yonder, they gonna be askin' your opinion on matters and wantin' you to stay and hep out and they'll be some white woman, sure as hell, without no man, and she'll be sashayin' around a-winkin' and a-gigglin' and a-wigglin' this and that and knowin' you, boy, you'll be trapped down there for the winter." Which was a long way off, since it was early spring.

The mountain man called Preacher shook himself like a big dog and stared down at the settlement. It was either '38 or '39 — he wasn't sure. So that made him about thirty-five or thirty-six — he wasn't sure about that either. Close enough.

There was a grimness on his tanned face as he stared at the homes below him. He could just about predict with deadly accuracy what was going to happen to them folks down yonder. And that was something he didn't like to think about because of the kids. Preacher rubbed his smoothly shaven face. He'd shaved his beard off, leaving only a moustache. This time of year fleas tended to gather in a woolly beard.

Preacher had gotten shut of people last fall, leaving them over to Fort Vancouver. Missionary types, come to spread the good word to the savages. He'd spent a quiet and peaceful winter holed up in a favorite cabin of his and he was in no mood to put up with another bunch of silly pilgrims who should have stayed back in Pennsylvania or New York or wherever the hell they came from.

Movement caught Preacher's eyes and he shifted his gaze without moving his head. Hammer's head came up and his ears were pricked. "Steady, ol' hoss," Preacher said. "They ain't Injuns, but I 'spect they ain't up to no good. Not the way they're movin' so quiet like."

The half dozen riders were approaching the settlement from the northeast, keeping the line of trees along the creek between the buildings and themselves.

And taking great pains to do that, too, Preacher noted.

The buckskin-clad mountain man remained where he was, watching the valley below him. Pretty little valley it was, too. The settlers had them plowed-up gardens about to sprout, and milk cows and goats and chickens and the like. Sure looked to Preacher like they'd come to stay. During the time he'd squatted on the knoll, he had counted five growed-up men, eight filled-out females, four good-sized teenagers, and what looked to be a whole tribe of kids. Two of the women were ample ladies. Didn't appear to Preacher that none of them folks down yonder had ever missed a meal; but them two ladies in particular would near about take a whole bolt of cloth to make just one of them a dress. Well . . . not quite, but close. Howsomever, ample ladies could keep a man warm in the winter and cool in the summer. They give off lots of shade.

Preacher leaned against his Hawken rifle and watched as the half dozen riders reined up, still hiding behind the line of trees, and dismounted, just like if anyone was watchin', it would appear that they was gonna have them a drink and a rest by the creek. But Preacher didn't believe that for a second.

"They ain't up to no good, Hammer," he said. Then with a sigh, he stood up and stepped into the saddle, taking up the lead of his packhorse. Staying in the timber, Preacher angled around and headed toward the creek. When he reached the banks, he cut north and headed into the cottonwoods and stopped. He was curious as to what the suspicious-acting riders were up to. But he thought he had him a pretty good hunch. Preacher was close enough to the settlement to hear the sounds of children playing and the laughter of a woman. He could also smell bread that was fresh baked. Got his mouth to watering, for he was mighty low on supplies. He could just about taste hot bread all smeared with butter and a tall glass of milk from the coolness of the well ledge.

"Well, hell, Hammer," he said as he moved his horse out of the trees and toward the cabins. "Might as well go on up and be sociable. I ain't forgot all my up-bringin'."

The riders had moved out of the trees. "If they was decent folks, Hammer, they'd have already made their presence known, so I got to figure they ain't nothin' but a pack of highwaymen who run out of highways back East and come out here to rob and kill. I reckon we'll see about that in a short enough time."

Preacher sat his saddle and waited. He had him a hunch the riders would pretty soon ride on into the settlement, all smiles and howdy-do's, and then when the settlers was unexpected of it, they'd jump them.

Then it came to him. Six riders. The Pardee brothers. Sure. That pack of no-counts from Ohio. Least that's where they claimed to have been whelped. Preacher wasn't sure about that. The Pardee brothers was so sorry, he doubted any woman would have the nerve to lay claim to them.

He heard their ponies splash across the creek, and leaving his packhorse in the trees, Preacher rode Hammer straight up into the clearing on the knoll, arriving a couple of minutes before the Pardees could make it. Men and women and kids all rushed up to meet him. Once they saw he wasn't an Indian. Preacher noticed with some degree of satisfaction that the men were all armed. That meant they wasn't all totally ignorant.

"You got a bunch of scalawags ridin' up here, folks. Don't trust 'em and don't present your backs to 'em. I think it's the Pardee brothers. And them's the sorriest pack of white trash that ever sat a saddle on a stole horse."

The children all stared wide-eyed at Preacher. They had probably never seen a mountain man before, for if that breed of man did not wish to be seen, he wasn't. Preacher's old black hat was battered and had a musket-ball hole in it. He was dressed all in buckskins and wore high-top leggin's. Behind the sash around his lean waist were two .50 caliber pistols. On holsters attached to the saddle were two more pistols of like kind. He carried one of the biggest knives any of the children—or the adults—had ever seen. It had been hand made for him by a top knife maker in New Orleans. The scabbard for the razor-sharp blade was beaded and very elaborate.

"Riders coming, Pa," a boy who looked to be about fifteen said.

"Yep," Preacher said, twisting in the saddle and eye-balling the riders. "It's them damn worthless Pardees all right. Do anyone here know what year it might be?"

"It's 1838, friend," a man said.

"I was close," Preacher muttered.

"Hallo the settlement!" came the call from down on the flats. "We're friendly and white."

"Just like I figured," Preacher said. "They comin' in all smiles and grins, and when they get you to trust them, they'll cut your throats and have their way with the women." He looked at several girls, ten or eleven years old. "And with them, too. Don't doubt it none."

"Why should we believe you?" a haughty-sounding lady asked. One of the ample ones.

"Ain't no reason to," Preacher told her. " 'Ceptin' I'm known from Missouri to Oregon as a man of my word." He swung down from the saddle, Hawken in hand, and flipped the reins to a youngster. "Stable him safe 'fore the shootin' starts. If it starts. And be careful. He bites and kicks." He faced the line of approaching riders. "Malachi Pardee!" he shouted. "Hold it right there, you snakehead."

The riders abruptly stopped. "Who you be, friend?" the call came from the line.

"I damn shore ain't your friend, Malachi," Preacher called. "You or none of them damn worthless brothers of yours. Now you hear me, Malachi, you'll not snolly-goster these good folks like you done them poor movers

14

up on the Paintrock."

"I don't know what you mean, friend!" Malachi called, standing up in the stirrups, trying to see who was hurling the insults at him.

Movement down by the creek caught Preacher's attention. "All your people gathered here?"

"Yes, sir," a woman said. "Why?"

"More of 'em down by the crick. I heard that Malachi had him a regular gang now. All the petticoats and kids in the buildings. You men see to your families. Move. I think we're only minutes, maybe seconds from bein' attacked. If they're stupid, that is. And they is."

"They all appear to be nothing more than harmless vagabonds to me," the haughty, ample lady said.

Preacher looked at her. Or as much of her as he could in one settin'. "Lady, you best get movin'. As much as you got to tote around, you're gonna be the last one in the house anyways."

She huffed up. "Well! I never!"

Preacher let that alone . . . with an effort on his part. "Move, people."

"It's that damn meddlin' Preacher!" one of the Pardees hollered. "Where in the hell did he come from? I thought he'd be down at the rendezvous."

The line of men and women and kids stopped suddenly and slowly turned around. Everybody from St. Louis to Vancouver knew that name. "The mountain man . . . Preacher?" a man questioned.

"I been called that. Get in the buildin's, damnit!"

"Pa," a boy said. "He's famous."

"And vulgar," the ample lady said. "Besides being an uncouth ignoramus."

One of the Pardee brothers let loose a ball that whined wickedly close to the lady. She let out a squall, jerked her dress up past her knees, and went up the grade like a buffalo headin' toward a wallow. Whoopin' and hollerin' and huffin' all the way up. She was the first one inside the big building.

Preacher ducked down and took shelter behind one of the wells the men had dug. "Stay in the stable, lad," he called to the boy tending to Hammer. "If you can shoot, they's a brace of pistols on the saddle."

"At a man?" the teenager questioned.

"Forget it," Preacher said. He eared back the hammer on his Hawken. "Pilgrims," he muttered. "They gonna be the death of me yet."

But the one shot appeared to be all the Pardees wanted to give this time around. They had lost the element of surprise and they hadn't counted on Preacher being anywhere within five hundred miles of the settlement. Preacher listened to the splash across the creek, then he ran up the slope to the flats where the buildings were located and climbed up on the sod roof of a cabin. He stood and watched the Pardees link up with half a dozen more men and ride off.

"Scum and trash," he muttered darkly, hopping down to the ground.

A settler came out of the community building and stood by Preacher. "They'll be back, won't they?"

"More than likely. You got food, clothin', possessions, and fair females. Yeah, they'll be back. You men stand ready. You had any problems with the Injuns?"

"A bit. But once they saw we would fight, they left us alone."

Preacher grunted as the others gathered around. "That didn't have nothin' to do with it, pilgrim. Injuns is notional folks. They might have taken a likin' to you. They do that sometimes. Maybe on that day they felt their medicine was bad. But out here in the Big Empty, you always stay ready for a fight with the Injuns. More and more people comin' out here is really gonna stir 'em up. This is Cheyenne and Arapaho country mostly. But at one time or another, you'll have bands from a dozen tribes wanderin' through. Any of them can and will lift your hair. Exceptin' maybe the Crow. They'll just steal your horses, usually. How long you folks been here?"

"We arrived last summer and just managed to get our homes built before the winter came. I'm Robbie MacGreagor and this is my wife, Coretine."

"Pleased, I'm shore. I'm Preacher. Y'all got anything to eat?"

The children sat on the floor and watched in awe as Preacher ate. They had never seen anybody his size eat so much. When he was through, he belched loudly and wiped the grease from his hands onto his buckskins. "Helps keep 'em soft and waterproofs 'em, too. You ever get invited to eat in an Injun camp, you be sure and belch like I done when you're finished grubbin'. If you don't, the Injuns'll think you don't like what they served you and be offended."

"Where is your home, Mr. Preacher?" a lady who had been introduced as Rosanna asked. She was married to a Millard somebody or other.

"Just Preacher, missy. My home? Anywhere I want it to be, I reckon. I left my folks' home back East when I was just a tadpole. Twelve, I think I was. I been out in the wilderness near 'bout all my life. Why'd you folks come out here?"

"To settle the new land," a man called Efrem said. His wife was the lady who bore a striking resemblance to a buffalo. Maddie did not like Preacher and made no attempt to hide her feelings. They had four kids — two boys, two girls. Fortunately, they took after their father.

"It's too soon, folks," Preacher tried to caution them. "Besides, this ain't farming country."

"Oh, but I beg to differ," Efrem said. "I think it is. We shall certainly see, won't we?"

"You might, I won't."

A man who was named Gerald Twiggs opened his

17

mouth to speak. A young girl of no more than three or four who was standing in the open doorway said, "Daddy? There are a whole bunch of wild red Indians in the front yard."

TWO

"Easy!" Preacher said sharply as everyone reached for weapons. "If they'd wanted us dead, we would be. Just stand quiet and ready." He walked to the open door and stood there looking at the dozen or so Cheyenne who had silently walked their ponies up the slope and onto the flat of the settlement. Preacher breathed easier. He knew the subchief leading this band. "Lone Man moves as silently as ever." Preacher spoke the words in Cheyenne as he made the sign of peace. "It is good to see that he is too great a warrior to make war against women, children, and peace-seeking men."

A smile flitted across the Cheyenne's face. He grunted and spoke in rapid-fire Cheyenne. What he said, loosely translated, was that while Preacher was still as full of buffalo turds as ever, it was good to see him.

Preacher was quick to notice the many hands painted on the Cheyenne horses. Each hand represented an enemy killed in hand-to-hand combat. The paintings were fresh and so were the scalps hanging from lances and tied into the manes of the horses. All were Indian scalps.

Lone Man had followed Preacher's eyes and said, "Crow. They have been warned many times to stay out of our land. Now these will—forever. I have not seen Preacher in two seasons. Have you now de-

19

cided to scratch into the earth?"

Preacher laughed at that and a twinkle appeared in the Cheyenne's eyes. He knew Preacher better than that. "I visit friends of mine here. These are good people who wish only to work the land and get along with all things of this earth. They cause no trouble."

"We shall see," Lone Man said. He turned his horse and rode out, the others following him.

"My God!" A man introduced as Charles Nelson had finally found his voice. "Did you see all the scalps?"

"Crow hair," Preacher told them. "They made one-too-many raids into Lone Man's territory. It's usually the Dakota—Sioux to you—that don't much get on with the Crow. But you get the Cheyenne all stirred up and you got yourselves a world of hurt comin' at you."

"What did they want here?" a woman asked.

"Curious. Injuns is mighty curious folks. They were just checkin' you out. Now, I told Lone Man that you all was friends of mine. He may or may not believe that, and it may or may not have some bearin' with him. But I've wintered with the Cheyenne and get along right good with them. They may leave you be. But they's renegades in every tribe. The Crow gets along fair to middlin' with the white man; but you always keep a gun handy. You be on the lookout at all times."

Buffalo Butt puffed up and haughtily announced, "We shall tell them all that we are God-fearing people and mean them no harm. We shall be perfectly safe here. It's people like you stir up all the trouble."

"Yeah," Preacher said dryly. "Well, I'll be long gone time you folks roll out of the bed come the mornin'. I'll be back this way from time to time to check on you and partake of your cookin'. Good night."

The next morning, as the sky was beginning to silver before dawning, when Robbie made his bleary-eyed way to the outhouse, Preacher was gone.

* * *

20

"Damn fool people," Preacher said, as he rode toward the trading post located near the Laramie and North Platte rivers. "Bringin' all them kids out here to the wilderness. Bunch of igits is what they is."

He was following the trail of Malachi Pardee and his gang, for as long as they rode toward the post, and while making good time, he was riding with caution. Malachi despised Preacher. They'd locked horns in the past a couple of times and Preacher had always come out on top. Preacher was no saint — far from it. But like most of his time, he operated under a strict code of conduct. And Malachi Pardee and his followers violated all the codes Preacher lived by. They were brigands and worse. As he rode, Preacher pondered what all he knew about Malachi, and none of it was good.

Pardee sometimes hooked up with a worthless bunch of Injuns who roamed about up in the Medicine Bow country. These particular Injuns were from all tribes, and they'd banded together after their tribes had kicked them out for one reason or another. But this time Preacher hadn't seen any Injuns in Pardee's pack. Just no-good whites.

The last time Preacher locked up with Malachi, Preacher should have killed him. He knew it then and knew it even better now. But Malachi had yielded and Preacher had stepped back and let him live. Big mistake.

Preacher nooned by a hidden spring — known only to about ten thousand Injuns and several hundred mountain men — and built no fire. He ate a thick sandwich he'd made that morning in the kitchen of the MacGreagor house. Hadn't woke a soul up as he did it. If they slept that sound, Preacher didn't give the pilgrims much chance of living very long out here. But most of them had seemed like real nice people. Except for Buffalo Butt.

Before eating, Preacher had let his horses roll and then picketed them and let them graze. Then he had

21

him a long drink of cold water and his sandwich. He stretched out on the ground and rested. He'd been doing a lot of ruminating of late, and decided this was a dandy time to do some more head thinkin'.

The future just didn't look real bright for men like Preacher. He'd predicted the trapping and the fur trade would play out, and it sure was doing just that. He hadn't done much of it the past couple of years anyway. But he knew he had to think about doing something. He was too proud not to work at something. Many of his friends had packed it in and gone back East. But most of them were coming back faster than they went out, all of them saying they just couldn't live back yonder no more. There wasn't no place for men like Preacher in the civilized East. Po-lite society, some was callin' it.

A mountain man name of Hogjaw had come back to the wilderness with a tale of horror. Seems like he was having him a drink in a tavern and a local called him a son of a bitch. Hogjaw whipped out his good knife and cut that citizen from brisket to breakfast. Damned if the constable didn't put Hogjaw under arrest and tote him off to the hoosegow. Charged him with murder. Hogjaw busted out of jail and lit a shuck for the Big Empty just as fast as he could flee.

After hearing that story, Preacher knew damn well he could never live back East. There was such a thing as being just too civilized.

Laying on the ground, Preacher heard the sounds of horses' hooves and got to his feet, moving to his horses. He calmed them and whispered to them so's they wouldn't whinny when they got the scent of other horses.

The Injuns passed close, and they was painted for war. Preacher made out several Crow, some Blackfeet, Mandan, and some he didn't recognize. A good-sized band of renegades, and they were riding the trail left by Pardee and his kin and trash. Preacher's tracks had blended in with the others and he'd been careful when he left the trail for the spring.

They were all gathering for some reason, and Preacher could guess what that reason might be: more settlers coming in. More damn fools heading this way, bound for the glory land in the Northwest.

Preacher said a very ugly word as he saddled up and pulled out. If there were more wagons coming, they'd more than likely stop at the post for supplies and for talk about the trail ahead of them.

Preacher had had his gutful of pilgrims and decided he'd head the other way and get himself back into the mountains. Then he stopped and, with a sigh, turned Hammer's head toward the post. The folks had a right to know what dangers lay ahead of them, he reckoned.

"Here we go again, Hammer," he said. "But this time, only part of the way."

When Preacher arrived at the post, he was startled by the size of the wagon train and relieved to see an old friend of his was going to be the man to guide the wagons westward. Jack Larrabee was a man to ride the river with. He was about fifteen years older than Preacher, and had been out in the wilderness for nigh on to forty years.

The two men hoo-hawed each other and whacked each other on the back a time or two and then went to the sutler's for a round of drinks.

Preacher nearly swallowed his cup when Jack said, "The movers ain't goin' on to Fort Vancouver, Preacher. They're going to settle just west of the Rockies."

"Wagh!" Preacher spat the word. He knocked back his whiskey and, when his vision cleared from the hooch, said, "Then they're fools, Jack."

"Maybe not. Long Hair's done told me personal that he wouldn't bother them."

"That's Long Hair. He's a Crow. Crows will steal

23

their horses and possessions, but Crows don't kill whites except in self-defense. Usually." Long Hair got his name because, when measured, his hair — and it was all his own — was almost twelve feet in length. Crows were known to take horse hair and attach it to their own to make it appear longer.

"For a fact," Jack agreed.

"How about the Cheyenne and the Arapaho and the Shoshoni and the Dakotas? To mention just a few who might lift some hair along the way?"

Jack shrugged his shoulders. "I warned the movers, Preacher. What else can I do?"

Preacher knew the fix the man was in; he'd been there personal. Jack was just trying to make a living and Preacher couldn't fault him for that. "And how about the Pardee boys and that gang of no-counts with them?"

Jack's eyes narrowed. "You seen them, Preacher?"

"I seen them." He told Jack what had happened at the little settlement and what he had seen while resting at the spring.

"Oh, they know about the wagons," Jack admitted. "But we're too many for them. This is the largest train to ever try to cross the Rockies."

Preacher looked out the open window at the fifteen-foot-high adobe wall that surrounded the trading post. Beyond it, a wilderness that seemed to stretch endlessly for hundreds and hundreds of miles. Preacher shook his head at the thought. And he had a right to be a doubter: he'd taken a train all the way to the Pacific the year past.

"They'll make it, Preacher."

"Oh, the hell they will!" Preacher said, pouring another cup from the jug. "They might make it 'crost the Rockies, but they ain't gonna survive alone where you're takin' them, and you know it, Jack. Who the hell do you think you're talkin' to? I know about them folks same as you. Maybe more. They's fleein' the bankrupt

24

eastern part of the country, that's who they is. Hell, I can read. I found me a paper last year. They done sold ever'thing they couldn't pile on them wagons and they can't go back. They got nothin' to go back to. And they got only misery ahead of them. Goddamnit, Jack, they're merchants and clerks and coin counters and the like."

"You're just upset 'cause the fur's gone and you can't abide crowds noway."

"That's part of it, yeah. But it's too soon for these folks, Jack. They got no protection from the government. A bunch of that territory's in dispute 'tween England and America. I snooped around, Jack. Them pilgrims just barely got enough shot and powder for their personal needs. What are you gonna do if you're attacked?"

"You know the odds of Injuns attackin' a wagon train of this size is slim, Preacher," Jack said stubbornly.

"Mayhaps you be right, Jack. Mayhaps you can get them movers 'crost the Rockies. But like I said: what happens *after* you get there and leave them? You know damn well good as me that's when the Injuns will hit them."

But the scout's jaw was set in determination.

"You know what would be smart on the mover's part, Jack? Huh? If you was to take these pilgrims about twenty-five miles from this post and settle them. Then the next bunch go twenty-five more miles past that, and so forth. Then you'd have, sooner or later, a supply line that ran all the way to the blue waters. But this way, Jack, is dumb!"

Jack stood up and looked down at his old friend. "We'll be leavin' at first light, Preacher. Feel free to tag along. The grub is better than passable."

Preacher shook his head. "No, thanks, Jack. But I'll wish you luck." 'Cause you're damn sure gonna need all you can get, he silently added.

The next morning, Preacher stood with several other

trappers and watched the long line of wagons stretch out. No one spoke for a long time. Finally, a long, lanky drink of water all dressed in buckskins said, "I got me a bad feelin' about those folks yonder, boys."

Preacher looked at the man. "So do I, Caleb. So do I."

The men turned as one and headed for the store. Preacher wanted to get him a jug and get rip-roarin' drunk and try not to think about those pilgrims heading into the raw and dangerous wilderness.

On a bright and clear spring morning, Preacher rolled out of his blankets and stretched the kinks from his joints and muscles. He was about two days' ride from the post and the whiskey he'd consumed was clear of his system. He had stayed in an alcoholic fog for near'bouts a week. He and Caleb and the other mountain men gathered at the post had swapped lies, jugs, thrown axes and knives at targets, and in general had them a high ol' time. Then, without anyone putting it into words, the men had drifted away, each hearing the silent call of the wilderness beckoning them back to the High Lonesome.

After carefully looking all around him and listening intently for several minutes, to the birds singing and the squirrels chattering, Preacher decided there were no Injuns about and shucked out of his clothes and jumped into a pool created by a cold, clear creek. He washed quickly, before he turned blue, and jumped out, running around the camp naked as a jaybird until he was dry. Then he put on fresh longhandles he'd bought at the post and slipped into buckskins a Mandan squaw had made for him. He fixed coffee over a smokeless fire and set about figuring just what he was going to do with himself and where he wanted to go.

Problem was, he'd been damn near everywhere there was to go in the wilderness. Preacher had been born restless, and in his more than two decades in the Big Empty, he had gained a reputation as not only a fierce and respected warrior, but also as scout and explorer, helping to guide many a government team through the seemingly impassable reaches of the mountains and the rivers.

Preacher saddled up and gave Hammer his head and let him go. Hammer soon began following wagon tracks and Preacher, with a sigh, let him have his way. He found no fresh signs of graves along the way for the next two days, so the pilgrims were staying lucky. So far. Two days later, he saw the buzzards circling. He checked his weapons and pushed on, steeling himself for the awful sight that would soon present itself to him.

He came up cautiously on what was left of the wagon train he'd seen back at the post. It was anything but a pretty sight. The men and women and kids had been hit whilst they were abed. Nearly all of them was dressed in bed clothes, which was something Preacher never could understand about pilgrims. They dress up to go to bed, then take off their dress-up-to-bed clothes to dress up again when they got out of bed.

Rifle in hand, Preacher walked among the silent and stiffened dead. The women and the girls had all been raped and the men tortured pretty bad. Preacher had seen sights similar, but not on this large a scale. A man might say it didn't bother him — as Preacher had often said — and a man might say that a man gets used to it — as Preacher had often said — but a man really don't get used to it. A man just steels himself for the task, that's all.

The buzzards were everywhere, many of them too bloated from human flesh and entrails to fly. They just waddled around and looked disgusting. Preacher found an intact shovel amid the wreckage and rubble and knocked half a dozen of the big, lumbering carrion eaters in the head until the rest of them got the message and waddled off a few yards away from the bodies, to stand out of harm's way and stare malevolently at the man who spoiled their dining.

Preacher began the laborious task of dragging what was left of the bodies off the trail and over to a ravine. There, he dumped them over the side. It wasn't very sedate, and certainly no one would call it Christian, but it was the best the mountain man could do. Damned if he was going to dig a lot of holes in the rocky ground. It would take him a week. By that time the bodies would be stinking so bad not even the buzzards could stand it. He really had no idea how many men and women and kids had been massacred, for they'd been dead several days and the buzzards and the varmits had been hard at work, dragging bodies and parts of bodies off into the woods to eat or stash for later.

Preacher changed out of his buckskins and into homespuns and worked all that day. It was late afternoon when he had nearly filled the small ravine with bodies and caved in the top to crudely cover the remains. He made a cross out of rocks, like a T on the ground, carefully working the rocks into the ground so's they'd stay put . . . at least for a time. He'd gotten used to the smell, but knew the vile odor had permeated his clothing and they'd have to be thrown away. Which was the reason he'd changed into homespuns. He found some soap amid the rubble and stowed the bars in his pack. He camped a mile from the ambush site and the next morning, after a bath, began casting around for sign. What he found disturbed him more than a little.

While he was gathering up a few stray horses that had wandered back to the ambush site and building a crude corral for them, he ruminated on the sign he'd found.

It appeared that maybe half a dozen or so people had escaped the slaughter and headed into the woods. And

28

from the size of their footprints, they either was women or kids or both. There wasn't a man-sized print to be found.

"Lord have mercy," Preacher said. "Little children adrift in the wilderness. If they was borned out here, they might have a chance. But these is town kids, and I bet most of them don't know left from right."

He went off the trail and into the timber, staying with the tracks of the survivors. It wasn't that hard to do. A piece of thread, a tore-off bit of dress that had snagged on a branch, a strand of blond hair hooked on a twig . . . all these things were easy to follow if a body knowed how, and Preacher knew how.

He finally concluded that there was six kids and one growed-up woman. Three boys, three girls, and one woman. Alone in the Big Empty, probably without even a weapon of any kind, and no flint to start a fire, for he hadn't found any sign of old ashes.

The renegades who attacked the train — and they were renegades, for he'd found several bodies — were long gone. Preacher had made sure of that before he started totin' off the dead. Red Hand's bunch, he was sure.

"Damn that renegade bastard!" Preacher said. "I just keep runnin' into that bad Injun."

Preacher found where the small party of survivors had stripped off berries and gobbled them up right then and there. He had to smile. He'd be catchin' up with them 'fore long. These berries would give a body the rear-end squirts real quick, and a belly-hurt, too. But Preacher knew how to fix that, once he caught up with them. Rhubarb was good, and so was honey. Dandelion was pretty good and chamomile was good for the bellyache.

But first he had to find them that got away. And then that very thought sobered him as he muttered, "What the hell am I gonna do with them?"

29

THREE

Preacher spotted the group and hunkered down in the brush, taking a slow and careful look around to be certain that no renegades were using them as bait.

Then he stood up and the small group spotted him. Before he could open his mouth, the girls started screaming and shrieking to high heaven and the boys started chunking stones at him. They must have had quite a pile of them. The air was filled with stones of various sizes. Preacher hit the ground.

"Wait a minute!" he hollered. "Damnit, I'm here to help you. Stop throwin' them rocks at me."

The stone barrage ceased and Preacher carefully got to his feet and cautiously moved forward, not wanting to get conked on the bean by an apple-sized stone, for these people were still some bad scared.

"I found what was left of the wagon train," he called, approaching the group. "I done my best to bury the dead."

"I saw you back at the fort," a boy said. "You're the mountain man called Preacher. Mr. Larrabee said you were famous."

"I wouldn't know about that," Preacher replied. He looked at the group. Boys and girls about the same age. Ten to twelve, he figured. The woman was a looker. Maybe twenty-one or -two years old. Fine figure of a female, mussed up hair, dirty face, and all.

Poked out in all the right places. Defiant type, too, for she met his appraising eyes with no blinking. "Come on. I found horses back yonder and corralled 'em. I found food that wasn't touched by the Injuns—"

"It wasn't just red Indians," the woman said. "There were whites among them."

"That don't surprise me none, missy. The Pardee brothers probably hooked up with Red Hand like Bum and his boys done last year. I killed Bum and his bunch; should have tracked Red Hand down and kilt him too. Sorry I didn't now. I will this time, you can bet on that. You kids line up and stay behind me. Sister, you bring up the rear and don't let none of these babies stray off. Come on."

It was not far back to the ruins of the wagon train, only a few miles, and Preacher set an easy pace because he could see the group was very tired. "What's your name, sister?" Preacher called over his shoulder.

"Betina. Betina Drum."

"You lose family in the attack?"

"No. I was traveling with a family, but they were no relation to me."

"You ain't got no man?"

"I'm spoken for. He's back East. He is to join me later."

Preacher muttered darkly and profanely, not quite under his breath, about the caliber of men who sent their women alone into the wilderness. The girl behind him giggled at his words.

Preacher stopped the group in the timber and brush a few hundred yards from the still-stinking wreckage of the wagon train and told them to stay put. From the edge of the timber, he checked out the ruins and then waved the group forward.

"Betina, you take the girls and see what you can salvage from this mess. Clothing and food and money that might be hid in secret compartments in the wagons. Movers do that. Red Hand and Pardee might have missed some of it. Most Injuns ain't got no use for money. Don't know what it is. These children got to have something to get them back East. I'll take the boys and do the same. Now, there might be some bodies I missed under some tangle, so be careful."

He stood for a moment, watching her walk away, and admired the sight for a few seconds. Then he remembered the boys and got them busy digging and pawing through the rubble.

They found food aplenty and articles of clothing and underthings and the like. Several knew where their parents had hidden money and they brought it to Preacher. He shook his head.

"We'll put it in the saddlebags and let Miss Drum see to it. That's a lot of money and I don't want no part of it. Come on, let's get saddled up and get gone from this place."

"We want to conduct a memorial service first, Mr. Preacher," Betina said. "Over the mass grave. It's the Christian thing to do."

"All right. You have at it, lady. I'll just see to the horses."

The horses were all riding stock, and that had surprised Preacher, but obviously the outlaws and renegade Injuns had been too busy raping and torturing and looting to gather up all the livestock. They had driven off the cattle to eat later. Preacher had found saddles among the rubble, and had repaired those that had been slightly damaged. The attackers had made only a half-hearted attempt to torch the wreckage.

Preacher waited with the horses while the little band of survivors had them a prayer service over the grave site. But he did take off his battered hat.

Preacher did some thinking while the others was prayin' and singin'. Sounded right nice, too. The girls had good voices.

Preacher figured he was closer to that little settlement he'd come up on than he was to the post. So he'd head there and see if those good folks would take in the kids for a time until they could see their way to get back to the post. Betina had told him she was a trained schoolmarm, so maybe she could stay there with them until her man come out from the East.

Preacher was amazed at how well the kids were holding up in the face of all this. But then, he knew that kids really had no grasp of death. When you're young, you think you're gonna live forever. One girl had cried when she found the body of her little dog. She had carefully and lovingly buried the arrow-shot pup. Those had been the only tears shed so far. That Preacher had seen. Maybe nothing had really set in yet, he figured.

That got Preacher to thinking about when he was a little boy and the dog he had. Got him to feelin' plumb emotional there for a few minutes.

"Come on, people," Preacher muttered, looking at the little group. "We're losin' daylight."

The group was silent as they rode away, the females riding astride just like the boys. Preacher figured the settlement was about two days' ride away from the ambush site. They'd have to spend at least one night on the trail. And he had no way of knowing how near or far away the renegade Injuns and Pardee's bunch might be. But he had been watching and had spotted no signs of smoke.

"I sure can get myself into some pickles," he muttered.

Once, on the crest of a long hill, while the coffee was boiling and the meat cooking, Preacher rested his charges and pointed out to the seemingly empty vastness. "That's the way I remember it," he said to Betina, a note of wistfulness in his voice. "Not a white man as far as the eyes could see. It'll never be the same no more."

"Civilization is moving westward. It's called progress, Preacher."

"Pain in the butt is what I call it."

"It's so . . . big," one of the girls said.

"It's that, all right, button," Preacher told her. "You get lost out yonder and we'd never find you. Remember that." He watched as the heads of the horses came up and their ears pricked. "Get out of sight," he told Betina and the kids. "Stay low and quiet no matter what happens. Take the horses and move into the timber. If anything happens to me, you know where to go, Bet. So move. Right now."

A moment later, the little party and their mounts had vanished into the timber and brush. Preacher kicked some dirt over a mess of little shoe prints and waited by the fire, his Hawken at hand. It wasn't a long wait. Four men rode slowly toward him, coming from the west. Preacher knew only one of them, a no-good who called himself Son. But if the other three had tossed their lot in with Son, they were just as sorry as he was.

"Hi-ho, the fire," Son called. "That shore smells like coffee to me."

"What the hell else would I be boilin'?" Preacher said sourly. "Hot water to bile my socks in? I ain't got no socks so it must be coffee water."

"Preacher," Son said, walking his horse up to the edge of the tiny clearing. "I thought it was you. You just as ill-tempered as I recall."

"I ain't ill-tempered neither, Son. I just don't like you. So don't bother dismountin'. There ain't nothin' here for you or them with you."

"You wouldn't let no poor tarred travelers git down

34

and stretch the kinks out whilst partakin' of coffee and that there fine-smellin' meat, Preacher?" Son asked.

"No."

"Then by God we'll just take it!" one of the men with Son hollered. "And if you don't like it, Slim, you can just go to hell!"

Preacher slowly turned his head. The mouthy man had no way of knowing it, but he was only heartbeats away from sudden and violent death. He should have expected it; that was the way he had lived. "You think you'll do that, huh?" Preacher asked.

"Yeah," the man said with an evil grin. His teeth were blackened stubs. "But first I think I'll kick your ass around this camp just for the fun of it."

Preacher shot him with the .54 Hawken. The big ball slammed into the man's chest and knocked him out of the saddle, his arms flung wide. He hit the ground and lay still, his heart shattered. His horse trotted off a few yards and stopped. Son and the other two were in momentary shock.

Preacher was on his feet, a cocked pistol in each hand. "They's both double-shotted, boys. Who wants it?"

Son and the two others stared at the dead man for a moment, their faces pale under the whiskers and dirt. Outlaws and scum, they were accustomed to always having the upper hand. They were not accustomed to this. They tore their eyes from the dead and stared at Preacher.

"I just flat out ain't got no use for you people," Preacher told the trio. "Now flop your friend acrost his saddle and get the hell gone from here."

"You're a mean man, Preacher." Son had found his voice and croaked out the words. He cleared his throat. "That was an unchristian and turrible low thing you just done. That poor wretch was

35

only funnin' with you."

"I didn't see no joke to it. Man pushes me, I just ain't got no sense of humor. You got any idee what's in the Hereafter, Son?" Preacher asked him.

"No."

"You want to find out this day?"

Son shook his head. "I reckon not."

"Then get off your horse and get that dead man and yourselves gone from here. I ain't got no time to waste with the likes of you people. And keep them hands away from your guns. I might mistook sudden movement as a hostile thing and lose my patience with you boys. I don't think you'd like that."

"You're a cruel and vile person, Preacher," Son told him, slowly and carefully dismounting, all the while being very careful to keep his hands clear of the pistols stuck behind his wide belt. "I say this to you as a man who fears the Almighty's wrath. The Lord will not smile kindly upon you come the day of the trumpets' sound."

"You best worry about your own salvation, Son. I'm recallin' all them widder women you robbed back East, before you run from a noose back yonder and slithered like a snake to the wilderness, and all them trappers out here you kilt for their pelts. You want to deny any of what I said?"

Son glowered hate and fury at Preacher, but made no attempt at rebuttal.

The two with Son stepped down and gingerly hoisted the bloody body of the dear departed across his saddle and tied him down. They mounted up and looked at Preacher.

"Ride!" Preacher told the three of them. "I don't never want to see your ugly faces again. And I mean it, boys. Son, you come ridin' in here with evil thoughts and bad intentions. I could smell the nastiness in you 'fore I smelled the stink of you personal.

36

I ought to do the world a favor and kill you here and now. But you can ride. Now go 'fore I change my mind."

When they had ridden off, Preacher put away his pistols and charged his Hawken. "Stay hid," he called softly. "They might work up some courage and decide to come back. They know I wasn't here alone. They ain't stupid. They's enough meat cookin' for a damn army."

"You're a violent man, Mr. Preacher," Betina called from the brush. "You could have shot to only wound that poor man."

"Yeah, I could have. But I didn't, did I? Now sit still and hush up."

Preacher ran up a hill and climbed a tree, watching Son and his party fade from view. He had him a hunch he'd see them someday, but for this day they'd had enough. Preacher also figured they wouldn't take the time to bury the body—they'd just dump it along the way.

"Let's hurry up and eat and get gone, people," Preacher told Betina and the kids.

Preacher ate with one eye on the trail Son had taken. He hadn't told Betina or the kids, but there hadn't been enough bodies back at the ambush site to match up with all the wagons he'd seen leave the post. And Jack Larrabee had not been among the dead. Preacher had made sure of that. He took into account that some women and girl kids might have been taken for hoppin' on later, but he was pretty sure that some others had taken to the woods and the brush and had made it clear. If possible, he would leave the woman and the kids at the settlement, and then head for the Lonesome and try to find some of those who had escaped the slaughter. He had him a notion that Jack was on the trail of the ambushers, and outnumbered or not, as he surely was, Jack was

37

riding to take his vengeance.

As for any of the others who escaped the massacre, Preacher could only wish them the best. Grown-up men could look after themselves and try to stay alive. But the thought of little kids wanderin' around hurt, scared, and hungry didn't set well with him.

Preacher halted the parade an hour before dark, built a small fire, and fixed bacon and bread and coffee. Then he moved several more miles before bedding the kids down for the night in a cold camp. He made sure they were safe and had cover aplenty, then sat with his back to a tree, his Hawken across his knees.

"Those men back there in the clearing," Betina asked, sitting close to Preacher in the darkness. "Why — ?"

" 'Cause they're no good," Preacher cut her off, knowing what she was going to say. Or he figured he knew. "Anyone who hooks up with Son just ain't no good. Son's a murderer, a thief, and a rapist. If he was to ever go back east of the Mississippi, the law would hang him."

She paused a moment and then said softly, "I see."

"No, you don't neither, missy. It's different out here than back where you come from. You told me you was from Albany. That's in New York State. Town's real old; maybe two hundred year old. Used to be called Beverwyck, I think. Missy, I ain't entirely stupid. Whenever I can get my hands on a newspaper or a book, I read it. But them things is kinda scarce out here. Back where you come from, you got uniformed constables, right? You can walk the streets and be safe at night, right? You can sit on your front porches, enjoyin' the cool of the evenin' drinkin' tea and eatin' cake and a-passin' a gentle time talkin' to friends and neighbors. You should have stayed back yonder, missy. But you didn't. So here you are with

38

your man more'n two thousand hard miles away. And for the second time in less than a year, I find myself explainin' to pilgrims that this is wild country. There ain't no law out here 'ceptin' the gun and knife and arrow and war axe, and there ain't likely to be none for many a year to come. Probably not much law will ever be out here in our lifetime. So what are you goin' to do, missy?"

"Stop callin' me missy. My name is Betina. Friends call me Bet. Do? Why . . . teach school."

Preacher was silent for a moment, listening to the sounds around him. "You mean you don't have no noble thoughts about educatin' the savages?"

"Heavens no."

"Well, that's a relief. 'Cause the so-called savages got they own way of life and don't want nobody tryin' to change them. You might make it out here after all."

A wolf flung his howling message into the night sky and then another called and then the pack all began singing. Betina scooted a little closer to Preacher and he chuckled softly. "Afeard of wolves, are you?"

"Shouldn't I be? Everyone else is."

"Stupid people are. There ain't no reason to be afeard of wolves. They won't bother you if you don't mess with them. I like wolves. They're good company as long as you know their ways."

"*Wolves* are good company?"

"Sure. I've took up with several over the years. And I've had several take up with me. They're social critters. Strong family bonds. Devoted to their mate. Some folks say that a wolf won't never mate up again ifn they lose a mate. I don't know about that. I like to think it's true. Wolf ain't like a human person. It won't kill 'ceptin' for food, family, territory, or self-protection. They better than humans in that way. Wolf eats what it kills and keeps its family fed and

39

protected. They a persecuted animal and there ain't no need for it. I been out here in the wilderness all my life, near 'bouts, and I ain't never heard of no healthy, full-grown wolf ever attackin' a human bein' unless that human bein' messed with it first. Injuns will tell you the same thing." Preacher smiled in the night. "Ain't that the God's truth, ol' feller?"

Betina looked at his shadowy shape. "Just who are you calling an old fellow?"

"That big ol' lobo wolf right over yonder at the edge of the timber. See him? He's lookin' right at us."

Betina squealed and got so close to Preacher he could feel the heat. Right nice feeling, too. Then he chuckled.

"Oh . . . *you!*" She scooted away.

Preacher laughed softly. "Bet, for ever' time you seen a wolf, a wolf has seen you a hundred times. They real shy critters. Relax, you're safe enough here. We'll be at the settlement tomorrow afternoon."

Movement at the edge of the small clearing cut Preacher's eyes. He saw the cold and unblinking eyes of a big gray wolf watching them from the timber. Preacher and the wolf stared at each other for a moment, then the big gray vanished silently into the night.

"What if the settlement isn't there?" Betina asked, unaware of the wolf's presence.

"I done give that some headwork."

"And . . . ?"

"I don't know. Cross that bridge when, or if, we come to it. Ain't no point in worryin' 'bout something that might or might not have happened."

"Preacher, what about the people in the wagon train who got away from the ambush?"

Sharp little gal, Preacher thought. "What people, Bet?"

"Don't fun with me, Preacher. You are perfectly

40

aware that men and women and children got away from the attackers. Just as I am aware of it."

"I seen signs of that, yeah."

"Mr. Larrabee was not at the train when it was attacked. He had gone on ahead to scout, or something. They struck us just after everyone had settled in for the night."

Preacher had not pushed her to talk about the attack. This was the first time she had offered to say anything about it. He let her talk softly while the children slept the deep sleep of the exhausted.

"We all wondered and thought the worst when Mr. Larrabee didn't return before dark."

That's it, then, Preacher thought. More'n likely, Jack's dead. They nailed him 'fore he could get back to the train. Arrow or lance, probably. A gunshot would have alerted the pilgrims. But if the renegades hit the settlement, they didn't come this way. And this is the easiest route.

"They dragged some of the younger women away," Betina continued after a moment. "The white outlaws were ripping the clothing from them as they rode off. It was awful. I had not taken off my dress to sleep. Just laid down on the blankets under a wagon. Melinda and Lorrie were sleeping next to me."

We're in bigger trouble than I first thought, Preacher mused. That smoke I seen this afternoon . . . or thought I seen. It was comin' from the direction of the settlement. Or what's left of it. Damn!

"The boys had gone into the bushes for personal reasons," Betina said. "I grabbed Jody as she was running past the wagon and the four of us made the woods and ran for our lives. But I saw others made it to the woods. What happened after that, I just don't know."

But I more'n likely do, Preacher thought. Them folks that made it away from the ambush is either

41

dead or lost and scared out of their minds. And a scared person will get turned around faster than a whirlwind.

"I hope that settlement is there," Bet said, covering her mouth as she yawned.

So do I, Preacher thought. But I'll wager it ain't.

FOUR

The large meeting building was the only structure that had not been burned.

Preacher had circled wide and come up with the creek and line of trees between the settlement and himself. He had smelled the unmistakable odor of charred wood long before he reached the creek. Leaving Betina and the kids hidden in the line of trees, Preacher rode on up to the settlement — or what was left of it. It was an ugly and savage sight.

"Lord God A'mighty!" Preacher had whispered.

The bodies of the dead lay naked, stiffening and bloated in the yard. The men and teenage boys had been tortured, scalped, and mutilated. What had been done to the women and girls was even worse — as bad as anything Preacher had ever seen. And Preacher had just about seen it all.

Preacher turned to see Betina riding up the slope. "Don't come up here!" he shouted. "Get back. Stay with the kids."

Naturally, she came riding up. And promptly fell off her horse and got sick all over the place. She got to her feet and staggered around blindly for a moment before she could take her hands from her face.

"Take a good look at it, Bet," Preacher told her in a hard voice. "And then don't ever lecture me again

43

'bout shootin' a man out of the saddle."

"Horrible!" she gasped, wiping her mouth on the sleeve of her dress. "Do you . . . can you recognize any of them?"

"Yeah. I think that's Efrem and Maddie something-or-the-other over there. She's got the heft to her."

"What did they do to the man?"

"Held his head in a fire. Brains cooked, built up steam, and the head busted open. I've seen it before a time or two. That's Gerald Twiggs and wife Pauline over yonder. I don't know the names of them little girls. I think them two boys there belong to Efrem and Maddie. The renegades took the rest of the girls and womenfolk. I'll start gatherin' up all the bodies. You see if you can find a shovel, Bet. We got some holes to dig."

"What type of human being would do this to another? Filthy, horrible, despicable . . ." She threw her bonnet to the ground and broke down and wept.

Preacher hunkered down and let her squall. He was not unfeeling or uncaring. It was just that he had seen it all before. He let her bawl for a time and then grabbed her and stood her up and shook her as he would a petulant child. "Now, listen to me, Bet. Damnit, *listen to me!* We ain't got the time for this. We got to get these people in the ground and get the hell gone from here. They ain't been dead more'n a day, so that means that whoever done it ain't far off. Now you go find us a couple of shovels and then you hump your back heppin' me dig. Then—"

"Mr. Preacher?" The small voice spun the mountain man around and filled his hands with pistols.

The MacGreagor kids, Andrew and Mary, stood

by the corner of the meeting house, hand in hand, staring at him with wide eyes set in dirty faces.

"Lord God, kids!" Preacher said, shoving his pistols back behind his sash. "Did anyone else make it out alive?"

"Our mother's hid out in the tater cellar out back. Mr. Nelson is alive, but he's been hurt real bad. He took an arrow in the belly. It poked out his back."

"He's gone, then," Preacher told Betina. "They'll be pison spreadin' all through him. I've seen it. It ain't pretty. Go with the girl and see what you can do. Me and the boy will dig the holes. Come on, lad. Let's find us some shovels."

Betina took Mary's hand and walked around the only building left standing and Preacher and the boy started looking for shovels. As they dug, Preacher asked, "What about your pa, boy? You ain't said nothin'."

"He's over yonder in the cornfield. He was plowing when the savages and the white men struck. He never had a chance. I saw some white men shoot him down while they laughed and whooped and hollered like it was a game. But he had told us kids and Ma what to do should the savages come. You see, Pa dug a tunnel from the house to the cellar out back. It's small, but reenforced right good. Ma yelled for me and Mary and we slipped into the tunnel and hid. I guess we was lucky that we couldn't hear much of the screamin'."

"I'd say so," Preacher replied, as he rolled Maddie into the shallow grave and put her husband in on top of her. At least he thought it was her husband. His condition, it was kind of hard to tell. He looked across the flats from the ridge. "Yonder's a pony, boy. And two more to the north of that one."

"It's Heck!" Andy said. "He's mine."

"Well, go fetch him and the others and get them kids I told you about down at the crick. We got to look around for any food left here and then get the hell gone."

"My pa didn't hold with cussing, Mr. Preacher," the boy admonished.

Preacher looked at the boy. He started to tell him he wasn't his pa. He bit back the words and said, "When you get a few more years on you, boy, then maybe you'll be big enough in the poot to tell me what I can and can't do. For now, do like I tell you."

"Two to a grave, Preacher?" Betina asked, walking up behind him.

"Less work. They can comfort each other on their way to wherever it is they're goin'. Grab a shovel."

"The man died, Preacher."

"Figured he would. You and Coretine drag him out here whilst I go out in that stupid cornfield and get MacGreagor. I told them all to tie a rifle boot to the plow and to keep a brace of pistols handy. Can't tell a goddamn pilgrim nothin'. They think they know it all."

She studied his face. "And that makes you angry, doesn't it, Preacher?"

"Mighty right it does. 'Cause it's a waste of good human life. These was decent people we're plantin'. Even Maddie, and she didn't like me worth a whit. For some reason. But she weren't no bad person. And she shore deserved a better end than what she got. Betina, you can't put eastern ways of life to work out here. Maybe someday, but not now. It's wild and untamed and savage. You lookin' at what I mean. I tried to tell these folks that. It was like talkin' to a tree stump." He threw down his shovel and swung into the saddle. "I'll go fetch Mac-Greagor. We got to get gone from here. Red Hand's bunch done this, and that's one bad Injun."

"You know him?"

"I know him."

Preacher took a tattered and somewhat scorched blanket and went after MacGreagor. Hammer was not real thrilled about totin' any dead body and he let Preacher know this by trying to bite him. But Preacher was ready for it and jerked his arm away just in time.

"I don't like it either, Hammer. So just calm down and let's get this done."

MacGreagor had been scalped and mutilated, so Preacher made sure the blanket covered the man's head so Coretine and the kids couldn't see what all had been done to him. Preacher didn't want the kids to have to carry that image of their pa all the rest of their days.

The bodies covered with the earth they had traveled a thousand miles to work and live on, Betina and the others prayed while Preacher kept a lookout. He'd caught a glimpse of smoke to the west, and wanted to get gone from what was left of the small settlement.

The women and the kids all started bawlin' and carryin' on something fierce and Preacher could do nothing except let them squall. He figured the full load of grief had finally overtook the kids from the wagon train. So while the survivors whooped and hollered, Preacher tightened cinches and made certain what supplies they had managed to salvage were secured down tight for the ride.

Finally, Preacher had to break it up. Each second they delayed was a dangerous one. "Get on them horses!" he said sharply. "We ain't got time for no more of this. Can't nobody here do nothin' for them that's in the ground. That's all up to God now. So let's ride."

About five miles from the ruins of the settlement, Preacher found the remains of Millard and Rosanna whatever-their-last-names-were. Both of them had been stripped naked and tortured long and hard.

"Filthy red savages!" Coretine said.

"This was white man's work. Injuns got more style than this," Preacher told her. "This is the work of Malachi Pardee and his no-count brothers and them other white trash with them. And all Injuns ain't the same, lady. They's just as many peaceful tribes as there is warrin' tribes. One of you boys fetch them shovels from the packhorses and let's get these folks all covered up."

"Smoke to the west, Mr. Preacher," Josh said.

"I seen it, boy. You're doin' real good. Keep your eyes sharp, now."

What Preacher didn't tell the others was that the smoke was not from campfires. It was talking smoke. It might mean that they had been spotted. It might not. No way of knowing. Yet.

The tortured bodies buried, Preacher took the lead and moved them out. He had him a place in mind that just might mean their salvation. If he could get to it. There would be graze for the animals and plenty of water. There was one way in and one way out of the little valley, and one man with two or three rifles and a brace of pistols could hold off an army, if he had people reloading for him.

"The children are tired, Preacher," Betina called from the rear of the line. "They need to rest."

"You can rest when you're dead," Preacher called over his shoulder. "Keep moving."

He pushed them hard the rest of that day. Some of the girls began to cry from exhaustion. Preacher remained stoic and did his best to ignore them. Their whimperings touched him, and he truly felt sorry for the kids. Maybe they'd never forgive him, but that was no matter if they were kept alive. Betina and Coretine were giving him dark looks, but he could live with that, too. He pressed on.

An hour before dusk began settling over the land, Preacher saw the upthrustings of rocks in the distance and turned in his saddle. "We're almost there," he called. "A few more minutes and we're safe."

He stopped at a line of trees and told the exhausted party to dismount and wait—he'd be right back. Preacher disappeared into the trees and was back in five minutes. "Lead your horses and follow me," he told them. "Quick now. We ain't got no whole lot of time."

"But we're safe!" Coretine protested. "You said we were safe here."

"Lady, move!" Preacher told her. "I got to clean up where we stopped here. They's horse droppin's and hoofprints and footprints all over the place."

There was just enough light left to show the weary party the lushness of the peaceful little valley, although it was more like a well-concealed box canyon. Preacher didn't waste a moment of precious time.

"Strip the saddles and pack frames from the horses and let them roll and drink and graze. Let them wander where they will. I'll fix the pass so's they can't get out. You people lay out your bedrolls and eat cold this evenin'. No fires. We're in a lot of trouble, folks, and I can't make that no plainer. We could easy be trapped in here if we're not all real careful. So stay quiet. I'll be back."

Preacher moved quickly to clean up the area where they had stopped outside the hidden valley. He worked fast, but thoroughly, using twigs and leaves and handfuls of fine dirt and sand. He'd come back at first light to do a better job of it, but for now, he felt he'd done all he could do.

Back inside the towering rock walls, Preacher longed for a cup of coffee, for he was a coffee-drinkin' man. Instead, he bellied down at the spring and contented himself with a long pull of icy cold water. He noticed that the younger kids had already rolled up in their blankets and were sleeping.

He squatted down beside the women and said, "Tomorrow, we'll gather up some dry wood and build a small fire back yonder under a cave over-hang. We can have a hot meal and coffee. We got plenty of supplies—last us ten days or more with nobody on short rations. By that time, Pardee and Red Hand will have done their evil deeds in this part of the country and be gone. Then I'll get y'all to the post."

"I'm sorry I was so testy with you today," Coretine said. Her voice was numb with grief and exhaustion.

"It don't matter," Preacher told her. "Forget it. I was pushin' you folks pretty hard. And I was mad 'cause I had to bury some decent folks back yonder."

"Yes. I know. My husband was a decent man. Would it have made any difference if he had mounted a musket boot on his plow, Mr. Preacher?"

"Might have. Folks see a gun, they think twice about startin' trouble. Least he might have gotten one or two of the attackers and the shot would have alerted the others. Don't make no never-mind now. What are you going to do, Mrs. MacGreagor?"

"I guess I will return to the East. I don't like this

dreadful country."

Preacher smiled gently. "I can understand how you might feel that way, Mrs. MacGreagor. But tell me this: the feller who come back East talkin' up the new promised land, what all did he have to say about this country?"

"That the land was free and it was ours for the taking. That it was lush and lovely and so rich that crops seemed to just leap out of the ground with hardly any work at all. Of course, we didn't believe that last part, but we did pay him, signed on with the forming-up wagon train, and left a few months later."

"And nobody asked nothin' about how Injuns was gonna take to a whole bunch of people movin' in on them?"

"Well . . . yes. But Mr. Sutherlin said that the Indians were peaceful and liked the white man. They welcomed the whites coming and settling. He said the Indians were anxious to learn the white man's ways."

"Did he now?" Preacher shook his head. "Mrs. MacGreagor, your Mr. Sutherlin fed y'all a bunch of bull. You know that now, don't you?"

"Yes. Certainly. But he was such a grand figure of a man, in his homespuns and buckskins. He was so tanned and fit and looked to be the very essence of a frontiersman."

"Probably never been west of Illynoise," Preacher said sourly. "A damned huckster and snake-oil salesman. So he took your money. Did you ever see him again?"

"No. He was supposed to meet us in Missouri, but he sent word that he'd be delayed and for us to push on. He would try to catch up with us."

"Sutherlin." Preacher rolled the word around.

"Seems to me like I've heard that name before."

"Oh, he is a very famous mountain man. He has written much on the West and its people."

"He ain't no famous mountain man out here, Mrs. MacGreagor. Least not under that name. I know them all. Lots of folks has read words written by men who come out here 'fore I did and in their minds twisted them words all around. Others has writ words about this place who ain't never set foot near here. I 'spect your Mr. Sutherlin is one of them . . . and maybe worser. He'll get his comeuppance. Bet on that. Now you go wrap up in your blankets and get some rest. We're reasonable safe here."

Preacher was alone with his thoughts for a time, and then Betina come to where he sat, his back to a tree. She spread a blanket on the ground and sat down beside him. "Coretine is a *very* nice person, isn't she, Preacher?"

Something in the way she said it warned Preacher that he'd better be careful how he answered. Betina had taken to battin' her eyes at him of late, and a-wigglin' this and that, too. And he'd seen her givin' them both sharp and hard looks as they sat together, talkin' low. "I reckon," Preacher replied, choosing his words careful. "She says she's headin' back East just as soon as possible."

"Attractive, too, isn't she?"

"I ain't paid no attention to that, missy." Which was a lie he hoped he could pull off. Coretine was a mighty handsome woman. Not near 'bout as pert as Betina, but full-figured and handsome.

Betina decided to give it a rest. She sat quiet for a time and then said, "You think they're out there, don't you, Preacher?"

"Yeah. I do. Not far away, neither. I think Red

Hand has people out lookin' for us. The next few days are goin' to be chancy ones, Bet. It'll be up to you and Coretine to keep the kids quiet at all times. No runnin' around and playin' and carryin' on. They's a cave about five hundred yards over yonder. It runs about two hundred feet into the rocks. First light, I'll check it out for critters and you and Coretine take the kids in there. And don't come out until I tell you to."

"All right, Preacher. You get some rest. You've got to be as tired as the rest of us."

"I'll catch me a few winks."

Preacher slept close to the canyon entrance that night, and slept very lightly. He'd found a few pistols and rifles at the ambush site and had taken them and what powder and molds and lead he could find. Before he'd laid down for the night, he'd loaded a few of the weapons and stashed them for the ladies in case of trouble. He didn't know about Betina, but Coretine had shocked him slightly when she said she would gladly shoot any savage red Indians or trashy white bastards who bothered them.

Preacher believed her, too.

At first light, Preacher checked out the cave and moved the people into it. Then he slipped through the narrow passageway and stood for a time near the hidden mouth, all senses working hard. He could neither hear nor smell anything out of the ordinary.

Moving slowly, Preacher went over the area where they had stopped the afternoon before and cleaned it up. Satisfied it would pass any quick inspection, he slipped back into the passageway and into the canyon.

He gathered up dry wood and twigs and carried them to the cave. At the mouth, under the over-

53

hang, he built a small, nearly smokeless fire and told the ladies to fix coffee and something to eat, and then put out the fire.

"They're close, I'm thinkin'," he told them all as they gathered around the fire, waiting for the meat to cook. "They've lost our trail and know we're somewhere nearby. The next couple of days will tell the story."

Preacher looked at the group, eyeballing each of them for a moment as he waited for the coffee to make. "Y'all was complainin' yesterday 'bout bein' tired. Well, you gonna get lots of rest durin' the next few days. Except for one lookout here in the mouth of the cave, I want you all to stay back in the cave unless you got to come out to do your business. Stay quiet. Do what I tell you to do and we'll come out of this pickle barrel alive." I hope, he silently added.

Preacher ate his bacon and drank his coffee. He allowed himself a short smoke from his old pipe and then checked his weapons. He told Andy to take the first watch at the mouth of the cave and went to sit at the entrance to the canyon. One thing Preacher had learned early on was patience, and he had a deep well of that to draw on.

He wasn't at all sure about the others.

After several hours of sitting very still near the entrance, Preacher picked up the very faintest of sounds. He waved at the lookout and the boy disappeared instantly into the blackness of the cave. Preacher eased his way through the narrow passageway—just wide enough for a horse to make it through—and knelt down in the sand, listening. He could hear faint talking, but could only make out a few words.

Renegade Utes, Preacher finally concluded. Three

of them. And they were very close. If he was going to take them out, it would have to be with knife and war axe. He couldn't risk a shot. Others were probably within hearing distance of the canyon.

He leaned his rifle against the wall of the passageway and slipped out into the brush and timber. Preacher, he thought, you sure can get yourself into some high-lacious predicaments. He heard movement behind him and spun around, coming face to face with a big, war-painted Ute.

FIVE

The Ute was startled for a split second and did nothing. Preacher was startled and killed the brave, slashing out with his long-bladed knife and nearly cutting the man's head off. The Ute's scream died soundlessly in his ruined throat. Kneeling beside the cooling body, Preacher looked around. There was the Ute's pony, a short distance away, its mane thick with tied-on scalps. Some of them, Preacher noted, were very fresh. And two of them were hair from women.

"Brave son of a bitch," Preacher muttered, as he wiped his blade clean on the Ute's shirt and then sheathed it. "I'll call you Killer of Women."

He heard the sounds of a walking horse draw closer. He shoved the dead Ute under some brush and jumped up into the lower branches of a thick-trunked old tree.

Preacher pulled his tomahawk from behind his sash and waited amid the leaves. He had every intention of opening up this Ute's head with his war axe. Might have worked out right well if the limb hadn't broken off just as the Indian was walking his horse under the tree.

When the limb cracked it sounded like a gunshot, and the horse bolted, leaving the startled brave sitting on his butt on the ground for about one second before Preacher and the limb landed on him and broke his neck. The third Ute charged his pony at the noise and Preacher just had time to roll away from the axe in the brave's hand.

Grinning savagely, the renegade Ute leaped off his pony's back and ran to face Preacher just as he was getting to his feet. Both Preacher and the Ute held war axes in their hands. They slowly circled each other, each one attempting to see just how good the other was.

The Ute called Preacher a very uncomplimentary word and Preacher responded by calling him a low-life son of a bitch whose mother slept with prairie dogs.

The Ute cried out and pulled a knife. Preacher pulled his own knife out with his left hand and the Ute frowned at that. The blade looked just about as large as the long knives the horse soldiers carried. Almost.

The Ute leaped silently as Preacher and the steel heads of the axes clanged as they met. Preacher took a wicked swipe with his knife and drew first blood as the razor-sharp blade cut the Ute's belly, although not deep enough to be called much more than a serious scratch. The Ute jumped back as warm blood oozed out of the cut.

The men once more began warily circling each other. The Ute insulted Preacher again and Preacher replied in the buck's own language, calling the Injun something slightly less than a rotting piece of maggot-infested skunk meat. It loses something in the translation. The Ute hollered and jumped at Preacher. Preacher sidestepped, leaped, and kicked the buck in the balls, doubling the brave over in sudden sickness and pain. That was all that Preacher needed. He brought the tomahawk down and split the Ute's skull open. The brave died with his eyes staring in astonishment that this could happen to him.

Preacher caught his breath and then quickly gathered up all the bows and quivers of arrows from the dead. He kept the best of the bows — it was a dandy — and filled one quiver with the best arrows. Then he ran back into the canyon and up to the cave.

"I'll be gone for most of the day and maybe part of the night. Stay absolutely quiet and away from the mouth of the entrance. I'll be back, but I can't tell you rightly when. So don't worry about me. I got to leave a false trail for the renegades."

Out of the canyon, Preacher did some fast work in cleaning up the area and then tied the dead Utes across the backs of their horses. On foot, he led them several miles from the killing site, staying in a meandering creek most of the way, then across a rocky bank. The Indian ponies were unshod, so they would leave no slashes on the rocks.

Preacher scalped the Utes and mutilated the bodies before stringing them up with rope by their heels from a tree limb. He then jumped onto the back of a pony and, leading the other two, set out on a hard run across the grass. He walked and ran the horses for miles before jumping off and heading back to the valley on foot.

Preacher almost ran right into a Cheyenne war party, but this was not a band of renegades. And it was a war party returning from battle, not going into it. While he got along well with the Cheyenne, most of the time, he did not feel like pressing his luck this time. It would be sometime in the future before Preacher would learn that this Cheyenne war party had struck at a Kiowa camp and, during the battle, two chiefs had been killed, Gray Thunder and Gray Hair. That battle would start negotiations between four tribes: Cheyenne, Arapaho, Kiowa, and Comanche. They would later make a peace that has lasted to this day. A pact of nonaggression between their tribes.

But on this day, all Preacher wanted to do was save his white butt. He jumped into a muddy ravine and hugged the mud until the war party had passed. Slipping and sliding and cussing, Preacher made his way back out and on to the valley. It was full dark and he was tuckered when he reached the entrance.

He told Betina to stoke up the fire and fix him some coffee and food whilst he cleaned up at the spring. Then, with the mud washed off of him, and over bacon and bread and coffee, Preacher told the group what had happened.

"You *killed* three right outside the entrance?" Betina gasped.

"Yeah. One of them by accident." He told the kids about the limb breaking and his falling out of the tree and onto the Ute and that got them all giggling.

Even Preacher smiled at his own antics.

"How many miles did you run today, Mr. Preacher?" a girl asked.

"Oh, mayhaps twelve or fifteen, I reckon. Not far enough for me to get my second wind though. I like to run. Keeps a body in good shape. I usually win all the footraces at the rendezvous. Which I was goin' to this year," he added glumly. "On the Wind River."

A little girl snuggled up close to him. "Don't be sad, Mr. Preacher," she said. "We'll all see that you don't get lonesome."

Preacher was at first startled, then amused. He was not a man to whom emotions such as gentleness and compassion came easy. "I 'spect you will, button," he said with a gentle smile. "Yes sirree, I 'spect you will at that."

The group stayed in the valley for a week, with only Preacher venturing out daily to check for signs and smoke. If any renegades came close, he did not hear nor see them. The group was running low on supplies, and Preacher decided it was time to head for Fort William, which was a trading post, not a military fort.

"Are the bad people gone, Mr. Preacher?" a girl asked.

"Bad people will never be gone, honey," the mountain man told her. "They'll be bad people around you all your life. You just got to keep one eye out for them all the time. Let's pack up and get gone, folks."

With Preacher in the lead, Hawken across his saddle horn, the party started out across the Lonesome Land, as some called it. Short-grass and sagebrush country. The name Wyoming came from the Delaware Indian term *maughwau wama*, meaning "big plains." In the late 1830's, Fort William — named after William Sublette, William Anderson, and William Patton, later to be called Fort John, for John Sarpy, and then later to be designated a U.S. military fort and renamed Fort Laramie — was a busy, bustling place. In 1836, the rotting logs that made up the outer walls were replaced with a fifteen-foot-high adobe wall, with higher bastions. Friendly Indians traded there, and it was a safe haven for weary travelers, of which, Preacher had noted sourly, there was a-plenty of lately.

All work stopped when a lookout spotted Preacher and his party approaching the fort and gave out a shout. The men, and the few women at the fort, all turned out to stand and watch silently. They all could accurately guess at what had happened.

Preacher looked around for a face he might know and spotted the mountain man named Caleb. "Where's the soldier boys, Caleb?"

"Gone out chasin' Blackfeet, Preacher. This all that's left of the wagon train?"

"Yep." Preacher swung down and took the jug offered him by Caleb. He took a deep pull and sighed as the whiskey hit his stomach. "Mighty refreshin', Caleb. Good goin' down." He cut his eyes to the bedraggled party of boys and girls and two women. "Three of them yonder in that pack is all that's left of that settlement I told you about. Woman and her two kids. Red Hand and the Pardee brothers hit them. It was bad. I don't know what in the hell any of 'em is gonna do. I'm right glad to be shut of them, personal. I've 'bout had my fill of people for a month or so."

"I do know what you mean. I was fixin' to head out in a couple of days. Figurin' on headin' up towards Pierre's Hole. You shore welcome to travel along if you like."

"Since you ain't no hand when it comes to flappin' your gums, Caleb, I'll take you up on that invite. I best get these poor sad pilgrims settled in. I'll catch up with you later on."

"I'll be around. I got to supply."

Preacher walked over to Betina and Coretine. "Ladies, I plan on pullin' out in a couple of days. So I reckon I'll get my goodbyes said here and now."

"How can we ever thank you?" Coretine asked.

61

"Ain't no thanks needed from nobody. I done what most any man out here would have done. Y'all got your mind made up as to where you're goin' from here?"

"We're . . . talking about it," Betina said. Preacher picked up on the hesitation but thought nothing of it.

"Luck to you all," Preacher replied, and then he walked away after waving at the kids. He was no hand at prolonged goodbyes. He headed to the store to get him a jug and then settle down for a night of serious drinking.

Preacher and Caleb pulled out two days later, long before dawn touched the skies. Preacher had deliberately avoided all contact with Coretine and especially with Betina. He didn't know what the ladies had in mind, and wasn't all that interested in finding out. Preacher had years back decided that his was to be a solitary existence in the Big Lonely. While he enjoyed an occasional dalliance with the ladies, red or white, there was no room in his life for a permanent female companion. By noon of the second day on the trail, the mountain man had put Betina and Coretine out of his mind.

Preacher and Caleb started out for Pierre's Hole, but as mountain men are wont to do, they got sidetracked, piddlin' around, lookin' at this and that, and running into a friend or two they hadn't seen in months or even years.

"Another year," Caleb said, breaking the silence that had lasted for hours as they rode along, "furrin' will be all gone. Done. Two year at the most."

"Seen it comin' three, four year ago," Preacher replied. "That's why I quit. Mainest reason I quit when I did. You know we're bein' followed?"

"Yep. Blackfeet."

"I sold me a pelt at the rendezvous back in '33 for six dollars," Preacher said. "Two year ago same quality fur brought one dollar. Knew it was time to quit. How many you figure they is tryin' to sneak up on us?"

"Too damn many people comin' into this country ain't heppin' none," Caleb replied. "I swear this country's gettin' crowded. Oh, 'bout ten, I reckon. Three, four of 'em done broke off and circlin'. I figure they'll set up an ambush at the pointy rocks."

The two mountain men had headed west from Fort William, riding for the Sweetwater Crossing. Once past that, they had planned on heading through the Rattlesnake Range and then on up to the hot springs. Maybe. Who the hell knew for sure? Neither man had anyplace in particular to go and nobody waiting on them should they decide to head there.

"You primed and ready to blow?" Preacher asked.

"I'm ready to bang all the way around."

"I have done everything I know to do to be friends with the Blackfeet," Preacher mused aloud. "And I have made a few friends. But them and the Pawnee has wooled me around for years. I'm a-gettin' right tired of it. Did you gleam how they was armed?"

"Arrows, mostly. Some old muskets."

Until the repeating rifle came to be, most Indians preferred to stay with bows and arrows or lance, for eight to ten arrows could be aimed and let loose in the time it took to reload a musket. And the Indian never had enough powder or shot.

"I'd rather not have no trouble," Preacher said. "If they'll just go on and leave us be, I'll not be the first to fire a ball." He chuckled. "Ol' John Colter finally had his belly full of the Blackfeet. Way I heared it, after they grabbed him and stripped him nekked as a newborn, they made him run. Chased him for hours. Wasn't long after that John give it up and said he'd never come back out here again."

"He didn't, neither," Caleb said. "Died back in '13, I think it was. St. Louie."

Preacher nodded his head and cut his eyes. "Them Injuns done vanished on us, Caleb. We best be ready."

"Yeah, you be right there, ol' hoss. They gonna be 'spectin' us to take the easy way through the pointies. So how you want to play this?"

"We'll take the south end when I holler. By the time them hid in the rocks get over to the south side, we'll be around the rocks and sittin' there cocked and ready to re-duce their number considerable."

"We there."

"You ready?"

"Give a shout."

"Now!" Preacher yelled, and their mounts and packhorses leaped forward. From the rocks, shouts of disgust and anger rose from the throats of the Blackfeet as they realized they had been tricked.

Preacher and Caleb slid to a halt, leaped from their mounts amid a jumble of boulders, and waited. The Blackfeet, unable to tell where the mountain men had gone, were confused for a moment, shouting at one another. Two leaped nimbly to the highest point of the maze of rocks and carelessly sky-lined themselves for just a moment. Two Hawken rifles roared, their huge balls tearing great

64

holes in the chests of the braves.

"Reload," Preacher said, pulling out his two pistols.

A brave came screaming around the south end of the rock pile and Preacher shot him off his pony. Another jumped down from the rocks and Caleb smashed his face in with the butt of his rifle. Preacher's second .50 caliber pistol belched fire and smoke and another buck's days of warfare ended.

Caleb rammed home ball and patch and cocked his rifle just as a Blackfoot flung himself inside the circle of rocks. The mountain man dropped the muzzle of the Hawken and pulled the trigger, the muzzle only inches away from the buck's face. The brave was unrecognizable as he hit the ground.

To any Indian, fighting what appears to be a losing battle is stupid. The attack broke off and the remaining Blackfeet vanished. Preacher and Caleb quickly reloaded and got the hell gone from that area. They left the dead where they had fallen, knowing their friends would be back for them. Neither Preacher nor Caleb felt any rancor for the Blackfeet. No hard feelings. It was just one way of life clashing with another. Other tribes, such as the Crow, were working with the white man and making peace. But the Blackfeet would remain hostile for years, as would the Cheyenne, the Comanche, the Dakota, the Apache, the Kiowa, and many other tribes.

The mountain men were the first to see the writing on the wall, so to speak, although had it been really visible in print, many would not have been able to read it. The white man was coming, and in many cases bringing his wife and kids with him; they were coming just as surely as one season follows another. And the Indian would have no more success in stopping that westward advance of the whites than he would in stopping the snow that fell or the sun that shone. They would kill a few, but for every one killed, fifty, a hundred, a thousand would take their place.

And to the mountain man, it was sad, in a way. For their way of life was being taken from them as well.

Preacher and Caleb moved on, once more assuming their northwesterly course. Just wandering, hoping to see a valley they had not yet seen, or to belly down by a cold, rushing creek for a drink of water from a mountain runoff. They were of a breed whose time had just about run out. They had made their mark upon a land and the land would always bear that signing. Many mountain men would simply disappear into history and never be heard from again. No one would know what happened to them, or where they were buried, or if they were buried. For in the wilderness, death in a hundred different ways waited around every bend and twist in the trail. Some would go back East and write about their adventures for an eager public.

But not Preacher. Preacher would go on to become even a larger legend. He would be a larger-than-life guide, tracker, scout, warrior.

Miles from the site of the brief but deadly battle with the Blackfeet, Caleb whoaed and sniffed the air. "You smell that, Preacher?"

Preacher did. "Yeah." His words were softly spoken. "That smell don't never change. Death up ahead."

66

Six

It was Jack Larrabee. His back was to a tree and his weapons were by his side. They had been carefully placed there. Two arrows protruded from his chest. Blackfeet arrows. Out of respect for his fighting ability, the Blackfeet had not scalped or mutilated the body of the mountain man. They had left his eyes in his head so he could see his way into the land that lay beyond earth life.

Casting about the battle site for sign, Preacher found four blood trails and Caleb found two more.

"He put up one hell of a fight," Caleb remarked. "Two musket balls in him and two arrows 'fore they brung him down. They'll be singin' songs about Jack come this evenin' and for many more evenin's to come."

"For a fact."

The Blackfeet had also left his horse and his possessions, meager though they were.

The man had escaped the renegade attack on the wagon train only to be ambushed by the Blackfeet.

"He was trackin' the Pardees and another small group," Preacher called, studying the sign on the ground about fifty yards from where Jack lay.

Caleb looked up from his digging in the rocky ground with a small shovel and nodded his head.

"We'll take it up," he said quietly. "What do you think about that, Preacher?"

"I reckon so, Caleb." Preacher walked to his own pack horse and got a shovel. "Ain't no law books nor constables out here. Seems to me like if any sort of decency is gonna pre-vail, those of us who are at least tryin' to do some right has got to act as the law."

"They's a word for that."

"*Vigilante*. Do it bother you?"

"Cain't say it do, mainly 'cause I don't know what it means or how to spell it. Somebody's comin'."

"I know. I been watchin' Hammer. But he ain't all that upset. Must be somebody whose scent he's familiar with."

But just in case, the men dropped shovels and picked up rifles.

"There ain't no need for nothin' like that." The voice came out of the rocks and brush.

"Hell, it's Windy," Caleb said, lowering his rifle. "Come on in, Windy. You can hep us plant Jack. You alone?"

"Rimrock's with me. You boys got airy coffee?"

"Shore," Preacher said, easing the hammer down on his Hawken as the two mountain men came into view. "But we ain't gonna boil none here. Let's get Jack decent, or as decent as he'll ever be, and then move on a few miles."

Windy and Rimrock were just about as disreputable looking as two men could get, and just about as opposite. They were shaggy and woolly and had fleas, but their courage was limitless and they knew the country from Canada to Mexico. They dismounted and walked over to where Jack lay, looking at the body, the arrows still sticking out of the body.

"Goddamn Blackfeet," Rimrock rumbled.

"Get something to dig with," Caleb told the pair. "But don't stand too close to me and Preacher. We had us a bath last week and we're still fairly fresh and pure. Did you never heared of no soap, Windy?"

"I run out. But you take Rimrock here, I don't think his mamma ever introduced him to soap."

"Rimrock never had no mamma," Preacher said. "He was found as a child in the woods and bears raised him."

Caleb stopped his digging and looked at Rimrock. "Come to think of it, you and a griz do favor."

Rimrock just smiled. He was one of the easiest-going people in the mountains, until he lost his temper, which wasn't often. Then he was awesome. Rimrock stood about six and a half feet tall and weighed about two hundred and eighty pounds. His horse was huge, looking more like a dray animal than riding stock. Windy, on the other hand, would have to stand on tiptoes to hit five feet two inches, and probably weighed about a hundred pounds . . . but it was all muscle and gristle and bone. To get on his pony, Windy usually had to find a large rock to climb up on. If one was not handy, Rimrock would just pick him up and throw him into the saddle. The two men had been partners for years, only occasionally going off on their own.

"Two musket balls and two arrows, hey," Windy said, shaking his head. "He give them a run for it, I'll say that. And they respected him for it."

Preacher told the newcomers about the wagon train and the settlement.

"We been up north, along the Powder. We ain't heard nothin' or seen nothin'," Rimrock rumbled in a deep bass voice. " 'Ceptin' movers comin' in. Why, we seen five families 'tween here and the Powder. Place is gettin' all crowded up with folks. I never seen nothin' like it. Gettin' to be a regular city out here."

"Trappin' up there?" Caleb asked.

"Naw. That's about over. We're just ramblin' around," Windy told him. "I wonder how many made the rendezvous?"

"Probably a goodly number," Preacher said, breaking off the arrows and trying to fold Jack's arms across his chest. They were locked in place. He gave up. "But I'll wager that in two, three years, there won't be no more rendezvous, nowhere. Anybody want to take me up on that bet?"

"You don't mean that!" Rimrock said, aghast at just the thought of it.

"It's over, Rim," Caleb told the man. 'Furrin's done. We all got to find something else to do. Me and Preacher, we're travelin' light. No traps."

"We don't have none either," Windy said quietly. "It ain't worth the bother no more."

"Gimme Jack's blanket over yonder," Preacher said, pointing. "Rim, help me wrap him up. He's done stiffened up tight as a drumhead."

They placed the mountain man on his back in the hole and buried his weapons with him.

"Put his blade in there with him," Rimrock said. "He might meet up with a big-assed griz on his way. Windy, strip the saddle offen his horse and turn the poor animal a-loose. He was wild when Jack caught him, so he'll cut wild again."

The men buried Jack Larrabee deep and covered him up and then layered the mound with heavy rocks to prevent the animals from digging up the body. Then the mountain men stood in silence around the mound for several minutes.

"Jack was a good man." Windy finally broke the silence.

"He didn't have no back-up in him," Rimrock said.

"He went out a-clawin' and a-scratchin' and a-bitin'," Caleb added.

Preacher put his battered old hat back on his head and said, "See you, Jack." Then he turned and walked toward Hammer.

The others fell in line with him.

"Ain't gonna be no one left 'fore long," Rimrock muttered, after tossing Windy into the saddle.

The men had settled in for the night, some miles from where Jack Larrabee lay cold in his grave. A hat-sized fire kept their coffee hot while they lay in their robes and blankets and drank coffee and jawed of men they had known and places they had been and sights they had seen.

"I heared you saved some pilgrim and then took them folks and their wagons all the way to the blue waters last year, Preacher," Rimrock said.

"I did. Me and Nighthawk and Jim and Dupre and Beartooth. I can't say as I ever want to do nothin' like that again."

"I'd left 'em along the trail," Windy said. "Damn pilgrims."

Preacher smiled. Windy would have done no such of a thing and everybody around the fire knew it. He just liked for people to think him sour and jaded and coldhearted. Preacher said, "If you'd a seen them fine-lookin' females I took over the mountains and rivers to the blue waters, you'd a still been out there with 'em, Windy."

"Women!" Windy snorted. "I ain't got no use for women. Always wantin' to tie a man down."

"What about that little Crow gal up on the Yellowstone?" Caleb asked with a smile.

Windy glared at him from across the fire and everybody hoo-hawed at him. Windy had come back to the lodge after too long a stay runnin' his traps and she had throwed all his possessions out on the ground, moved the tipi, and took up with another man.

Windy had been sorta testy about women ever since.

A fallen branch snapped out in the darkness and the four mountain men were out of their robes and blankets in a heartbeat, grabbing up rifles and flattening out behind cover, well away from the small fire.

A moan reached their ears. The mountain men did not move. They waited, rifles cocked. Something stirred in the brush, then another moan.

"I'm hurt, boys." The words came weak and in no more than a whisper. "I'm Shields. Tom Shields."

"I know him," Windy whispered. "He's all right. Can you make it to the fire, Tom?"

"If it's the last thing I ever do, and it just might be. I'll make it. Them damn Pardees got lead in me."

"You stay put," Rimrock called, getting to his feet. He went out into the darkness and carried the badly hurt man into the camp and laid him down by the fire, his back against a rock. Preacher started to open Tom's bloody shirt and the injured man's hand stopped him.

"Don't waste your time, t'ain't no use in that. . . . Say, you be Preacher."

"Yeah. Now I 'member you. You was at the rendezvous up on Horse Crick back in '35, I think it was."

72

"Yeah. Just give me some of that coffee, boys," Tom said. "And talk to me whilst I pass. I got lead hard, high and low. One lung's gone and my innards is on fire. I thought for a time I was gonna pass with no one clost to hear my tale."

"The Pardees did it?" Caleb asked.

"Mighty right. Them and their kin and followers. They was drunk and mean and fixin' to burn my feet for fun when I broke and run. I been runnin' for might near two days. Walkin' and crawlin' and staggerin' is more like it." He took a big gulf of coffee and all could see that the hand holding the cup had no fingernails.

Preacher looked at the hand and felt a killing coldness creep over him. "The Pardees tear out your fingernails?"

"Yeah. They did. They got some poor women and girls with 'em, too. And them poor creatures is bein' abused so's it's a mortal sin, it is. It's the most pitifuliest sight I ever did see. I 'spect they all dead by now. They'd shore be better off if they is." He took another slug of coffee and drew a long, shuddering breath. "Them men is worser than any Injun that ever lived." He coughed up blood.

"Where be they now, Tom?" Rimrock asked.

"Oh . . . I wouldn't have no idee. They said something 'bout attackin' some wagon train of pilgrims somewheres. But I was in so much pain the words just didn't register in my head." He closed his eyes for a moment and then said, "It's funny, boys. The pain is plumb gone. My head is real clear now. I was just then thinkin' how it was when we all furst come out here. You could ride for months and not see a white man. Now they's cabins a-poppin' up all over ever'place. They must be two hundred people out here now."

Tom began to ramble and Windy took the cup from his hand before he could spill the hot coffee. He met the cold, dangerous eyes of Preacher staring across the dying man at him and sensed that their wandering was going to come to an end. He'd seen that look in Preacher's eyes before.

"Mighty peaceful, boys," Tom said. "Things is all misty and sparklin' lights and blue like. I guess the Good Lord has decided to let my clock wind down."

"We're goin' after the Pardees, Tom," Caleb said. "At least, I am."

"Count us all in," Rimrock said, his face hard with anger. "We'll avenge you, Tom. You can go out knowin' that much. You got my word on that."

"It's a good thing to have friends, I swear it is," Tom said. "Gimme another swaller of that coffee 'fore I pass, boys. Say, you reckon they got coffee over on the other side? I've often wondered about that. I'm a coffee-drinkin' man."

"Shore they do, Tom," Windy said, his voice very gentle. "I'd bet on it. As a matter of fact, I want you to keep a pot hot for us. Will you do that?"

"You know I will," Tom whispered. "It's all dark boys. I can't see nothin'."

Rimrock took one of the man's tortured hands into his own big paw. "It's all right, ol' hoss. We're here with you."

Tom Shields smiled and died.

The men stood around the rock covered mound in the new light of day. Preacher took off his hat. "Lord," he said. "We done buried two good men in the past few hours. We ask You to receive them with kindness and charity. They wasn't perfect, but

74

they were men to ride the river with. And I can't say no more good about a man than that. Amen." He plopped his hat back on his head. "Let's ride, boys. We got some snakes to stomp on."

Seven

Preacher held the razor-sharp blade to the renegade's throat. The renegade was wearing the buckskin dress of a Ponca *berdache*. A homosexual. Many Indians believed that the moon appeared to boys during puberty and offered both a bow and a woman's pack strap. If the boy hesitated in reaching for the male symbol, the moon gave him the pack strap, and a female life-style. It was as good a theory as any.

"I ain't belittlin' your way of life, Pretty Little Fallin' Star," Preacher said sarcastically, speaking in the *berdache*'s tongue. He had no way of knowing what the Ponca's name was, but he wanted him to know that he spoke it and knew all about him. "But if you want to continue your way of life, you better not tell me no lies."

The Ponca was no coward, for he was a veteran of many battles, but the look in Preacher's eyes spoke silent volumes. And the Ponca knew about the mountain man called Preacher. Many in his own tribe — before he got kicked out — called Preacher White Wolf. The Mandans called him Man Who Kills Silently. The Dakotas called him Bloody Knife. The Crow sang songs about his bravery and fierceness, as did most of the tribes, including the Blackfoot.

"I will not lie," the Ponca said.

"The Pardees and Red Hand. Where are they?"

"Red Hand has left Pardee for a time. Probably half a moon or more. They will meet again when the next wagons try to cross. I do not know where Pardee and his people have gone, nor do I care. I left them and Red Hand. Their viciousness sickened me. War is one thing, but they go too far. A puking vulture would make better company."

Preacher pulled the knife away from his throat and stood up, sheathing the huge blade. "Get out here," he told the Ponca. "Go on back to matchmakin' in your tribe."

"I cannot," the Ponca said. "They have banished me forever. I am nothing. I am nobody. They even took my name. I would be better off dead."

"All right," Windy said, hauling out a pistol and cocking it, ready to give the Ponca his desires.

"Wait a minute," Preacher said. "He leveled with us. Let him go his way."

The Ponca stood up from the ground, straightened his dress, and then swung onto his pony, showing a lot of leg. It was not a thrill for any of the mountain men. He looked at Preacher. "They plan to steal children from the next train."

Rimrock's face grew hard. "To sell them to slavers?"

The Ponca shook his head. "To use them and then kill them." He rode away without looking back.

"We might not be able to wipe out Red Hand's bunch," Preacher said. "But we can damn sure put a dent in the Pardees' operation."

"Providin' we can find them," Caleb said, mounting up.

Preacher stepped into the saddle and picked up the reins. "We'll find them. 'Cause if we don't, a lot of kids is in for a rough time of it."

* * *

The Pardees and their followers left the abused and tortured body of the last woman captive dead on the ground. The carrion birds and the varmits would soon take care of the body. To the best of their knowledge, no one was now left alive to connect them with any atrocities. The gang of cutthroats and brigands saddled up and headed out.

The Pardee gang had long been a scourge in the wilderness. They were a totally ruthless, savage, and lawless pack of degenerates in a land that had never known any type of law except for tribal law . . . and no tribe would have anything to do with the Pardees. Only tribal outcasts, like Red Hand and those that followed the renegade.

Miles and days behind the Pardee gang, four men rode. They rode with rifles across the saddle horn. Small bands of Indians saw the four men and did not bother them. A band of warring Blackfeet saw the four men and let them pass without trouble. There was something in the way the men sat their saddles and held their rifles that caused the Blackfeet to hesitate. And they knew that one of the men in the group was the man the Blackfeet called Killing Ghost. The band of warriors who watched the four men ride on were not afraid of Killing Ghost, known to the white as Preacher, but they respected him. They knew that should they attack, there would be heavy losses and no gain for them. So to attack was foolish.

The Blackfoot raiding party sat their ponies and watched the four men ride out of sight.

"They ride after the white renegades," one brave said.

"Good," the subchief said. "I hope they catch

78

them and kill them all." He turned his pony's head and the others followed.

"Wonder why them Blackfeet back yonder let us go?" Caleb asked, during a break for water.

"By now, that Ponca's spread the word that we're after the Pardees and no one else," Preacher said. "Most Injuns hate the Pardees as much as we do. But they're 'feard of them. I had a Pawnee tell me one time that the Pardees had good medicine workin' all the time. And there ain't never no less than ten or twelve of them."

"A Pawnee?" Windy questioned, knowing how Preacher felt about the Pawnees. "You actual had a conversation with a Pawnee?"

Preacher smiled. "I had my good knife to his throat. He had to talk to me."

The great monetary collapse of the late 1830s was sending people westward by the hundreds. Most were cautious enough to populate states and territories east of the Missouri River. But there were others who heard the westward-ho call and ventured on. Naturalist Henry David Thoreau wrote: "Eastward I go only by force; but westward I go free."

Most of those who went west knew very little about the country into which they were traveling. Much of what they did know was wrong. Actually, very little was known about the wilderness west of the Missouri River. There were those movers who turned back, telling tales of savage hordes of wild red Indians, and of terrible sicknesses and bad water that killed when tasted. Still others told of the awful loneliness of the great plains that drove some people mad.

But still they came. For whatever reasons, they

came. Alone, in pairs, often entire families. The story is told about the pioneer who, when he glimpsed the Pacific Ocean, fell to his knees and wept because he could go no further west. No one knows if the story is true or not, but it is attributed to the British novelist Charles Dickens.

By the late 1830s, cabins were beginning to dot the wilderness. Many of them belonged to trappers, but many were also family dwellings of easterners who headed west and, for one reason or another, came to a spot and went no further. All too often in the early days, they were never heard from again.

"That's a damn cabin down yonder!" Rimrock said.

The four were resting their horses on a ridge.

"It wasn't there last year," Preacher commented: " 'Cause I come this way." He stared at the lonely cabin. "Anyways, it ain't much of a cabin."

"You be right about that," Caleb said. "But it's new. I don't think they's anybody to home. The day is cool and they ain't no smoke from the chimney."

"Why would anybody build a cabin here?" Windy questioned.

"Who knows why an easterner does anything?" Preacher posed the question as he gave Hammer his head and started down the ridge. The others followed.

The men stopped just out of good rifle range of the cabin and spread out, studying the lonely cabin set well back from the banks of a creek.

"I'm goin' in," Preacher said, and kneed Hammer forward. He stopped in the weeded-up front of the cabin and hallooed it several times. His shouts of greeting echoed back to him. Preacher swung down and walked up to the front door, noticing that it was hanging slightly open on its leather hinges. The hinges were cracked and dried nearly useless.

Standing to one side, so the logs of the wall would stop any ball, he pushed open the door with the muzzle of his rifle. Before he could step inside, Rimrock called, "I'm going around back."

"I'm goin' inside for a look around," Preacher said.

Dust covered everything. But not one thing was out of place. A musket hung over the fireplace, and a brace of pistols in holsters were hung on the back of a chair. The table had been set for a meal, with four plates and four cups and real silverware. Preacher picked up a dust-covered spoon and hefted it. Good quality stuff, too. He looked in the blackened kettle hanging over the long-dead ashes in the fireplace. Something had been cooking in the pot, but all that was now left was a hardened glob of whatever it had been.

Pack rats had been at work; their sign was evident. But by and large, everything was as it should be.

There were three rooms and a loft. Preacher climbed the loft ladder and looked around. Nothing out of order. Two floor pallets had been made up and they had not been disturbed by any human hand. He climbed back down and walked out into the back.

"We got some skeletons out here," Caleb said.

"This is spooky, boys," Preacher said. "Damn strange. Any arrows about?"

"Nothin'," Caleb said. "And we been castin' about for sign. Critters got at the bodies, o' course, but none of the skulls has been cracked open by war axes."

"Pox might have got them," Preacher opined. "The reason the house was untouched might be 'cause the Injuns consider this an unnatural place of death and won't go near it." But he really didn't believe that. If they had the pox, why would they all run out into the backyard? He had no idea what had happened to the pioneer family and realized that, like so many other mysteries, he probably would never know. And it really didn't matter.

"What about the bones?" Windy questioned.

"I reckon we can scoop them up and plant them," Rimrock said. "That skull over yonder probably belonged to the man, and that one there is the woman. Them two over yonder was the kids."

The men got their shovels and started digging. "Seems to me like we're shore buryin' a lot of folks this go-around," Caleb remarked.

"You should have been with me at the wagon train," Preacher said, ending that topic.

No one knew where the Pardees hid out when they weren't rampaging around the ever so slowly populating wilderness, stealing and killing and raping. Preacher and his friends looked for the gang, but they had dropped out of sight.

In the wilderness, if one wished not to be found, it was easy to disappear within the millions and millions of acres of plains and timber and mountains. But not so easy for a large gang. They had to cook, had to have coffee, and that meant more than one fire for a dozen or so men. Somebody would see the smoke.

"Have not seen them, Preacher," a Cheyenne called Big Belly told him. "But Red Hand went north and west, to the mountains. This much I know is true."

"Why so far away?"

Big Belly shrugged his shoulders. "I cannot say what I do not know."

Preacher and his friends pushed on, all sharing the feeling they were chasing a will-o'-the-wisp. They headed west, and when they came to a spot that seemed familiar to them, they made camp. The Indians knew they were there, of course, but the mountain men had long ago made friends with most of the tribes . . . except for the Blackfeet. Most of the Indians looked upon the mountain men as being one of them, wanderers and hunters and lovers of the earth. But the men kept a sharp eye out nevertheless. You just never could tell.

"No point in us wearin' ourselves out looking for the Pardees," Preacher said. "They got them a hidey-hole and they's dug in tight. If there is any wagon trains headin' west, and I pray they ain't, they'll be loathe to leave the safety of the fort with all the killin' goin' on."

"You hope," Caleb said, as he dug a shallow pit for the fire and lined the rim with rocks. "Movers bein' what they is, some of them would walk through the hellfires to get west. I never seen the like."

Windy brought back a battered and blackened coffee pot filled with water and set it to boil. "Reckon what month this is?" he asked.

"May, I think," Rimrock said. "Since I give up furrin', I don't pay much attention no more. Preacher, we best be mindful of what that driftin' Mandan told us about them Contraires."

Preacher nodded his head in agreement. The Cheyenne warrior society called Contraires were extremely unpredictable. If they meant no, they said yes. They washed in dust and dried off in water. Nearly everything they did was backwards, except in battle. They was nothing backward about them in battle. The Cheyenne believed they possessed magical powers, but Preacher knew from personal experience that they bled and died just like anyone else. But they were fine warriors and to be feared.

"You got somethin' gnawin' at you, Preacher," Caleb said. "You want to spit it out?"

"Yeah, I do," Preacher admitted. "Any of you boys ever heard of a man named Sutherlin?"

Caleb, Rimrock, and Windy exchanged glances. "How come you ask that?" Windy inquired.

" 'Cause I think he's crooked as a snake. I think the bastard's workin' with the Pardees."

The men chewed on that for a moment. "I heard of him," Windy said. "He lives back East. Ain't he some kind of organizer of wagon trains west?"

"That's him. Betina told me he was the one who spoke to her and them others back East. He was supposed to meet them for the trip west, but backed out. Now I got me an idea that he's done this before."

"Sounds reasonable to me," Rimrock said. "But you ain't got no proof of that."

"Not a bit. Just a gut hunch is all."

"Who would know that we could ask out here?" Caleb questioned.

"One of them damn Pardees, that's who," Preacher said.

"They ain't likely to be givin' that up easy like," Windy pointed out.

"I 'spect not. But you let me get my hands on one of them, and I'll make you a bet I get the news out of him. Count on that. Dump in the coffee. Water's boilin'."

"That would be a low thing for a man to do, if this Sutherlin's doin' it," Rimrock said. "A terrible mighty low thing."

The men sat silent with their thoughts for a time. Then, strong black coffee poured, they leaned back against their saddles and relaxed. "I knowed it," Rimrock said, breaking the silence. "I knowed I been here 'fore. Right here in this same spot. It just now come to me." He looked around. "Yep. Right over there is where I buried Jake Maguire. Right over yonder on that rise in that stand of cottonwoods."

"I 'member him," Caleb said. "Injuns get him?"

"Nope. He started complainin' 'bout his stomach hurtin' and it just got worser as the days wore on. We stopped right here on this very spot and he passed the next mornin'. His belly was all swole up. Something went wrong with his innards, I 'pose."

The men followed Rimrock as he walked over to the stand of trees and up the rise. "Right there," he said, pointing. "I scratched them words in that big rock."

JAKE M. DYED 1821
OF INNARD SIKNES.

"I didn't know how to spell his last name," Rimrock confessed. "But I got them other words right!"

Eight

The eyes of the mountain men popped open and everyone lay still in their robes and blankets, alert and listening as the very faint and unnatural sound came out of the night and to the now-wide-awake camp. The fire had burned down to only a few embers and the night sky was cloud-filled, limiting vision to no more than a few yards. With their hands on their weapons, the mountain men waited. They could smell the wood smoke and grease from the bodies and clothing of the Indians and knew from long experience in the wilderness that when the attack came, it would come either in a silent deadly run or in a wild screaming rush of killing frenzy. They also knew the Indians were very close. No one had to ask if the others were awake. These were men who had lived all their adult lives on the cutting edge of danger.

Preacher cut his eyes to the bulk of Rimrock, who was lying only a couple of yards away. He could see the whites of his eyes and practically feel the tenseness in the big man's body.

Across the dying embers, Windy had his hands outside his blankets, and both hands were filled with pistols. Caleb lay on his side, one hand on his rifle.

Any second now, Preacher thought. They're as close as they dare come before they leap. If we make every ball count, we can break the attack at the first rush . . . maybe. If they get inside the circle, we've got a fight on our hands.

Preacher knew that every man there was thinking the same thing. He also felt that these were Red Hand's renegades rather than the Cheyenne Contraires the Mandan had warned them about; but he wasn't quite certain why he thought that. Then he knew why. The smells were many, signifying men from different tribes. Not all tribes ate the same thing, hence their body odors were different. Some Plains Injuns, such as the Blackfoot, Crow, and Comanche, would not eat fish, considering it taboo. Apaches would eat a horse, but Plains Injuns worshipped the horse, oftentimes staging elaborate burial ceremonies for a favorite. A few tribes would eat dog, but most would not; some even worshipped the dog as a minor god. Some Injun tribes considered the coyote as sent from the beyond, so they revered it.

Just some of the dozens of little things a man must learn quickly in the wilderness . . . if he plans on keeping his hair for any length of time.

Then there was no more time for thinking as the renegades came screaming out of the darkness, charging the camp with rifles and war axes and knives.

Preacher threw back his blankets and rose to his knees, cocking and leveling one pistol. He fired, the ball taking the brave in the chest and stopping him cold. Before the dying attacker hit the ground, Preacher turned and leveled his second pistol. The night blossomed with muzzle flashes and Preacher's second shot hit a brave in the face. The Injun's face exploded and he was flung backward, dead before he stretched out on the ground. Preacher grabbed for his Hawken.

A buck jumped on his back and rode Preacher to the cold ground. Preacher flipped him off and jumped into the middle of the man's chest with both feet. He heard bones break under his feet. The renegade screamed in pain as Preacher rolled away, grabbing up his rifle and cocking it as he came to his knees.

The rifle was torn from his grasp and Preacher ducked a savage blow from a war axe. On his back in the dirt, Preacher got his feet all tangled up in the Injun's feet and ankles and brought him down. Kicking out, Preacher's foot smashed the buck's nose and the other foot caught him in the throat. The Indian started gagging and gasping for breath through his ruptured throat.

Rolling to his feet, his rifle lost in the dust, Preacher hauled out his big blade and went to cuttin'. He nearly severed the head off of one buck. The man went down, blood squirting with every beat of his heart. Turning, Preacher drove the blade into the throat of another warrior, abruptly stilling the wild cries. He jerked the blade free and jumped to one side, avoiding the screaming charge of a brave with the hair knot that some Cheyenne favor. Preacher stuck out a foot and tripped the buck, sending him rolling and sprawling. Preacher jumped on the man's back and drove his blade into the buck's neck.

Rimrock had dropped his empty pistols and snapped the back of an attacker, and he was now wrestling with a huge brave. He clamped one big hand around the buck's throat and squeezed with all his might. Blood erupted from the buck's mouth and Rimrock let him drop to strangle on the ground.

Windy had fired his last charged weapon and was now fighting with a lance he'd taken from a dead Sioux. He impaled a buck, and when he jerked to free the lance, the tip broke off. Windy started using it like a club.

Caleb was swinging his empty rifle and doing some fearful damage with the heavy weapon. Dead and dazed Indians lay all around his feet.

Preacher grabbed up a war axe and planted it in a Cheyenne's head.

Suddenly, as it nearly always is, the attack was over. Indians ran back into the timber and rode out. The mountain men found their weapons and quickly charged them, working fast but smoothly from years of practice. One Indian rose up and tried to stab Windy in the back. Preacher shot him in the chest.

Windy built a small fire and soon had the coffee hot. The men began dragging the dead Indians out of their camp area. Then they sat back down and caught their breath. When they had swallowed some coffee, each took a firebrand and inspected their grisly work.

"All renegades," Preacher said, as they walked around the area where they'd dumped the bodies. They were not worried about the Indians returning this night. This bunch had taken a terrible beating at the hands of the mountain men, and wanted no more of them. And since they were renegades, they would not be back for the bodies. But the men weren't careless, either. They quickly broke camp and moved about a mile. Since it was nearly dawn, they did not attempt to sleep.

"I killed a Ute," Caleb said. "And I seen Preacher drop him a Cheyenne. Rimrock killed a Dakota. Something big is in the works, I'm thinkin'."

An Indian with blood all over his face and chest

staggered into the camp and fell down before he could do any damage with his axe, and before any of the men could shoot him.

Preacher squatted down beside the dying brave and tossed his axe into the graying early morning. "You a damn Kiowa," he said. The dying Indian glowered up at him. "You sort of out of your territory, ain't you?"

The Kiowa cursed and spat at him, showing Preacher that he was not afraid. But also giving away that he spoke some English. He had taken a ball in the chest and his head was busted wide open, the skull bone showing.

"You better talk to me," Preacher told him. " 'Cause if you don't, when you die, I'll cut out your eyes and take your hands and feet. You'll never find your way to the beyond and you won't be able to see it if you do stumble into it."

The Kiowa's eyes narrowed at that. Finally, he said, "What is it you wish to know?"

"You're part of Red Hand's bunch?"

"Yes."

"Where is he?"

"That I do not know. We broke from him for the time he spends away from the wagon trail. In this I speak the truth." He coughed up blood, pink and frothy, and that was a sure sign that he was lung-shot.

When he had finished coughing, Preacher asked, "Where is the Pardee hideout?"

"No one knows that. Not even Red Hand. I know only that it is in the mountains."

Preacher believed him. He didn't know why, but he did. "How do you want to be treated at death?"

"You would do that for me?"

"Why not? I ain't got nothin' ag'in' you."

The brave sighed, the expulsion of air sounding

more like a death rattle. "I wish to be left to rot. That is all I deserve." His head lolled to one side.

The men drank coffee and waited for the Indian to die. He died about an hour after dawn. "I wonder what he done to get banished from the tribe?" Windy asked.

"Don't have no idea," Preacher said. "Must have been something awful." He rolled the Indian up in a tattered blanket he was going to throw away and secured it. "We'll wedge him up yonder in that thick fork," he said, pointing to a huge old tree. " 'Bout the best I know to do."

The men packed up and pulled out. A mile from where they'd left the dead Kiowa, they found the body of another Indian. They did not dismount, just looked at the body and rode on. That made fourteen renegades the mountain men had killed in one brief battle. When the news reached Red Hand, it would make the renegade leader much more wary of the four, pointing out to him that their medicine was very strong.

The men pushed on, heading for the high mountains in the faint hope they could find the hideout of the Pardee gang. Chances of them doing that were slight, something they all knew, but all four felt it was something they had to do. They cursed the ever-growing numbers of movers that were heading across the Great Plains to the Pacific, and cursed those who were stopping to settle in the wilderness. In all the days they'd been in the saddle, they'd seen two new cabins. Place was really getting crowded. But the curses were mainly without rancor. The men realized it was progress, and like the Indians, they could do nothing to prevent it. But unlike the Indians, they could live with it and try to adjust to it.

"This here's where the pilgrims cross," Preacher

said, dismounting and stretching.

They were west of Three Crossings, standing on the east side of the Sweetwater River.

"If somebody was ambitious," Preacher continued, looking around him, "they'd build them a post right here and make a fortune sellin' to the movers."

"Tend store?" Windy said. "Wagh!"

The mountain men all shuddered at the thought. Just the idea of being trapped inside four walls was disgusting. And having to deal with people was even more disgusting. Especially pilgrims. Pilgrims didn't appear to have a whole lot of sense. If they did, they'd stay to home and hearth.

"But that ain't for the likes of us," Preacher said, summing up all their feelings. He looked around him at the silent loneliness. "The Pardees got to be just west of here. Somewheres between the Wind River and South Pass. Or at least they got lookouts close by."

"Mayhaps you be right, Preacher," Caleb said. "Let's split up. We're all gettin' a tad sick of each other's company, and that way we can cover a lot more territory and be shut of one another for a time."

The mountain men parted company that day, agreeing to meet back at the crossing in a week or so. They rode the land, going into areas where few white men had ever been. They searched for sign and inspected the horizon for smoke. They could find nothing. They all came back more than a little disgusted. None of them had found hide nor hair of the Pardee gang.

"They ain't within no twenty-five or thirty miles of this place, Preacher," Caleb said. "Or if they is," he amended, "they ain't cookin' 'ceptin' after dark and under a tent or in a cave."

That last part triggered something in Preacher's

brain. But he couldn't pin it down. He let it lie dormant for the time being. It would come to him.

"Hello, the camp!" The call came out of the late-afternoon air. "I'm uncurried and mangy and got fleas, but I'm told I'm right friendly."

"Carl Lippett," Caleb said. "I'd know that voice anywheres. Come on in, Carl."

Carl sure wasn't lyin'. He definitely was uncurried and mangy. He looked and smelled like he hadn't had a bath in weeks. And as for the fleas, Preacher started scratching five minutes after Carl joined them around the fire. But he did have news, so the men could scratch in exchange.

"Big doin's at the post, boys," Carl said, after taking a swallow of coffee. Since he came from the east, the post would be Fort William. "Got some pilgrims who pulled in and some of them wanted to sell their wagons and possessions and head back to home. Had some pilgrims there who jumped right in and bought the wagons. But here's the funny part: these pilgrims ain't goin' over the mountains west of here. No sirree. They're sayin' they're gonna settle just north of here. Permanently. Up where the Wind River bends."

Preacher leaned back against his saddle and drank his coffee. He dismissed what Carl had just said. He didn't believe a word of it. Carl must have had his head in a jug of whiskey and got things all twisted around. Nobody in their right mind would settle anywhere near this location.

". . . And kids," Carl continued. "Lord, I have never seen the like in all my borned days. Looked like a herd of midgets. And they was two women travelin' without no men; they had about ten kids 'tween 'em."

Preacher sat up and looked at Carl. "*What* two women travelin' alone, Carl?"

"Well, I disremember their names right off. But they was both comely ladies, I can tell you that. One a few years younger than the other. The younger one was the real looker. And they must have had a right smart poke to buy them wagons and outfits."

Preacher stared at him, a sick feeling in the pit of his stomach. It just couldn't be. "What . . . ages . . . were . . . the . . . kids?" he asked in a low and slow tone. Caleb, Windy, and Rimrock all gave him strange looks.

"Why . . . I'd have to say they run 'tween nine and thirteen," Carl said. "And that puzzles me. How do you reckon them ladies done that? I can't figure it out. There wasn't no twins amongst 'em. It's a mystery to me."

"Done what?" Rimrock questioned.

"To be so young and to have all them younguns so close together? Don't none of them kids favor a-tall."

"Well, hell, igit!" Windy said. "They probably adopted 'em. Any fool could figger that out."

Rimrock and Caleb shook their heads. Preacher's face was a real study.

"Oh," Carl said. "Mayhaps you be right. I never thought of that."

"What else in the way of important events has you got to tell us?" Caleb asked.

"They left the post about a week 'fore I did. They ought to be along in about ten days. Oh, Preacher. I do recall one of them females' names. Drum, it was. Betina Drum."

NINE

It took the men about fifteen minutes to calm Preacher down. They were all pretty good cussers, but after listening to Preacher unload, they all had to admit that he could probably outcuss anyone they had ever been around. Preacher stomped around the camp, kicking this and that and hollering and running off any animal within a five-mile radius who wasn't picketed. He did make an exception for a small band of friendly Shoshoni who had silently walked their ponies up on a ridge above the camp and sat listening to their old friend Preacher rant and rave.

"I ought to throw you in the damn river!" Preacher told a startled Carl Lippett.

"Me? What'd I do, Preacher? Now you just calm down. Me and water don't get along."

That was the wrong thing to say but spoken at just the right time. Preacher scratched at a flea bite and glanced at Rimrock, who smiled and looked at Windy, who grinned and winked at Caleb, who had a wicked look in his eyes.

Preacher said, "You got airy soap in your possibles bag, Rimrock?"

"Brand new bar I bought up north. Strong soap hand made by some movers."

"I seen him buy it," Windy said. "It's strong all

95

right. Man can get clean just by standin' near it."
Windy scratched at a bite. "Carl, you got en-tarly
too many varmits on you. I'll fetch the soap."

Carl began looking wildly around him for a way
out. There was none. The men had him blocked.
Carl spotted the Shoshoni warriors on the ridge and
yelled for them to help him. They laughed and
pointed at him.

"Weasel Tail!" Preacher shouted. "Keep an eye out
for us, will you?"

"You have your fun, Preacher," Weasel Tail
shouted. "We watch good."

"Now lookie here, boys," Carl protested. "I had
me a right good wash back some months ago.
That'll do me for the rest of the summer."

"Now!" Preacher yelled, and the men grabbed
him, one to each arm and leg. They carried him
squalling to the river. They all piled into the water.

The Shoshoni were laughing and pointing. They
would have stories to tell when they returned to
their village.

"Goddamnit!" Carl roared. "Unhand me, you heathens! Too much water ain't good for a body. Rots
the skin."

Carl was dunked into the water several times and
Rimrock lathered his long hair with the strong lye
soap. Fleas were leaping and hopping for their lives
by the hundreds. If they could shriek, they would
have been doing that, too. But since those bathing
Carl had just about as much soap on them as did
Carl, the fleas were exiting the other mountain men
as fast as they landed on them. Articles of clothing
were tossed on the bank and soon the men were all
as naked as the day they came into this world. Tell
the truth, they all needed a good scrubbing,
and they got it, in addition to some black eyes,
busted lips, and various other contusions and

abrasions from Carl's fists.

"Halp!" Carl hollered.

Windy jammed a fistful of suds into his mouth and that closed that.

For the mountain men, it would have been a terribly inopportune time for a band of outlaws or renegade Indians to come along. But Weasel Tail was a mighty war chief of the Shoshoni, and it would take a large band to attack him.

But they were lucky, for the Shoshoni were enjoying the show and more than happy to guard over the rambunctious and frolicking men of the mountains.

The men finally decided that Carl was clean enough—probably the cleanest he'd been in years—and allowed him to exit the water, which he did with great haste, running around the camp drying himself off and cussing the other men.

"I'll probably die of phew-moanee!" he hollered at them, frantically looking around for his clothing. "Where's my damn clothes?" He had not noticed when Preacher tossed all their clothing into the river. Windy grabbed them and commenced washing.

"I got 'em!" Windy hollered. "I'll get the varmits out of them, too." He waved at the Shoshoni and they waved back. "Look at Weasel Tail, Preacher. He's gettin' a real laugh out of all this."

Preacher waved at the five Shoshoni and motioned for them to come on down, pointing at the coffee pot and making the sign for eat. They did not need a second invitation. While the mountain men were drying off and dressing in spare clothing—except for Carl; he didn't have any spares and Caleb loaned him some britches and a shirt—the Shoshoni dismounted and sat around the fire, waiting patiently for their hosts to join them. To eat and drink first would not be at all polite. They ignored the rantings and ravings of Carl.

Over coffee and venison steaks, the men ate in silence—no talking until the food was gone. Finally, Weasel Tail belched and spoke. "You all look very hard for something, Preacher. What is it you seek?"

"Band of no-good white men. The Pardees."

"They live in caves in the mountains. Just across the Wind River." He pointed and that little worrisome thing that had popped into Preacher's mind was now clear. He knew now the general area of the Pardee gang. "But the way is guarded. Two men with rifles could hold back an army."

"How many ways in and out?" Rimrock asked.

"I do not know. It is a bad place and Indians do not go there."

No one asked why. That would not be polite. Probably something terrible had happened there, perhaps centuries back, and the story was passed down through the generations by the keepers of those things.

"I have to tell you that more whites are coming," Preacher said.

"From out of the fort to the east. Yes. We know. They won't be bothered by my tribe. I cannot speak for the Sioux or the Cheyenne." He spat on the ground. "Who would want to?" The Shoshoni were bitter enemies of the Sioux and the Cheyenne, and didn't have a whole lot of love for the Crow, either, since neither the Sioux or the Crow would admit that any other Indian tribe had the right to exist anywhere.

"Red Hand?" Preacher asked.

"Red Hand will die if he attempts to fight us. So he does not. I do not know where he is."

Preacher figured Weasel Tail was lying about that. But he didn't push the issue. Preacher waited, sensing something else was on the subchief's mind and that he would get to it in his own good time. Preacher took out tobacco and they all smoked.

"There will be no stopping the whites, will there, Preacher?" Weasel Tail asked.

"No. If all the tribes in the West came together, you would only stop them for a little while." Preacher wasn't sure about that, either, but he figured he'd better plant some doubt in the brave's mind. And his remark would be repeated, he knew that.

"What is it like where you came from, Preacher?"

"I couldn't tell you now," Preacher admitted. "I been out here since I was just a boy. I ain't never been back. I had a person tell me last year that they got great iron steam engines that run on steel tracks. They're all over the place. Call them trains. Some folks say that they'll be out here 'fore long."

"Trains," Weasel Tail repeated. "What do these trains do?"

"Carry goods and people, I reckon. Be a right interestin' sight to see, I 'pose. Some folks back East even got toilets in their houses."

"Inside the lodge?" Weasel Tail was appalled.

"Yep. 'Fraid so."

Weasel Tail shook his head at the thought. "That would not be a good thing. I cannot imagine why people would want such a thing."

"Me neither."

"What are you going to do now, Preacher? You did not trap this season."

"I don't know," he admitted.

"You could come live with us," Weasel Tail suggested, his face brightening. "Preacher is always welcome in our lodges. Why not? You are a great hunter and provider and my village has some fine-looking young women and you could choose one

99

and she would make you a good partner. Your way of life is almost gone, Preacher, and . . ." His voice trailed off and he sighed his frustration. "I mask my own fears, Preacher. I am afraid I will live to see the end of my own way of life. The whites just keep pushing westward and bringing sicknesses that we have never known before and do not have the power to combat. Many tribes have been nearly wiped out. Tamsuky of the Cayuse is already making talk against the Bible shouter Whitman west of us. The Cheyenne and Ute and Arapaho and Sioux and Blackfoot say we must fight to keep the whites out. I do not want to fight the whites."

"We would rather be friends," a young warrior said. "But it is hard to be friends with whites who come now. They are not like you men. They are fearful people and they leave great mounds of stinking garbage behind them when the wagons leave."

Preacher knew that to be fact. He'd personally seen it. He nodded his head in agreement. "The Nes Percé?"

Weasel Tail met his eyes. "They are as we. They do not wish to fight the whites. But a fight is coming, Preacher. If the advancing whites do not respect our land, and our way of life, and you know they will not, there will be war."

Preacher was a simple man; he did not have the words to be profound, even though he was considered fairly well educated among his peers, being able to read and write and do sums. He could but shake his head in agreement, for he knew the words of Weasel Tail to be true. Already, many of the tribes along the West Coast had been wiped out, had succumbed to sickness, or, for the most part, had been tamed. But Preacher, despite his gripings about the steadily growing numbers of people moving west, knew that many of the folks back East who moaned about the plight of the Noble Red Man did not know all the truth. The truth was that the whites were not stealing the land from the Indians, for the Indians didn't own it. Most did not believe that anyone could really *own* part of the earth. They could not comprehend that. And the Indians were not poor, simple savages. They certainly could be savage — to the white man's way of thinking — but on the plus side, many Indian tribes had very complex societies and laws and rules.

"I don't know what to say to you, Weasel Tail," Preacher replied. "I ain't no educated man, but I know that what you say is true. You and us here, we think alike on most things. That's why we can get along. We respect your way of life and don't try to change it. But these new folks comin' out . . ." He sighed, wishing he could tell the Indian about how the movers felt. But to tell the truth, he didn't understand them either. "Yeah, you gonna have to change, Weasel Tail. They gonna make you change — or kill you."

Preacher had heard the stories about the Fox and the Sauk, and how back in '32 a warrior named Black Hawk tried to lead about a thousand of his people back to their homelands, part of which included western Illinois. His original intent had been peaceful, not warlike. Black Hawk and his followers just wanted to go home. What they got was slaughtered as they fled, trying to swim across the Mississippi River back into Iowa.

"Now Preacher is sad," Weasel Tail said.

"Yeah, I reckon I is. Farms and factories now are where the Ojibwa, Menominee, Iowa, Winnebago, Ottawa, and Potawatomi once lived. And that ain't altogether right."

"What is a factory, Preacher?" a brave asked.

"Well, it's a place where people work to make

101

things. Sort of like when your women all gather to sew together skins for a tipi."

"Ahh! And then when what they make is made, they go back to . . . what?"

"Well, they ship them goods out and then they start all over makin' more goods."

"Why?"

"So's the people . . . ah, so's other people don't have to make the goods that are made in the factory."

Weasel Tail sighed and shook his head. "These other people, what do they do that makes them so important that other people must do their work for them?"

Preacher smiled. "Well, it ain't that they's so important. It's just that the people in the factory makes things for the people in the other factory . . . sort of."

"Ayee!" Weasel Tail cried. "My head is reeling from confusion. Let me see if I understand all this. When both factories have finished making whatever it is they make, they all get together and trade, correct?"

"Not exactly," Preacher said—his own head was beginning to reel from confusion. "You see, white people use money. You've all seen the metal coins. Well, they have value to white people. So they give the coins for the goods that are made in the factories."

"There is more than one or two factories?"

"Oh, yeah. Hundreds of 'em."

The Indians looked at one another. Weasel Tail said, "There are not that many things that have to be made."

"There is in the white man's world."

"What makes these co-ins worth something?" another brave asked.

"Well, I ain't real sure about that," Preacher admitted. "But it boils down to gold and silver is valuable."

"To who?"

"The white man."

"Why?"

"I . . . don't know. It just is."

Weasel Tail picked up a rock. "Could this be as valuable as gold or silver?"

"If enough people thought so, yeah."

"So if enough people thought this rock was the worth of twelve horses, and I had twelve horses, they would give me this rock for the horses?"

"Yeah . . . that's about it, I reckon."

"What would I do with the rock?"

"You could use it to buy more horses from another person."

"There is no one in my tribe that stupid."

"Yeah . . . well, you do have a point. I think."

"Will we have to use these co-ins you speak of?" a Shoshoni asked.

"Probably. Someday. Yeah, you will."

"And how will we get them?"

"You work for them."

"Where?"

"In the factories and on the farms and things like that."

Weasel Tail stood up. "My head is aching from all this confusing talk about co-ins and factories and rocks that are worth twelve ponies. Why don't whites just give a sack of potatoes for a shirt, or a horse for a wooden box that whites live in, or a gun for a shoe and be done with it?"

"Well, because not all whites have a gun or a horse or a sack of potatoes."

"But they have co-ins?"

"Well, yeah, some of them. Most of them."

Weasel Tail looked down at Preacher and shook his head. "Your people are very strange. Your people want to possess so many things that are useless that you complicate your society so you must carry around pieces of metal to purchase more things that you really do not need. I think I will never understand the mind of white people. They make my head hurt. White people live in houses that cannot be moved. What do the white people do when they get tired of looking at the same thing all the time?"

Preacher chuckled. "Well, they sell their houses, I reckon."

"Then the people put the co-ins in their pockets and go chop down more trees to build another wooden box they cannot move."

"That's . . . just about it, Weasel Tail."

"Well. That is very foolish. What happens when all the trees are gone?"

"Weasel Tail, the trees ain't never gonna be *gone!*"

"What will prevent that from happening? I have been told that there are so many whites they cannot be counted. If that is true, if they all cut down trees to build their useless wooden houses, soon there will be no more trees, am I not right?"

"Now he's got me worryin'," Rimrock said.

"Me, too," Windy said. "He's got a point, Preacher."

"I don't even know what in the hell any of you is talkin' about," Caleb said.

"These clothes smell funny," Carl said. "I'm gonna smell like a laundry for a week."

"Oh, hell!" Preacher said. "They's trees all over the damn place. They grow up out of the ground natural. Stop worryin' about trees."

"Somebody better worry about them," Weasel Tail said somberly. "Trees are life. Indians know this.

Whites do not. I am afraid that someday white people will cause the earth to die. Then see if you can buy another earth with your co-ins." He waved his hand, and without another word, he and his party left the encampment.

Rimrock took the empty coffee pot down to the river for more water. Windy placed another stick on the fire. Caleb leaned back against his saddle and looked reflective. Carl was fanning himself, trying to dispel the soap smell.

Preacher shook his head. "Maybe Weasel Tail is right and we're wrong. Hell, I don't know. I just wish everybody would get along. Might as well wish for the moon." He lay down and pulled a blanket over him. "Wake me up when it's time to eat."

TEN

All they could do was wait, and that was something they could do well. Carl pulled out a few days after Weasel Tail's gloom-and-doom talk, saying he'd see the men around . . . when they got shut of that damn bar of soap.

"I still smell like a laundry," he muttered as he rode away. "At least the fleas was company."

"What's your plan, Preacher?" Windy asked, as the men lay around the fire, drinking coffee.

"I really ain't got one. I know the wagons got to pass right by here. So mayhaps I'll see to it that they get clear of the Pardees. I don't know exactly what I'll do. I'll damn shore try to talk them out of cuttin' north and settin' up yonder. That's plumb foolish."

"Well, I don't mind waitin'," Caleb said.

"You boys want to pitch in with me and see to the needs of a bunch of hammerheaded easterners, hey?"

"It ain't as if we had a whole lot of pressin' engagements, Preacher," Windy said.

"We ain't got nothin' else to do, Preacher," Rimrock said. "Throw another stick on that fire, Windy. It's our lazy day."

The men did nothing but eat, sleep, hunt for game, fish, and tell totally outrageous lies to each

106

other and about each other. The days drifted by and blended in. Time was unimportant. They could almost make themselves believe it was very nearly like when they first arrived in the Big Lonesome. But they all knew it was not. Already, wagon ruts were being carved in what some were calling the Oregon Trail.

Then one morning the men heard the very faint sounds of bullwhips and the shouting of human voices.

"Yonder come the pilgrims headin' to the promised land," Caleb said.

"Yeah," Rimrock said. "They in for a jolt, I'm thinkin'. 'Cause they ain't no milk out here and the only honey usually has a bear close by it."

"One thing about it, though," Preacher said, recalling last year when he led a party of pilgrims to the West Coast, "by now they'll have gotten rid of much of the stuff they thought they just couldn't live without. And they'll be plenty trail wise, too."

"What I can't figure out is just exactly where they think they'll settle up north of here," Rimrock mused. "And what they're gonna do oncest they get there."

"That's a mystery to me, too," Preacher said. "But I reckon we'll know directly."

"I wonder why the scout didn't come up on us hours ago?" Windy said.

"The fools probably don't have one," Preacher replied. "And don't nobody go lookin' at me."

The men and women and children stared at the four mountain men. And stared. Finally a man mounted on a fine bay horse stepped out of the saddle and pointed a finger at Preacher.

"You there!" he shouted. "Come here."

The mountain men looked at each other and all smiled. Preacher raised his voice and told the man,

"You got something you want to say to me, get over here and say it. The distance is the same for you as it is for me."

The man flushed a deep red. "I am not accustomed to such impudence, sir," he called. "My name is Samuel Weller."

"I'm proud you know your name," Preacher told him. "If a man don't know nothin' else, he shore ought to know his name. I fought a bear oncest in the woods and lost, so he took my name. Folks started callin' me Preacher. So if you run into a bear with a Christian name, leave him be. It's me."

Weller stared at Preacher for a moment. Then he walked toward the men, stopped, and shook his head. "That is utter balderdash, sir. Are you mad?"

"I ain't even upset. Are you?"

Several of the men and women in and alongside the wagons at the front of the train started laughing, and Weller's face again turned crimson. Preacher figured right off that he hadn't made any points with Weller. Not that he gave a damn.

"You there!" Weller pointed his whip handle at Rimrock. "We are in need of an experienced guide to lead us to our final destination. Are you interested?"

"I ain't even curious," Rimrock told him.

Weller opened his mouth, then abruptly closed it as the name Preacher began sinking in. *Preacher!* The man who had rescued the missionaries and then led the wagon train to the Pacific. My word! The man was a living legend.

Weller walked over to where Preacher and the other mountain men stood, rifles in hand, pistols and knives hung all about them. Good Lord, he thought, facing the men, but they certainly were a disreputable-looking bunch. But they all seemed . . . quite capable. He looked at Windy. For a man

108

of his small size, he certainly had a bold and reckless demeanor about him.

Weller looked at the bulk of Rimrock. The man was very nearly a giant. Certainly capable of breaking a man in two. Rimrock grinned at the man.

Caleb was a long and lean and lanky man, but Weller knew those types of men could possess extraordinary endurance and strength. Preacher was, well, Preacher. Wide shoulders and hard-packed muscle in his arms. Huge wrists. The man had only a stubble of beard, so obviously he shaved quite often. But there was one more thing about Preacher that Weller had missed at first glance, but not now. The man was dangerous. Not dangerous in the unpredictable sense, but dangerous in that he would be a bad man to have as an enemy.

Weller cleared his throat and was about to speak when a woman's voice cut him off.

"Oh, Preacher!"

Miss Drum came rushing up, quite unladylike, Weller thought, and threw her arms about Preacher's neck and boldly kissed the man right on the *lips!* Weller was taken aback by the utter brazenness of it.

"Preacher! I just knew I'd see you again," she exclaimed, and kissed him again.

Preacher's eyes were wide with shock. Embarrassed, he disentangled himself from the woman and held the well-endowed young lady at full arm's length. "Betina. You're lookin' well."

"To say the least," Rimrock muttered.

"Amen, brother," Windy whispered.

Caleb stared at the woman.

"I just knew we'd meet again, Preacher," Betina gushed. "Were you waiting for us to come along?"

"Well . . . tell you the truth, yes. I was wantin' to talk you folks out of this crazy notion of headin'

109

north, and point you either west to the Oregon Territory or back home."

She shook her curls. "Preacher, we are going to build a town just north of here. Along the banks of the Wind River. We shall have shops and stores and a church and a school. Isn't that right, Mr. Weller?"

"That is correct, Miss Drum," the man said—a bit stiffly, Preacher thought.

Preacher took off his hat and rubbed his forehead with a hard and callused hand. "Betina, listen to me, girl. There ain't nothing up there where you're talkin' about 'ceptin' Injuns. It's too soon for all this, girl. You've had you a taste of how wild and savage this land can be. But you ain't seen nothin' until you winter out here. That is, providin' you and the rest of these good folks *survive* 'til the winter. Betina, there ain't nothin' up yonder. No trails, no roads, no civilized folks, no nothin'. There ain't nothin' 'tween Fort William and Fort Hall 'ceptin' wilderness, Injuns, and renegades. It's a fool's errand you're on, girl."

She stared at him for a long moment and Preacher knew he had not dissuaded her. "I am determined, Preacher. We shall have our town to the north."

Then Weller had to stick his mouth into it. "We shall trust in the Lord, Preacher," Weller said. "He has guided us this far, and we shall continue to bask in the light of His providence."

"Mayhaps you be right, Weller," Preacher said.

Weller beamed his delight at that.

" 'Cause I reckon that old sayin' holds true," Preacher added.

"And what might that be, sir?"

"That the Good Lord looks after drunks, children, and fools!"

* * *

"This ain't right what you're doin', Preacher," Rimrock bluntly told him.

Preacher stopped in his rolling of blankets into canvas groundsheet and looked up at the man. "You don't mean to tell me that you're stayin'?"

"I got to, Preacher. These people ain't got a prayer out yonder on their own."

Preacher stood up. "Rim, there ain't even no good *trail* that leads up yonder to where these fools want to go. You know that as well as me. We've all been there. There ain't nothin' there. So why there, Rim? Answer me that."

"I don't know the answer to that, Preacher. But that there little gal thinks the world and all of you, and if you turn your backside to her at this time of need, then you a mighty sorry excuse for a man."

Preacher's eyes narrowed and he cocked his head to one side and stared at the man. "I've killed men for sayin' a hell of a lot less than that to me, Rimrock."

Rimrock met the stare without blinking. "I don't think you ever kilt no man just 'cause he spoke the truth," the big man said calmly.

That stung Preacher. He frowned and shook his head in disgust. He'd been friends with these men for too many years to have something like this drive a rift 'tween them. He sighed heavily. "All right, Rim. All right. Hell, I'd a probably been back come the mornin' noways. I'll help you take these people into the wilderness. Has any of 'em told you exactly where it is they want to go?"

Preacher listened and his eyes grew wider. When Rimrock finished, Preacher said, "Now I know they're all plumb crazy. That ain't farmin' country. That country ain't good for nothin'. Are you sure about this?"

"He had the location all writ now and he read it off to me."

"Something is bad wrong with this, Rim. That's a good thirty-five or forty miles north of this trail. The only visitors they'll have will be them lookin' for scalps."

"I done pointed that out to them. Weller said the Lord would see to their safety."

"Is he a gospel shouter?"

"If he ain't, he shore ought to be. Are you goin' to talk to him about this folly?"

Preacher shook his head. "No need. We ain't gonna change their minds. But I thought Betina was boundened and determined to reach the Oregon Territory and that Coretine person was headin' back East with the kids?"

"I reckon they changed their minds."

"I reckon they did at that. When do they want to make the turn north?"

"Right here, come the mornin'."

"Lord help us all." Preacher nodded his head and secured his bedroll behind the cantle of his saddle. "You know the way, Rim. I'll leave sign along from time to time. I'll see you in a couple of days. I want to travel light, so see to my pack animal and possessions, will you?"

"I'll do it, Preacher. See you."

Preacher swung into the saddle and rode out, past Betina's wagon. She was tending a small fire and had coffee on. She smiled up at him. "Coffee, Preacher?"

"Thank you kindly, but no. I got to push on. I'll see you in a couple of days. Then we'll talk."

Her face brightened. "I'm looking forward to that."

"Yeah," Preacher said dryly, then rode away.

He made a lonely camp that evening not too far

112

from a slow-moving little creek. If it had a name, Preacher didn't know it. "Fools," he muttered to his tiny fire hidden in rocks. "Someday this might be a settled land. But it's too damn soon now for people to even try."

He emptied his coffee pot and put out the fire as the shadows began creeping in. Drinking his coffee and munching on a biscuit he'd swiped from a mover's wife that morning, Preacher tried to make some sense out of this move. He'd asked Weller, but the man turned mum on him. No sense in that either. He could understand people wanting to go to California or the Oregon Territory — sort of — but this move . . .

Then it came to him.

"Shore, there it was, right there in front of me all the time," Preacher muttered to the shadows. "So damn plain I couldn't even see it."

He could see Sutherlin's fine hand in this. Had to be. And the reason the Pardees couldn't be found was 'cause they wasn't back at their mountain hideout . . . they was waitin' up on the Wind River. Or at least was headin' that way. Had to be it. Sutherlin would have the wagons leave the more-or-less-established trail west and head north to settle in a country that only mountain men, a few Army scouts, and Indians had ever seen. Then when the movers was busy with building cabins and such, they'd hit them, Pardee's gang and Red Hand. They wipe them out, burn the wagons and structures, sell the women and girls for slaves and whores, and then vanish. The movers wouldn't be missed for months, at least until spring, and by that time, their bones would be bleached white and scattered by varmits. And the odds were, no one would ever know what happened to them.

"Quite a plan, if I got it figured out right,"

113

Preacher muttered. "But how did Sutherlin get tied in with the Pardee bunch? And what did he get out of this?"

Preacher knew the answer to that immediately. The fee for organizing the train, of course. But how many times could he get away with something like this?

"Plenty, if he's smart," Preacher said aloud. "Let two or three trains through, and hit the third or fourth one." And Preacher knew then why the Pardee bunch was sometimes not heard of in the Big Lonesome for months at a time: they staggered the territories where they operated. They'd ride hundreds of miles to strike, and then beat it back to the Lonesome with their booty and hide out for a time. Then they'd move to another location to strike again.

"Quite an operation," Preacher muttered. "This Sutherlin must have a lot of men workin' for him. He organizes a train back East, then sends riders west with the news." And, he thought, no tellin' how long this has been goin' on. Preacher shook his head at the vastness of it.

Preacher had known some cold-blooded ol' boys in his time, but Sutherlin and Pardee and Son and men of that ilk took the prize for bein' pure evil. To date, those workin' with Sutherlin must have been responsible for the deaths of no tellin' how many men and women and kids along the trail. No tellin' how many young girls and boys had been sold into slavery, or indentured to someone, which to Preacher's mind was the same thing as slavery.

And so, he thought, summing it up in his mind, here I am stuck a hundred miles from nowhere, knowin' what's goin' on, and now what am I goin' to do about it?

He pondered that for a time, then nodded his

head as he came up with a plan. "Might work," he said. "At least I can give 'er a try."

Satisfied with it, he rolled up in his blankets, Hawken close to hand, and went to sleep.

The next day, he rode into Weasel Tail's camp and met with the Shoshoni war chief.

"A terrible thing," Weasel Tail said, after listening to Preacher. "I will help. Your plan is good one, I think. And you are right about the Pardees disappearing for long periods of time. Now we will eat and smoke and rest." He smiled sadly at Preacher. "Treachery knows no color or way of life, does it, my friend?"

"I'm afraid not," Preacher agreed. "We all got good and bad amongst us. When the time comes, Weasel Tail, you be careful what you agree to with the whites." He was silent for a moment, then added, "Some amongst us are prone to lie."

ELEVEN

Weasel Tail started sending out riders that day. They were to range as far out as they dared, talking to friendly tribes and gathering news of any wagon-train ambushes or of any recently built cabins and settlements being wiped out. Weasel Tail said his riders would be back when they would be back. Time was not that big a deal for an Indian.

Preacher expected the wagon train to make no more than five or six miles a day at best. Ten days, he figured, to that miserable spot somebody had conned them into taking.

Then Preacher leveled with Weasel Tail about the final destination of the wagon train. The war chief was neither angry nor surprised. Instead, he smiled.

"We have known that for weeks, Preacher," Weasel Tail said. "Some of my people slipped close to the wagons one night and listened to the men and women talk."

"They took a chance," Preacher told him.

"Not without someone of your caliber there," the war chief replied, with a twinkle in his eyes.

"You know where I'll be," Preacher told his friend. "As soon as you get some news, let me know."

As Preacher rode the land, he was once more reminded that this part of the country was not his favorite by a long shot. He never could figure out exactly what this country was good for. And he hoped that when the members of Weller's party got themselves a good taste of it, they'd see the folly in staying and either push on west or turn around and go back home.

But it was a faint hope and he was fully aware of that. He was beginning to understand the mentality of movers.

Preacher reined up and studied the land for a moment, looking all around him. Then he smelled dust. He and Hammer went immediately into a ravine. Ground-reining the horse, Preacher slipped from the saddle and climbed up the bank and sought a little cover behind a bush that was growing tenaciously in the rocky soil. That was the only thing that prevented his head from being exposed.

It was a small war party of Utes, and they had them a couple of prisoners. Preacher knew from experience that the Utes could be real inventive when it came to torturing prisoners. But from where he squatted, he couldn't see any way in hell he could help them poor men lashed to their saddles. Then he watched as the Utes stopped and swung down off their ponies.

"Hell," Preacher muttered. "They're gonna do the deed right in front of me."

There were six Utes, all young braves, a couple of them just into manhood, it looked like. None of them had rifles or pistols. Two carried long lances, the rest bows and arrows. All had war axes.

Preacher stared hard at the prisoners. He didn't know either of them. They looked and dressed like pilgrims. With a sigh, Preacher knew he just couldn't squat back behind a skinny bush and watch two white men get tortured to death. The screamin' and hollerin' tended to get on a person's nerves. So that left only two options: leave or fight.

He slipped back to Hammer and fetched his other two charged pistols, checking them carefully and hoping they wouldn't misfire when he most desperately needed them. He rubbed Hammer's nose and whispered to the animal, calming the big horse and taking comfort from him.

"I'm a-fixin' to stick my nose into the fire ag'in, Hammer. Way I see it, I ain't got no choice in the matter. Goddamn pilgrims is gonna be the death of me yet. So you just rest for a time and be here when I get back."

Preacher slipped up the ravine until it narrowed down to nothing. He crawled on his belly for a few yards until coming up behind another skimpy bush. There would have been nothing to this in the lushness of the real wilderness, with thick stands of timber and growth aplenty.

He peeked around the scrub bush and saw smoke beginning to rise. These young Utes were fixin' to have themselves a high ol' time with the prisoners. Probably going to start out by burnin' the feet of the men. That way even if the men did get loose, they couldn't run away. The backs of the Utes was toward him, so Preacher closed the distance by a few more yards, then a few more as a wild shriek of pain tore from the throat of one of the captives.

"Hell with this," Preacher muttered, coming up on one knee and leveling the Hawken. He let a ball fly. The big ball caught one buck in the center of his back and the brave pitched forward, landing with his face in the fire. His hair caught on fire and sent up a fearful odor.

Preacher dropped his rifle and jerked out two pistols, running toward the momentarily confused scene. One older Ute, reacting faster than the

118

others, quickly notched an arrow and let it fly. It missed Preacher by a good foot and he never stopped his running charge. He let a pistol bang. The ball struck the buck in the hip and turned him around, knocking him to the ground. He pulled the trigger of the second pistol and it misfired. Preacher added some pretty fancy cussing to the wild hollering of the Utes and jerked out the last brace of pistols, knowing that he was in real trouble now. There were four pissed-off Utes standing facing him, and he had two charged pistols.

One of the men all trussed up kicked out with his bare feet and caught a Ute behind his knees, knocking the buck to the ground. A brave with a lance in his hands and a scream on his lips charged Preacher. Preacher gave him a ball of lead at nearly point-blank range and the Ute's chest was suddenly smeared with blood. An arrow missed Preacher's head by inches and Preacher gave that brave his last ball. The shot knocked the Ute down, but didn't kill him right off. He lurched to his feet and staggered toward Preacher, a knife in his hand.

Preacher grabbed up the lance and met the brave, just as the Ute the man had knocked down jumped to his feet. The buck with the knife tried to fake Preacher out, but the mountain man was an old hand at this. Preacher gave him the point of the lance in the belly, driving through. The Ute screamed, dropped the knife, and wrapped his fingers around the shaft of the lance as he sank to his knees.

Preacher broke the lance off in him and met the two Utes charging him, screaming their rage and hatred at this interloper. Preacher swung the lance like a club and took one out with a wicked blow to the head. He jammed the broken end of the lance into the belly of the last Ute and the Ute fell back, jerking the lance from Preacher's hands. The last Ute standing faced Preacher with a knife. The trussed-up captives were methodically kicking the hip-shot Ute in the head with their bare feet.

Preacher could see out of the corner of his eye that the buck was unconscious and would probably not survive the vicious kicks to the head. But the prisoners were plenty mad and scared and taking that out on the Ute's head. Preacher knew their feelings very well.

The Ute facing Preacher told him in no uncertain terms what he thought of Preacher. Preacher replied in the warrior's own tongue that he pretty well felt the same about the Ute, then grinned and added that he felt the Ute looked like a stinking pile of buzzard puke.

The young Ute lunged and Preacher drew the first blood with his good knife. The wound was not serious, but it did give the brave something to think about.

The Ute cursed Preacher.

"You better sing your death song," Preacher told the war-painted brave.

The Ute leaped and Preacher's knife ripped into the brave's belly as Preacher's left hand clamped down on the Indian's wrist and held the knife hand firmly away from him. Preacher twisted the knife, ripping upward with the cutting edge. The Ute's face grimaced as the pain tore through his guts and the blade finally ripped into the heart. The pain turned to death. Preacher jerked out his knife and let the Ute fall to the bloody and churned-up ground.

He ran to the trussed-up men and sliced their bonds with the bloody knife. "Grab up a pony and let's get gone from here. Them gunshots was probably heard by other Utes. How come them Injuns didn't take your weapons when they overpowered you?"

"The first bunch did," the one with the slightly charred foot said. "Then they took off after our partners and left us with this bunch."

"How far back?"

"A good eight to ten miles," the second man said. "If our friends can find any kind of shelter, they'll off the savages. I'm sure of that."

Some of the tenseness went out of Preacher. The sounds of the shooting would not reach eight miles. Preacher gave the men a longer second look. Pilgrims. Their clothing was store-bought and their hats new. Burned Foot even had him a gold watch on a fancy fob.

"All right, you boys take it easy. Look around and strip you some moccasins off a dead buck and get you a knife from them. I'll get my guns and horse."

"One of these red savages is still alive."

"That's his problem. Either kill him or let him be. Don't make no difference to me." Preacher quickly reloaded and trotted back to Hammer, who was waiting patiently for him in the ravine. "Place is fillin' up with amateurs, Hammer." Preacher swung into the saddle. "Seems like all we been doin' is pullin' pilgrims out of trouble. It's gettin' to be a right wearisome thing."

"I cannot find footwear that fits me properly," Burned Foot complained as Preacher rode up.

"Well, my goodness!" Preacher told him. "I guess that means we'll just have to ride right out and find where them Utes tossed your boots, won't we?"

"There is no need for sarcasm," he admonished Preacher. "We are strangers in this savage land."

"I never would have guessed. And the land ain't savage. It just ain't worth a damn for nothin'

121

around here. Mount up. Let's go find the bodies of your partners."

"The *bodies?*"

"Yeah. The bodies. If they're still alive, I'll eat a raw skunk. Let's go."

Preacher turned Hammer's head and rode off, not waiting to see if the men were following. The trail left by the Utes was plain as the nose on a man's face, and he figured even a pilgrim could follow it.

The men caught up with him and Burned Foot said, "There are dead people back there."

"Do tell? What about them?"

"Well, it's the Christian thing to bury them, wouldn't you say? I mean, they did inflict some horrible pain upon my person, but they are human beings."

"I don't know whether I'm a Christian, or not. But if you want to bury 'em, you can just ride on back there and start diggin'."

The two men thought about that for a moment and said no more about it. "What were you doing out this way, sir," the second man asked. "Exploring?"

Preacher sighed mightily. He shook his head. "No, pilgrim, I was lookin' for the man in the moon. Do you two have names?"

"But of course," Burned Foot said. "I am Miles Cason and this is my best chum, George Martin."

Preacher looked at him. *Chum?* "Pleased, I'm sure."

The two men waited. And waited. Finally, George said, "To whom do we owe our lives, sir?"

"Your mamma and daddy, I reckon."

"My foot hurts like the devil!" Miles said.

"What is your name, sir?" George asked.

"Preacher."

"*Preacher?*"

"Yep. Just Preacher. See the smoke over yonder, boys?" He pointed. "Did y'all have wagons?"

"Yes. Two of them. To carry our supplies. We're out here hunting gold."

Preacher looked at the man. "Gold? Here? You're huntin' gold . . . *here?* Who told you there was gold around here?"

"A geologist."

"A *what* ologist?"

"What is that smoke over there?" George asked. "Is that a settlement?"

Preacher chuckled. "The next settlement west, pilgrim, is several hundred miles from here. That smoke you see yonder is the burnin' bodies of your partners and anything else the Utes didn't take. See the buzzards already circlin'? Now follow me down into this draw and don't ask questions."

"Why are we going into this ravine?" Miles promptly asked. "I simply must have a doctor see to my foot."

"We're goin' into this draw 'cause the Injuns is still over here havin' fun with your friends. Although I don't much imagine your friends is seein' no humor in it."

"How do you know the savages are still over there?"

" 'Cause of the damn dust!" Preacher said irritably. "They must be draggin' one of them."

"Are you going to their rescue?" George asked.

"Hell no! Even if I was a mind to—which I ain't, by the way—by now there ain't enough left to save. We will give them a proper burial, though. Tomorrow."

"*Tomorrow?*" Miles asked, horror in his voice.

"That's right, pilgrim. Tomorrow. If we're still alive, that is. You can bet your boots, if either of you had any, them Injuns over there is seasoned braves. Not like them young bucks that had you two. We can't risk movin' out of this draw 'cause we'll kick up dust in this goddamn godforsaken place. We'll just sit this out here and hope them over yonder don't take the same way back that we come. So just sit down, shut up, and don't ask me no more questions. I'm tired of it."

"I'm hungry," George said.

Preacher reached into his parfleche and tossed them some jerky and pemmican. "Stuff that in your mouths and chew on it. If it don't do nothin' else, it'll keep you quiet."

"You really are a very rude man," Miles said.

Preacher just looked at the man and said nothing. Although there were a great many words he thought about saying.

The men opened their eyes in the grayness just before dawn. Preacher was sitting on the ground, his back to the wall of the earth bank.

"The Utes pulled out hours ago," Preacher informed them. "Get the kinks out of your legs and saddle up."

"My foot hurts," Miles said.

"It'll either get better or it'll rot off," Preacher told him. "Good Lord, man. I've hurt myself worser than that cookin' breakfast. Quit your bitchin'."

"Are you sure the savages have gone?" George asked.

"Yeah, I'm sure."

"It's going to be a dreadful sight, isn't it?"

"Yeah, it is," Preacher replied, tightening the cinch on Hammer. "But if you're plannin' on stayin' out in this country, it's a sight you better get used to."

"I could never become that callous," Miles said,

his lip still stuck out over Preacher's mild castigating.

"Then you best run on back to wherever the hell it is you come from, pilgrim. 'Cause out here, you either toughen up or you die. And that's the way it is. Now saddle up and mount up. We got some buryin' to do."

George and Miles got the heaves as soon as they rode up to the site. Both of them staggered off a ways and fell down on the ground, coughing and gagging. Preacher prowled the still-smoking ruins.

Preacher had seen this many times. He kept his face impassive to the horrible sights around him as he looked at what was left of the men who had come west in search of gold. Preacher breathed shallow and through his mouth. The stench was terrible.

"That's poor Willie over there," Miles said, his face pale and drawn. "He came out here for the adventure of it. We went to college together. He graduated with honors."

"Didn't do him much good out here," Preacher remarked. Under a torn over bundle, he found a pistol and tossed it to Miles. "Start lookin' around for things that you might could use, you two. I seen some boots over yonder. And there's a shovel. I'll start diggin' the hole."

"You mean holes, don't you?" George asked.

"No. I mean a hole. One. Pile 'em in there together. We can't waste of whole lot of time tarryin' around here. Them damn Utes might decide to come back. You can bet they've found the ones I kilt yesterday and they'll be hoppin' mad."

"What you're suggesting is very indecent and most unchristian," Miles told him.

"But very practical," Preacher responded. He'd dealt with enough pilgrims to know that most of

125

them didn't use a lot of common sense once they got west of the Missouri. Not for a while, anyways. Then they either smartened up or got killed. "But you boys can take the time to speak some words over the grave," he told them.

"How very kind of you," George said.

"Think nothin' of it." Preacher let the sarcasm roll right off of him. "I do have my good points. Start rumblin' around and stop all this jawin'."

Preacher grabbed a shovel and started digging. "When you two get done grubbin' about in the rubble, start bringin' some rocks over here. Dump them yonder. We got to pile them on the mound so's the varmits won't dig up what's left of the bodies and eat on them."

"That's disgusting!" Miles said.

"Not to a varmit."

"Do you have a Bible, Preacher?" George asked.

"No. Had one. Give to me last year by a gospel shouter. I lost it somewheres."

"I hate this savage land," Miles said.

"Good. Glad to hear that," Preacher said, digging in the ground. "Maybe you'll go home now."

"We came out here for gold, and we won't leave until we have found it," Miles said firmly.

"That means you both gonna be here forever," Preacher muttered.

TWELVE

Preacher waited patiently while the two men conducted services over the large mound of earth. Sounded to him like both of them were part-time gospel shouters. They sure did praise the Lord and such. Didn't sound too bad, though; man needs a little gospel hollerin' every now and then. When the two had wound down and he got them back in the saddle, he headed them toward the wagon train. Preacher damn sure didn't want to be stuck with them out here all by his lonesome. Although he had to admit, they showed some spunk all trussed up and kickin' that buck down. It helped, for a fact, it did.

Windy was scouting far ahead of the train and whoaed up when he saw Preacher and the pilgrims. He eyeballed the two men, questions in his eyes.

"Gold hunters," Preacher told him.

"In *this* part of the country? There ain't no gold around here."

"A what-ologist told them they was. They had them a streak of bad luck by runnin' into a Ute war party not too many miles up ahead."

"Do you have a physician with your party?" Miles questioned.

Windy blinked.

"He means a doctor," Preacher said.

"I ain't scoutin' for no hospital," Windy told Miles. "You sick?"

"I have a horribly burned foot. I was tortured savagely by those filthy wild red Indians."

"Do tell? Lookin' at you, I'd have to say that you stood up to it right well."

"The Utes stuck his foot in the fire one time," Preacher said. "Stick a poultice on it when you get these lost sheep to the train, Windy. I'm gone." Preacher wheeled his horse and rode out without looking back.

"We certainly owe that person our very lives," George said. "But I have to say that he is the most irritable-behaving man I have ever encountered."

Windy smiled. He knew some mountain men that would make Preacher look like a cross between Solomon and Moses. "Come on, children," he said, lifting the reins. "Let's get you back to your own kind."

"And what kind is that, sir?" Miles inquired.

"Igits," Windy told him, and rode off.

Preacher snared him a big fat rabbit for supper, and after eating every scrap of meat and sucking the marrow from the bones, he carefully buried the remains, put out his fire, and moved on another couple of miles before he found a good spot to bed down for the night. He checked his guns carefully. That Ute war party would have long since found the six dead young braves and they would be angry and looking for revenge. And Preacher didn't think the ones who attacked Miles and George and the others was the main party—more like a splinter band. Right about now, they would be all linked up and there would be a whole passel of them whoopin' and hollerin' and singin' their songs and workin' themselves up into a killing frenzy.

Whether they would attack the wagon train was something he could only guess at. But if the main bunch was fifty or more, they'd try it.

But a man alone would be easy pickin's for them, so he'd ride careful come the morning. Not that he didn't always . . . but a little extra caution never hurt.

It sure paid off. Preacher had not ridden two miles from where he'd camped when he smelled dust. A lot of dust. Then from a draw, he spotted the Utes. And this was no small party. Preacher figured at least seventy-five strong. He pulled back off and walked Hammer slowly to an upthrusting of rocks and got behind the huge natural barricade.

"Now, Hammer," he told the big horse. "This ain't no time for conversin' with some long-lost cousin of yours. Since you with me, them Utes just might decide to eat you!"

Hammer looked at him mournfully.

"That's a fact, horse. So you just be quiet now. Be real quiet."

The Utes were riding with a purpose in mind, and did not have many outriders flanking them or none ahead of them that Preacher could spot. He thought that strange, but then the Utes probably figured they were in safe enough territory. As soon as they had passed by, Preacher headed back for the wagon train, since that was the direction the Utes were taking. He stayed several miles to the east of the war party. This bunch was going to hit the wagons, Preacher would bet his hat on that. And they just might do it at night. It was a myth that all Indians never attacked at night. It all depended on whether or not they felt their medicine was strong enough. Preacher had once opined, over a jug of whiskey, that a man ought to be always careful at night, 'cause supposin' you run up on a whole bunch of atheist Indians who didn't believe in no kind of afterlife. Man would be in a real pickle then.

Preacher rode hard, pushing Hammer, until he was sure he was ahead of the Utes; then he cut toward the train. They had just circled for the evening's camp when Preacher rode in and tossed the reins to Caleb.

"War party of Utes not more'n two, three hours away," he told Weller and the mountain men. 'Comin' down from the north and they ridin' with a purpose. I think it's the main bunch of that smaller party that hit Cason and Martin's friends."

"I was told that the savages never attacked at night," Weller said, then noticed all the mountain men smiling at his words. "Obviously, I was misinformed."

"Yeah, you was," Preacher said. "Best double the guard tonight. And have ever' man charge ever' weapon they got and keep them close by. Check powder and shot, too. Have the women break out the molds and get some lead heated up for balls."

When Weller had gone, Rimrock asked, "How many did you see, Preacher?"

"At least seventy-five, maybe a few more or less than that. Only a few of 'em armed with rifles, I'd say."

"Well, they'll hit us for sure," Caleb said. "There ain't nothin' out here 'ceptin' us."

"Did you ever make the spot where these pilgrims want to light?" Windy asked.

"I come close enough to it to know that it don't look like no farmin' country I ever seen and there sure as hell ain't gonna be no town there no time soon." He told him what he suspicioned about the

130

Pardees and Sutherlin and also what he had Weasel Tail's braves doing.

"Sounds right to me," Rimrock said. "You musta really put your head to workin', Preacher. This Sutherlin feller, he's shapin' up to be a real black-heart."

"He'll stop bein' when I put a ball through it," Preacher replied.

Preacher grabbed him a short snooze—'cause he didn't figure on dozin' none that night—and then ate a plate of stew that Betina brought to him. She sat on the ground beside him all google-eyed and watched him eat every bite. Made Preacher nervous. Female had marriage on the brain. He knew from experience. He had a squaw follow him around one time, actin' just like Betina was doin'. Preacher finally pulled out of that Cheyenne village in the damn dead of winter just to get shut her.

"I can hardly contain myself," Betina said. "I am so anxious to get our new town established. We'll have us a fine schoolhouse, too. I'll see to that."

"Betina—"

"Do you remember your school days, Preacher? Oh, my, but I certainly do."

"Ma mostly taught me writin' and readin' and figurin'. Betina, about this here town—"

"Schools are so dismal," she prattled on. "But ours won't be. I attended a great barn of a school. Sometimes, when the winters were very harsh, we would be dismissed because of the lack of proper heating. But that won't be the case with my school. We must educate our children and see to their comforts while doing so. Don't you agree?"

"Yeah. Sure." She had stressed *our* and that sent shivers up and down Preacher's spine. "Betina," he

131

tried again, "you gotta understand something about this town—"

"And I want to give each student some personal attention. I think that is very important, don't you, Preacher?"

"Oh, yeah," Preacher said wearily. " 'Specially with a good strong board when they act up."

"Oh, I don't believe in corporal punishment, Preacher. I believe that is the wrong approach."

"Wished I'd been in your school," he muttered. The brief times he had attended a regular school he got a lickin' damn near every day. And another one from his pa when he got home. He smiled. He had deserved every one of them and more.

"What are you smiling about, Preacher?"

"The hidin's and the knucklin's I got when I did go to a regular school."

"Was it horrible for you?"

"Hell no. I deserved twice that many for the stunts I pulled and didn't get caught doin'."

"They're out there, Preacher," Windy called softly. "And workin' their way in."

"I'm scared, Preacher," Betina admitted. "I've been prattling on like a magpie because I am scared to death. I don't want to go through this again."

"It'll be all right," he assured her. "You get into the center barricade with the others and try to keep the kids calm. Go on, now."

The livestock had been pulled inside the huge circle and several wagons placed there for the children and for those women who would take care of them. Brush and logs had been hurriedly pulled in to fill in the large gaps between wagons. Betina ran for protection and Preacher took up a position by the rear wheel of a wagon. He had four pistols and two rifles, all freshly charged. He had shoved his war axe behind his sash.

132

The women had good reason to be afraid, for it was Ute custom to repeatedly rape all women they took captive. They might let them go afterward, but the women would have a rough time of it while in Ute hands.

Preacher also felt that the party he'd seen earlier was only part of a larger bunch. The Utes were a little north of the usual territory, so that meant they had declared war against another tribe. The wagon train was just an added pleasure for them, and a chance to take more scalps and women prisoners.

Preacher also felt that many of the bunch he'd seen were made up of the highly skilled warrior society of the Ute tribe. They were fierce fighters and did not give up easily.

Weller came up to Preacher's side, moving quietly in the early night. He carried a rifle and had two pistols behind his belt. "We came this far without experiencing a speck of trouble with the savages. Now we may well be fighting for our lives at the next blink of an eye."

"We sure will be doing that," Preacher agreed. "In about two, three more minutes. And these Utes are tough. Believe it. Now let me tell you the real bad news. You've led these people into what might be a death trap."

Weller opened his mouth to speak and Preacher cut him off and shut him up.

"Shut up and listen to me, Weller. It's about time you listened to somebody. You and your damn town in the promised land. That's crap, Weller. Puredee crap. We're in trouble, man. We're cut off. Alone. There will be no help comin' our way. None. Do you understand all that? Injuns are the most patient people on the face of the earth. Especially Utes. I know. A band of Utes kept me and four other men pinned down tight for days when we was furrin' south of here. We had ample powder and shot and just wore 'em down. But we was in the mountains, Weller. In good cover. Not stuck out here on the flats like we are now. We're gonna lose some men, Weller. Women and some kids, too, probably."

Weller stood silent for a moment, his gaze shifting from Preacher to the unknown that lay waiting in the darkness outside the ringed wagons. When he spoke, his voice was filled with resignation. "I was told that the trail west would soon move to the north—to the area we hoped to settle. I was assured of that move."

"Why should the trail move north?" Preacher softly questioned. "It's been used for years right where it's at. Further on, it's the only logical way through the Rockies."

"Mr. Sutherlin—"

"I knew it!" Preacher said hotly. "I knowed it had to be him. I was right. I'll tell you later. If we live through this night, that is." Weller again opened his mouth and Preacher shushed him. "Go on back to your post, Weller. They're about to rush us. Move, man."

Weller was learning, for he asked no questions. He vanished into the canvas-ringed circle of night, moving swiftly back to his post. Preacher turned all his attentions to the vast expanse of dark that lay before him.

The Utes would be very close now. They'd had several hours of darkness to creep close, sometimes moving no more than an inch or two at a time. Preacher was just glad they were not Apaches. They were the best at making the most out of every scrap of cover. Or no cover at all.

Preacher had briefly spoken with most of the men in the wagon train. None of them had much experience when it came to fighting, for most of them came from the cities and towns back East. There were a few who came from rural areas, and knew something about fighting. A couple had actual combat experience, having fought with Jackson in the War of 1812. But fightin' Injuns was a tad different from fightin' the British, who for the most part just stood all in a line and let you cut 'em down. And the U.S. Army wasn't much better. Dumbest damn way of fightin' Preacher had ever seen. Injuns was a whole lot smarter when it came to fighting. And Preacher and the other mountain men had quickly adapted to their ways of stealth and ambush.

Then Preacher saw a bush that hadn't been in that spot a couple of minutes back. He lifted his rifle to his shoulder and sighted in. The bush moved a few inches and Preacher put a ball right through it, about six inches off the ground. A scream ripped the night and the bush flew up into the air as a mortally wounded brave reared up on one knee, a hideous wound pouring blood from his neck. He fell forward and was still just as other Utes charged the wagons.

Preacher picked up his other rifle and let a ball fly. A brave doubled over like he'd been hit with a thrown anvil. He bounced on the ground and jerked in pain. Preacher jerked out a brace of pistols, both of them double-shotted, and let them bang. When the smoke cleared briefly, he'd put two more Utes on the cool, rocky ground.

All around him, the night was exploding in gunfire. There was no breeze at all, and the gun smoke was thick and smarting to the eyes. Preacher's immediate area was momentarily clear of all living things, and he took that time to recharge his weapons, looking up and around him every two or three seconds.

The men of the wagon train had broken the first

charge and the Utes seemed to just drop off the face of the earth. But Preacher knew better. He knew they were out there, and very close. One Ute tried to drag off a wounded brave and Preacher cut his spine with a ball.

"Sing out!" Preacher shouted.

"One mover over here took an arrow in the chest," Rimrock called. "He's dead."

"Got one wounded over here," Caleb called out. "He'll be all right."

"Everybody's all right over here," Windy called.

Preacher looked left and right of his position. "Anybody hurt along here?"

"No," a mover said. "Just scared."

"Stay that way," Preacher told him. "It'll help to keep you alive."

"What's next?" another one asked.

"Probably fire-arrows if they stay true to form. Charge up all your weapons. Everybody got a hatchet or axe close by like I told you? Good. We might be hand to hand 'fore this is all over. And brothers, them Utes is good at that. Don't play around with them. Just whack off anything in reach. Arm, hand, head, anything at all."

"I don't know that I can do that," a mover said.

"You want to have your hair jerked off and live long enough to see your wife and daughters raped?" Preacher tossed that at the man.

"No."

"Then you'll do it."

"Yonder comes the fire-arrows," Rimrock called. "Grab the buckets and stand ready."

Preacher squatted down by the rear wheel and waited. He knew from experience that a rush would follow the fire-arrows. The Utes—among other tribes—had quickly learned that movers would drop their guns and grab up buckets of water in an at-

136

tempt to save their possessions.

"Let the women handle the water buckets," Preacher called. "Every man stay with his gun."

Fire-arrows zipped through the air, shot from well-concealed positions. The canvas on one wagon burst into flames and the women began tossing buckets of water on the fire. They had it out in half a minute. The other fire-arrows fell to the ground and burned out harmlessly.

Then the Utes came silently out of the night, some of them mounted, others running on foot, waving war axes and holding decorated lances.

"Fire, goddamnit!" Preacher shouted. "Don't let them get inside the circle."

Preacher felt if they could contain this charge, the Utes would feel their medicine was bad and break it off to talk it over. But it was a big if.

A war-painted Ute reared up in front of him and Preacher shot the brave in the center of the forehead, the big ball almost taking the top of the Indian's head off. He smashed the butt of the rifle into the face of another and then jerked out his pistols and fired into a mass of brown bodies just outside the circle of wagons.

And still the Utes came.

A warrior jumped his horse inside the circle, leaped off, and landed right on top of Preacher, taking both of them hard to the ground. The brave lost his war axe and scrambled for it. Preacher and the Ute rolled around on the ground for a few seconds until Preacher smashed the buck's head in with the butt of an empty pistol and then leaped to his feet, grabbing for his last two charged pistols.

More canvas had been set ablaze and the wind had picked up, fanning the leaping flames that highlighted a frantic life-and-death struggle amid the circle of wagons on the plains. A woman was smashing a brave's bloody head in with what remained of a wooden bucket. Several movers were locked in hand-to-hand combat with Ute warriors. One woman lay on the ground, an arrow in her chest and a crying child on the ground beside her. Preacher observed all this in a split second as he worked to charge his pistols. A wild scream turned him around. A brave was running toward Weller, his axe raised to crush Weller's head. Preacher shot him and the brave stopped in his tracks and stumbled forward, landing on his face. Weller looked at Preacher and nodded his thanks.

Windy had grabbed up the lance of a fallen Ute and had driven it through another brave, pinning the writhing buck to the earth.

Then, like it began, it was over, silence falling around them as the Utes vanished into the night.

"Reload," Preacher called. "Right now, before you do anything else." He left his post and walked toward the area where the kids and a few women were located in the center of the circle. He smiled at Betina. Her face was sooted up some and her hair all mussed, but she managed a wan smile.

"Will they be back?" she asked.

Preacher nodded. "If they feel their medicine is right, they'll hit us just at dawn."

"If their medicine is bad?"

"They'll leave."

"I'll say a little prayer."

"Shore wouldn't hurt none. While you're askin', tell Him to send some help, will you?"

138

Thirteen

Preacher took charge of the defense of the train and began posting guards, telling those not on guard duty to get some rest. He told the women to have coffee and hot food available at all times, and to work in shifts, some cooking while the others rested.

"Them Utes know we're total cut off from any kind of relief," Caleb said in a low tone as the men squatted down in the darkness, cups of coffee in their hands. "So it's my thinkin' they might try to wait us out."

"They might," Preacher agreed. "But we got food and a ready supply of water behind the train. They's maybe two days' graze for the stock if we limit them, and then another two days of grain for them on short rations. You all and me, we know this battle ain't gone unnoticed. Other Injuns has seen the fire and smelled the smoke and all the dust. Some might come to investigate. And that could be good or bad, depending on the tribe."

"If it's Crow they'd hep us," Windy said. "And so would Weasel Tail's bunch. But if the Snake and the Crow both show up, they'll start fightin' each other."

"I don't know," Rimrock said. "They been right friendly to each other the past couple of years. I think they might have made peace."

"Did you talk to Weller about this here Sutherlin

person?" Caleb asked.

"Just done it. Shocked him down to his socks, it did. To be a religious sort of feller, he done some right smart cussin'. Sutherlin is the one who told these pilgrims to cut north from the trail. I told Weller to take pen to hand and to write down the whole story and seal 'er good and give it to me. Later on, I'll take me a trip east. Maybe even go as far as the Missouri. Find me a regular Army fort, like Leavenworth, and talk to the generals and colonels about Sutherlin."*

"Maybe we'll all go," Rimrock said, as Caleb and Windy nodded their heads in agreement. "I ain't been back in so many years I forgot what civilization looks like."

"Take a look at these pilgrims," Preacher said dryly. "That's what it looks like."

"Maybe I won't go," Rimrock said.

"Gone," Windy said, after slipping back into the circle of wagons. It was not yet dawn and the little man with more guts than most had been gone for over an hour. "They pulled out durin' the night. Headed south."

"We hurt 'em bad, all right," Caleb said. "I reckon we killed a good thirty of 'em. Probably wounded another fifteen or so real bad. Injuns ain't gonna stand for that. They're headin' for home."

Preacher went to Weller and was as uncommonly blunt with him as he had been the night before. "You understand that you were on a fool's mission headin' north, don't you?"

"Yes," the man admitted. "I do. But Preacher,

*Fort Leavenworth was established in 1827 as protection for the Santa Fe Trail. It was originally called Cantonment Leavenworth. It is the oldest U.S. fort west of the Mississippi still operating.

we've come too far to turn back now. I . . . ah . . . would you lead us up to the Oregon Territory?"

"No. No, I won't do that. But we'll see you back to the trail and you can either wait there for another train to come along or I'll take you back to the post and you can wait there. Talk to your people and see what they want to do."

"They will not turn back to the post, Preacher. I can assure you of that. We would lose too much time. We have to get across the mountains before the snows come."

"You sure got that right."

"A rider coming from the west," a lookout shouted. "And he's alone."

Rimrock squinted and smiled. "That's Carl Lippett. I recognize the horse. If he sees us he'll run thinkin' we're gonna give him another bath."

"Does this man know the trails?" Weller asked.

"As good as any man."

"Perhaps then he might be persuaded to lead us on westward," Weller said with a hopeful note in his voice.

"He might," Windy said. "He's just about crazy enough to take the job."

Preacher faced Weller. "Weller, take these people on back a ways. Take them to Missouri or Iowa Territory. Wait a few years and then come on out. It's too soon, Weller. It's just too soon for this."

But the man would not budge from his decision. "We shall press on westward."

Shaking his head and muttering, Preacher walked back to the wagons of Betina, Coretine, and the kids. Betina took one look at his face and said, "No, Preacher. We shall not go back." It was spoken softly but firmly.

"Nor shall I," Coretine said, standing by her side. "This savage land shall not defeat me. My husband had a dream, and I shall see it come to be."

141

"No point in my sayin' nothin', then." Preacher walked away without another word.

Carl Lippett agreed to guide the party on to the Pacific and the wagons were made ready for the trail. The train turned around and headed back toward what some had begun calling the Oregon Trail. Preacher and the other mountain men tagged along.

"Way I look at it," Carl said, as Preacher rode along with him at the head of the stretched out train, "either I take them on west or they go in alone. Least with me along they'll have a chance. They won't get lost. Preacher, you took a train acrost last year. I'd 'preciate anything you could tell me about it."

For the next two days, Preacher told the man everything he could remember about the way west to Oregon Territory—the way a train could get through. When he had exhausted his memory, Carl shook his head.

"Looks like I just might have a mighty big job on my hands," Lippett said.

There was nothing Preacher could add to that statement.

A few miles before they reached the trail, Preacher and his friends left the pioneers and rode away without saying a word to anybody. Farewells had been said and there was nothing more that anyone could add.

"I said it back at the post some weeks ago," Caleb said, breaking the silence after a few miles, "and I'll say it again. I got me a bad feelin' about that train."

"We done all we could do to talk them out of goin'," Windy replied. "I ain't gonna feel bad about it."

But he did. They all did. Grown up men like Miles Cason and George Martin going into the wilderness was one thing (George and Miles had been

142

persuaded to join the train and press westward toward the Pacific)—they were men and could make choices, whether they be right or wrong. A woman usually followed her man. But little kids had no say about it at all.

Of late, the mountain men had buried entirely too many people who sought a new land and new life. And it did weigh heavily on their minds.

When they made camp that evening, the men were not in their usual joking and kidding mood. They all sat silent and reflective around a slowly dying fire, chewing on rabbit meat and drinking coffee.

"Feels like I'm at a funeral," Rimrock finally said.

"The only funeral I'm lookin' forward to attendin' is the plantin' of the Pardees and Red Hand," Preacher said.

Caleb tossed a stick on the fire. "It ain't that we're so damn busy doin' other more important things."

"What are you talkin' about?" Preacher glanced up.

"I know," Windy said. "And that ain't the point, Caleb. Point is, they was *told* that goin' on was crazy." He tossed the dredges of his coffee into the brush behind him. "Aw, hell! Them movers don't have to know that we're even about."

"I ain't gonna be about," Preacher said, catching on.

"I ain't neither," Rimrock said. He poured another cup of the coffee. Black as sin and twice as hot.

"Speak for yourself," Windy told his friend.

"What say you, Preacher?" Rimrock asked. "You changed your mind about the movers?"

"No," Preacher told him. "If a big enough band hit the train, either stretched out or circled, four more guns won't make no difference."

That the four mountain men were able to stay together this long was nothing short of a miracle, for the mountain man was by nature a solitary creature, and few of them made lasting bonds with others of

143

their kind. Only a few, like Rimrock and Windy, ever rode together on a full-time basis, and even they split up from time to time.

But as their way of life came closer to an end, and it would end almost abruptly, some mountain men looked up others of their kind and in twos and threes they wandered the High Lonesome until their deaths, finally wandering onto the pages of history and into oblivion.

"I think come the mornin', I'll just ride back to that train and tag along," Caleb said. "Food's good."

"I'm with you," Windy said firmly, surprising his longtime partner, Rimrock.

Rimrock stared at his small friend for a moment and then smiled. "You never did have no sense, Windy. But I wish you well anyways. Me, I'm for ridin' up toward Canada." He stretched out on his robe. "I ain't been up there in a while. It's nice up there this time of year."

"How 'bout you, Preacher?" Caleb asked.

"I ain't made up my mind yet," he replied glumly. Which was a lie, but what he had in mind he wanted to do alone. "I reckon whichever way the wind is puffin' in the mornin', that's the way I'll go."

Since it was dead flat calm when the dawning broke, Preacher lingered long by the fire, drinking coffee and watching his friends ride off. There was little conversation. Caleb and Windy rode toward the wagon train, Rimrock headed north. Windy and Rimrock would probably hook up again, but out here, you just never did know. They'd gone their separate ways before, but never for very long at a time.

As Preacher sat alone by the quiet fire, in the silent camp in the wilderness, the thought entered his mind that with furrin' all but gone, he didn't have the faintest idea what he was going to do for a living. He didn't know anything but the Big Empty. Couldn't imagine living anywhere else. He sat by the fire until it had burned down to coals. He watched an eagle soar high above him and listened to the birds sing and the squirrels play and chatter. Then he smiled.

He knew how the Indians felt. He could understand it. All this magnificence was his and all this was theirs. Nobody liked to see a way of life come to an end. Preacher had read somewhere that all things change . . . or something like that. And that to fight against change was useless.

Maybe so, he thought with a sigh.

Right now, shut of his friends, Preacher could more easily take the fight to the Pardees. For this was the way he liked it — alone.

The wagon train prodded on westward and Preacher hunted for the Pardee gang in the high country. They'd had time to run back there after the Wind River ambush fell through. So they lived in caves. That was well and good, but they had to come out of those caves, and whenever they did, they would leave tracks. More than that, they had to have a trail to follow in and out. Or they made one when they decided to make the caves their hideout. If there was a trail, Preacher would find it. He hadn't yet seen a river he couldn't cross, a range he couldn't find a way through, or a horse he couldn't ride. Preacher would find the Pardees.

"Preacher just don't give up," Radborne Pardee told his older brother. "We been hearin' stories 'bout Preacher ever since we come into these damn mountains. I hate him. He shore messed up a good thing back yonder on the Wind."

Malachi Pardee shook his head and tried to dismiss the talk of Preacher with a wave of his hand. A very dirty hand. "Preacher's just a man, like us. All them stories is a bunch of bull. Just bull. He's like all these mountain men, a wanderer. Preacher is long gone and nowheres near here. So just forget him, boys."

Renegade scouts of Red Hand's bunch had reported the wagon train had moved on west after the Ute attack. The Pardees were restless and apprehensive. They had not seen civilization for a long time. And Malachi didn't know if Red Hand was going to join them for the attack against the wagon train. Red Hand was getting a little spooky about Preacher's medicine.

Radborne was not to be put off. "Brother, we have stretched our luck far . . . maybe too far. We've got gold aplenty from the raids and no place to spend it."

"Radborne's right," brother Henry said. "Somebody's got to be addin' all this up and gettin' close to figurin' out what's goin' on. Hit's just a matter of time 'fore Sutherlin gets caught up to. And when he do, he'll tell all he knows 'bout us to save his neck. And then where'll we be?"

Malachi gave each of his brothers a long, hard look. "How about you, Ansel? Where do you stand? Do you want to ride back 'crost the Missouri?"

Ansel shook his head. "No, I don't. But I do want to go somewheres where they's real white women and whiskey and people to talk to and civilization. I'm gettin' tarred of humpin' squaws."

Valiant Pardee stuck his penny's worth in. "We got gold enough from the wagons to head to Californy and open us up a tavern. We can get some whores a-workin' for us and fleece the travelers like we done back in Ohio."

"Keep talkin'," Malachi said. "I want everybody to get it all said."

Kenrick Pardee said, "Whilst I am tarred of livin' in caves like moles, I think we ought to play this string out. Three or four more raids and we'll have enough gold so's we won't ever have to work agin. Not never no more. Not that we ever worked much," he added.

"Boys," Malachi Pardee said, standing up and pacing the cave floor. The cave smelled like a skunk's den, for the Pardee boys were not big on personal hygiene. "Let me see if I can't get something through your heads. Now I want you all to hear me good. We can't ever go back 'crost the Missouri. Not now, not tomorrow, not never. The onliest thing that's waitin' for us back there is a hangman's noose. We're known from Ohio clear through to the Pacific. I ain't sayin' that someday we can't quit this business and settle down. But what I am sayin' is that this ain't no time to do it. And when we do pack it in, we can't be nowheres near no settled place for a long time. That won't work a-tall. And if I have to explain the why of what all I just said, then I got to figure I got a bunch of igits for brothers."

The Pardee boys all looked at the floor of the cave and said nothing in rebuttal. Malachi walked out into the sunlight and let his younger brothers stew for a time. Tell the truth, Preacher did worry him just a bit.

Tell the truth, although Malachi would never admit it to anybody, especially his brothers, Preacher worried him a whole hell of a lot.

Malachi kicked at a rotten branch, sending bits and pieces of it flying. "Preacher," he muttered under his breath. "What a goddamn stupid name. He's about as much a preacher as I is."

What Preacher was, and Malachi was well aware of it, was a tough, mean, and dangerous fighter and a bad man to have on your trail. Twice he and Preacher had locked horns, and both times Preacher had stomped the snot out of him. Malachi had swore on his poor old mother's memory (even though she had been a mean old bitch and Malachi had hated

147

her guts) that he would someday kill Preacher.

"Be a fine day when that happens," Malachi muttered darkly. He squatted down and proceeded to think things out. And of all the brothers, he had to be the one to do that. That weighed heavy on his mind at times.

Malachi was no mental giant, but compared to most of his brothers, he was a genius. Malachi could read and write and figure some, as could Kenrick. The rest of the Pardee clan were all dumb as dirt. If Malachi wasn't around to look after them, he just couldn't imagine what would happen to the ninnies. Especially Ansel. Ansel was just plain stupid.

But his brothers had their good points. They would kill without hesitation on his orders . . . matter of fact, they liked to kill mayhaps a tad too much. And brutalize women! Lord, but them boys loved to put the hurt on a woman. They wasn't much left of a woman when his brothers got done with her. And they could torture a man in ways the Injuns hadn't even thought of. Malachi loved to watch them at work. But Malachi didn't fret too much about his brothers.

Basically, they were real good boys.

FOURTEEN

"Gotcha!" Preacher whispered, his eyes hardening and his smile becoming more like a wolf's snarl.

He had found a track. Just one. But that was enough. He pressed on, on foot, leading Hammer. He found where a branch had been broken. Another spot where a horse had dumped a load and the rider had been unaware of it. Preacher stopped and looked up. He had been on the trail for days before picking up the first hopeful sign.

The mountains loomed up majestic before him. The air was fresh and cool and scented. He was home. The mountains comforted him, and always pulled him back. And he knew them intimately. The Pardees had made a bad mistake if they were up there, and Preacher believed they were.

"Now, you child-killin', baby-rapin', torturin' no-count bastards. Now I'm gonna give you all some mountain justice and rid the world of you."

He searched carefully until he found a tiny valley nestled behind an almost impenetrable wall of brush. He was delighted to find the valley was lush with grass, belly-high to Hammer, with a deep pool of spring-fed water. Preacher stripped the saddle from Hammer and the rig from his packhorse and let the animals roll while he inspected the mountain meadow. There was another way out, and he blocked that carefully with transplanted bushes, watering them so they would live. He worked slowly and carefully, for he had time. He now knew the trail the Pardees and their ilk used from their caves high up, when they went on their murderous raids. As long as the lush grass and the water was plentiful, and it was, his horses would not attempt to leave the peaceful little valley. So Preacher had plenty of time to hunt the Pardees.

When he was satisfied his horses would be safe when he left, Preacher chanced a small fire under an overhang and boiled coffee and chewed on jerky. He had not seen one sign of Indians, and neither had he found any signs that this particular valley had ever been entered by humans, red or white. In his prowlings, he had not found a single trace of the ashes of old fires. Preacher had him a feeling that he was the first white man—maybe the first human—to ever enter this tiny bit of pristine wilderness. And that left him with a good feeling.

And that feeling stirred emotions within him that he had not experienced in years. The feelings he had had years back, when he stood on a ridge overlooking a wild and roaring river, or a lovely undisturbed valley, or a stretch of grass that looked so large and so long it seemed to be one with the sky.

"A little piece of what it used to be like," Preacher muttered, a little bit of sadness in his voice. He dumped the coffee into the boiling water, and then took the pot off the fire and tossed in some cold water to help the grounds settle.

Actually, it was still pretty much the way it was when Preacher and the other mountain men had arrived, years back. But they were feeling the first tentative push of pioneers westward. Only a ripple for now, but soon it would turn into a huge, roaring wave of humanity sweeping over the land. Preacher and the others hadn't seen a thing yet.

His fire out, Preacher slept soundly and dreamlessly

that night, his horses picketed nearby. Anything alien or out of place with nature moved in the valley during the night, they would wake him in an instant. Hammer was as good as any trained dog.

Up before the skies turned silver, Preacher carefully packed a few things in his blanket and groundsheet and rolled it, securing it with rawhide strings and slinging it across his back. He checked his pistols. The bright sash was gone, replaced by a wide sturdy strip of deerskin that tied securely. The pistols went behind that. His horn was filled with powder and he had plenty of shot. His bow was good and his quiver filled with arrows. His big knife was honed to a fine edge. He was ready to go hunting.

He was going to do his best to put the Pardee brothers out of business.

"Don't you get too fat now, Hammer," Preacher told his horse. "I'll see you in about a week, or less, the Good Lord willin'." He picked up his rifle and headed out of the lovely little valley in the mountains.

He had enough pemmican and jerky in his parfleche to last him a good long time, and he planned to once and for all rid the wilderness of the Pardee trash and anyone stupid enough to ride with their wicked way. Also any renegade Injuns he might chance upon.

Which was what he spotted not an hour after leaving the valley. Preacher recognized him as a Comanche, and this Comanche was a long way from home. He had evidently broken some hard-and-fast tribal rule and gotten himself booted out. And here he was, big as life. Which was going to end, very quickly.

The Comanche must have thought himself safe in these mountains, for he was not exercising much caution as he rode the country. Had him a fine lookin' horse, too. Preacher immediately coveted that animal.

"Might as well take him," Preacher muttered low, and climbed a tree to the lower limb that dangled over the nearly invisible trail.

When the renegade drew near, Preacher dropped and kicked the buck in the head on the way down. Addled, the renegade staggered to his moccasins just in time to receive Preacher's big blade in his belly, the cutting edge up. Preacher finished the Comanche and let him fall.

Looking around, he noted with disgust the scalps tied to the horse's mane. One of them was from a woman's head. Blond hair. He calmed the spooky horse and untied the scalps, throwing them into the brush. Then he stuffed the body of the Indian up into a hollow log. He'd let a bear work for his supper.

Preacher led the big horse off the trail and back to his little valley. Hammer snorted a few times and let the new addition know who was boss real quick. When they got all that settled, all three of them went to grazing.

The horse the Comanche rode to his death was an Appaloosa, and a big one for that breed. The renegade had either made or stolen, probably the latter, a buckskin pad saddle, stuffed with buffalo hair and grass. Preacher had read some accounts of the wilderness — written by eastern writers — which stated that Indians never used saddles. That was pure bunk. It all depended on the Indian. Many Injun women used a high-backed Spanish-style saddle made of wood, and they rode astride like a man. Lots of Injun men used saddles of all types and styles and descriptions for long journeys and for ceremonies.

Preacher again took his Hawken in hand and moved out of the valley, exiting this time using a different route. He walked for several miles, and just as he reached a point a few hundred yards below the timberline, he smelled smoke.

He squatted down and inhaled deeply. Somebody was broilin' venison steaks and boilin' coffee. Made Preacher's mouth start salivatin', and it made him mad. Here he was trying to do the right thing and just get along with them that would let him, and these murderin', thievin' bums was eatin' high off the hog. Or the deer, as it were. Well, by God, he'd put a stop to that, and do it right now.

Preacher followed the scent trail with his nose and almost stumbled right into the camp. It was very well concealed. If he had taken two more steps, he would have gone over the edge of a ravine, and before he'd stopped rolling, he'd have been shot to pieces by them below.

"Hurry up with that there meat," a bearded, burly lout of a man said, irritation in his voice. "I got myself a bad case of the hongries."

"Peacify yourself, Reed," the man at the fire said. "I can't git this far no hotter and I shore can't cook the meat no faster than I is."

Reed stood for a moment with a frown on his face. He licked his thick lips. "I just don't like you a-tall, Franklin," he said. "I never have. You're a smart-aleck son of a bitch. If you couldn't cook, I'd have shot you a long time ago."

Franklin cut his eyes. "You want this here steak rolled in dirt, Reed? 'Cause you say one more word to me and that's how you gonna get it."

Reed said something that Preacher couldn't catch and Franklin stood up from the fire.

"That's enough!" the third man said sharply. "We got enough troubles without fightin' amongst ourselves. Reed, you said something about takin' a crap. Go do it and then go tell Asa to come in and eat. You relieve him at guard. Now move!"

Preacher noted the direction that Reed was taking and Injuned his way over. He had already spotted Asa the guard.

Just as Reed was dropping his trousers and preparing to hang his butt over a log, Preacher sliced his throat wide open and held him by the hair, lowering silently to the ground. He stuffed the man's pistols behind his belt and then quickly scalped the man, cutting around the hair and jerking it loose. Preacher left the man and moved around to the guard. He notched an arrow and put one straight into Asa's spine. The man dropped as soundlessly as a child's rag doll and Preacher very quickly dragged him into the bushes and scalped him. He was getting loaded down with pistols, but no Indian would leave such fine weapons, so he took them.

"Goddamnit, Reed!" the shouted words came to him. "Will you hurry up with your crappin'? What's the matter with you?"

No reply. Naturally. If there had of been one, Preacher just might have decided it was time to take flight and get shut of these mountains.

"Asa!" the man called to the guard. There was a note of worry in his voice. "Where is you, boy?"

Preacher waited, another arrow notched and ready to fly.

"Something's wrong," the man said.

"Naw," Franklin said, not looking up from his broiling meat. "Reed's just a troublemaker and Asa's probably asleep, that's all. Nothin' to worry about, Simpson."

But Simpson wasn't buying that and Preacher could both see it and sense it. Simpson had a deep streak of suspicion in him. The man stood for a moment, listening, then picked up his rifle and stepped away from the fire.

"I'm goin' out to take a look for myself," Simpson said. "You 'member that Malachi said Preacher would probably be comin' after us."

"Oh, hell, Simpson!" Franklin said. "Preacher ain't nowheres nearer than five hundred miles. Y'all gettin' mighty spooky over nothin', say I."

"Just cook the damn meat," Simpson said. He began walking toward Preacher's location.

I'm gonna have to be quick and true if I pull this off,

Preacher thought. It was far too early in the game to risk a shot, and he wanted this camp's attack to be blamed on the Indians. He hauled back the bow string and let the arrow fly. He was notching another arrow before the man called Simpson took the first arrow in the center of his chest. He grunted and dropped to his knees just as Preacher stepped out of the thin brush and let another arrow fly toward Franklin.

It was a clean miss.

"What the hell!" Franklin yelled, jumping to his feet and leaping for his rifle, which was leaning up against a boulder across the clearing.

Preacher won the wild race by a second, leaping on the man's back just as his hand closed around his rifle.

Preacher rode the man down to the ground, pounding at his face with big hard fists. Franklin twisted and threw Preacher off his back. Preacher rolled and came up, his knife in his hand.

"Bastard!" Franklin panted, blood from a busted nose streaming down his chin. He reached for his own blade.

Preacher jumped at the man and kicked out, his foot catching the man on the knee and putting him down with a yelp of pain into a dusty heap. Franklin rolled and came to his boots, slashing out with his knife. Preacher sidestepped and cut the man's arm to the bone. Franklin screamed in pain and dropped the knife. He turned to run for the sparse timber and Preacher reversed the knife and let it fly, the big blade sinking into the man's back. The blade had centered Franklin's back, severing the spinal cord. Franklin went to the ground in an uncoordinated heap, falling almost soundlessly.

Preacher pulled out his knife and knelt down, quickly scalping the outlaw. He went back to where Simpson lay, the ground all around him wet with blood, and took his hair. It was not something Preacher enjoyed doing, but to pull this off, laying the blame on the Injuns, it had to be.

It didn't damper his appetite, however.

After he had finished his gruesome work, Preacher carefully hid the spare weapons and then returned to the fire, leaving the bodies where they lay. He washed out a cup and drank the coffee, then slowly ate the meat, savoring each bite and ignoring the dead men.

After he had eaten his fill and polished off the pot of strong coffee, Preacher turned the men's horses loose and then set about disguising his tracks to make it look like several Indians had attacked the camp. What he was doing would not fool anyone who had enough sense to sit down, think it out, and then carefully examine the signs. But Preacher was hoping no one among the Pardee gang would do that.

He left a piece of venison broiling over the fire so it would be burned to a crisp, only adding to the scene he hoped would convince the others of the suddenness of the attack. He knew he should mutilate the bodies and he tried to steel himself to do that, but he just couldn't bring himself to do it. It had been bad enough scalping the men.

When he was satisfied he had done all he could, Preacher stood for a moment, inspecting the surroundings. He had played hell here for a fact. Finally, he nodded his head and slipped away from the camp of the dead. It would not take the carrion birds long to find the bodies and it would not be long before the Pardee brothers or some of their followers took notice of the slowly circling flesh eaters and come to investigate.

He stopped at the edge of the camp and looked back. "Oh, to hell with it," he said. "That ain't gonna fool no one." He returned to the camp, found a piece of paper and the stub of a pencil, and wrote out a short note, smiling as he did so. It took him awhile 'cause it had been a long time since he had written any words.

He left the note stuck on the end of a branch and

then melted back into the Lonesome. He figured it was gonna get right interestin' when the Pardees discovered the camp and the note. He was hoping they'd follow him. That was why he was leaving a trail even a pilgrim could follow. A mile from the camp of the dead, Preacher paused long enough to carefully construct a booby trap. He smiled grimly as he worked. Somebody was going to be in a work of hurt when they hit this one.

He backed off and waited. All in all, he thought, it was starting out to be a right nice day.

FIFTEEN

"They never had a chance," Radborne Pardee said, after he and his brothers ran off the bloated carrion birds. The birds didn't go far from their snack. They waited and watched patiently. "Injuns snuck up on 'em and finished 'em."

No one had yet discovered the note. Very observant bunch of outlaws.

Malachi wasn't at all sure it had been Indians. He stood in the middle of the carnage and looked slowly all about him. "Something is wrong with this," he finally said. "I don't think this was done by Injuns."

"How come you to say that, Malachi?" his brother Henry asked, a stupid look on his stupid face. "What else could it have been? Them's arrows, ain't they?"

"I know they're arrows, Henry," Malachi said. "I can see that. But something's mighty wrong here. Mighty wrong. It's just . . . I can't put my finger on it."

"I'll say this," Kenrick Pardee said, looking at the trail. "Them Injuns, if it was Injuns, was either drunk or it's a setup. A blind man could follow this trail."

Malachi nodded his head in agreement, thinking that he was very grateful to have at least one brother with sense enough to come in out of the rain.

"What is all this scribblin' on this here paper?" Radborne said.

Malachi took the note from the branch and slowly

read the words. He and Kenrick were the only ones in the clan who could read. His mouth dropped open and his face darkened with rage. He started cussing and balled up the note and threw it to the ground, then jumped up and down on it. It had been unsigned, but he knew who wrote it.

"Nobody calls me a stupid son of a bitch!" he yelled. "Goddamn that Preacher."

"Preacher!" Kenrick said.

"Yeah. Preacher. He writ that note. I know it was him."

"Then let's don't take no chances, Malachi," Kenrick said. "Let's call in the whole bunch and take off after him. We try to go this alone and he'll pick us off one by one."

Malachi nodded his head. "All right. Put out the call, brother. Sound it long. We've got to get him. Before he gets us," he added grimly.

Preacher heard the mournful sounds of the hunting horn as it sounded around the high country. Malachi was calling his bunch together to come after him. He settled down for a wait.

"Come on, Malachi," he said. "I made the trail easy for you. But you'll have to look close to see this surprise I got rigged up down yonder."

Preacher had left the wider animal trail and worked his way into a stand of timber. Those following him would have to leave their horses and continue their tracking on foot, for Preacher didn't want to hurt anyone's good horse unless it just come hard to that. A horse couldn't help it if the man who rode it was a sorry son of a bitch. Preacher did know that most highwaymen took better care of their horses than they did themselves, for the outlaw's life often depended upon the speed and the stamina of the horse he rode.

Preacher waited behind the jumble of rocks and thin

brush. From his vantage point, he had a wide view of the area just below him, a fairly thick stand of timber, and there was only one way the Pardee gang could come at him—straight ahead.

Down the trail, Malachi Pardee had halted the gang and they had gathered. They moved out slowly, in single file, for the trail was narrow and rocky, with bad footing. Now they had halted. Ned Blum had volunteered to take the point, as Malachi had suspected he would. Ned hated Preacher, and his hatred spanned a dozen years. Ned had braced Preacher once and Preacher had tossed down the glove and then proceeded to stomp the bejesus out of the outlaw from Delaware, publicly humiliating him in front of a dozen men. Ned had sworn to kill Preacher.

"I don't need no help to take Preacher," Ned boasted to Malachi and the others. "Y'all just stay back here and let me handle this."

"You go right ahead, Ned," Malachi said, thinking: Maybe you'll really get lucky and get a ball in him.

Rifle in hand, Ned moved out, working his way carefully into the stand of timber, moving ever closer to the spike trap Preacher had laid out for anyone stupid enough to follow his trail. Ned was cautious, and he had good reason to be, for everyone in the wilderness knew that if Preacher was anything, he was a very dangerous man. But Ned figured he could take him now that Preacher didn't have his buddies around him. Not that his buddies had anything to do with Preacher whipping him that time, but Ned had convinced himself through self-lies that they had.

Ned dried his sweaty palms on his britches and once more gripped his rifle. He paused for a moment, looking around him. He could see nothing out of the ordinary. Damn that Preacher, he thought. He's a-layin' up yonder somewhere's like a stinkin' Injun. He's been out here in the Lonesome so long he ain't even a white man no more. He thinks like a damn Injun.

160

Ned moved on and up. After a few steps, he sensed something was wrong and paused, looking all around him. Something was wrong, but he didn't know what. He let his eyes linger on the trees, the brush, the rocks, the faint trail that Preacher had left. He looked behind him. The boys was clean out of sight. He took one more step, then another. He began to feel better. Maybe he'd been wrong. Maybe all them feelin's of gloom and doom was wrong. After all, Preacher was just a man, not no superbein'.

He took another step and felt the earth give beneath his foot. He tried to jerk back but it was too late. Ned screamed as the sharpened stakes tore through his foot and ripped into the flesh of his ankle and calf. He dropped his rifle as the pain became so intense he almost lost consciousness. He began screaming, over and over, the hoarse howlings echoing around the high country.

"I reckon Ned wasn't as good as he thought he was," Malachi remarked matter-of-factly, listening to the screaming.

"What you reckon Preacher done to him?" a thug called Van asked. He looked furtively all around him. That screaming was really unnerving.

"Why don't you go find out?" Malachi said, looking at the scared outlaw.

"Me?"

"I ain't talkin' to no damn tree, Van. Yeah, you. So move on out."

All the others looked at him as Van licked suddenly dry lips and hesitated for a few seconds. The wild screaming was now more animallike in nature. All of them were thinking that there was no damn telling what Preacher had done to Ned.

"Back him up, Dexter," Malachi ordered.

That made Van feel some better. Dexter was a good man and pure hell with a pistol, and in that stand of timber up yonder, a pistol was what a man was going to have to use. Van moved out, Dexter staying about twenty-five feet behind him.

As they slowly and cautiously closed the distance, both of them expecting a ball through the chest at any second, Dexter asked, "Van, what you reckon we've gone and done that's made Preacher so mad at us?"

"I don't know. I ain't never done him a hurt, that's for sure. Let's get Ned out of this mess first and then we'll tackle Preacher." They stepped into the timber. "Jesus, it's close in here. Watch yourself."

"Oh, may God help me!" Ned wailed. "My foot and leg is all tore up bad."

"Hang on, Ned!" Dexter called. "We're comin' in to hep you. Just hang on."

"Yeah," Preacher muttered, Dexter's words just audible to him. "Come on, boys. I got some surprises waitin' for the two of you, too."

Van was the first to reach the injured man and he almost got sick when he saw what Ned had gotten into. Preacher had dug a pit and rigged up sharpened stakes, with about half of the stake points up, the other half of the points down. Those pointed up had torn into Ned's foot, calf, and ankle. When Ned had tried to jerk his foot free, those stakes pointing down had ripped into flesh and trapped him.

"Good Lord," Dexter said. "Keep watch, Van. I got to somehow pull these stakes out. Damn a man who would do something like this. Christ, they's blood all over the place. I can't get no good purchase on nothin'."

Preacher had worked several hours in the building of his traps, and when Preacher wanted to be low down mean, he could be one mean son, for a fact.

Dex stepped back a foot or so and his boot hit a vine stretched tight. He had time to look up and open his mouth to holler before the heavy log fell on him. The log crushed his skull and broke his back and neck. But Dexter didn't mind. He was dead before he hit the ground. He would rape and rob and torture and murder no more.

Van had jumped back at Dexter's shout; now he looked at the mess, horror in his eyes. Ned had passed out, and that was a good thing for Ned, for one end of the heavy log had landed on his shoulder and bounced off. In addition to his other woes, Ned now had a broken shoulder and broken arm.

Van gingerly stepped back from the dead and badly injured and his boot slipped under and triggered another stretched-tight vine. A green and thick and limber limb lashed out and slammed into Van's face, breaking his nose and knocking out a couple of teeth and loosening a few more. Van screamed in pain and fright, struggled to his feet, and went staggering back down the trail, almost blind from the involuntary tears that were streaming from his eyes as a result of the busted beak.

"What the billy-hell . . . ?" Malachi said, hearing all the commotion and then seeing Van come lurching and staggering out of the timber.

A rifle slammed and Van went down bonelessly and limp, a hole about the size of a teacup in his back. Malachi and the others hit the ground and went scrambling on all fours for cover.

"Anybody see the smoke?" Kenrick called from his cover behind a skinny tree.

"No," a ne'er-do-well called Hall said. "But it's got to be comin' from up yonder in them rocks above the trees. Hell, that's a good three, four hundred yards."

"Preacher can shoot," Malachi said grudgingly. "This ain't no good, boys. We got to pull back from here."

"What about Dex and Ned?"

"You ain't heard no more sounds from up yonder, have you?"

"Well . . . no."

"They're dead. Come on. Let's pull back and get gone. We got to plan some."

163

They left Van where he lay and slipped back, far back, well out of rifle range. They went so far back they were out of cannon range.

Preacher watched them leave and left his rocks and drifted down to where Ned lay trapped in the stake pit. He ignored the battered and broken body of Dexter and squatted down beside the unconscious Ned. While Ned was out, Preacher freed his legs and hauled him out of the hole, stretching him out on the ground. He could plainly see that the man's arm and shoulder were busted. He poured a little water from his canteen on the man's face and Ned moaned and opened his eyes. They were bright with the pain that rippled through his body.

"Your pals pulled out and left you," Preacher told him. "Mayhaps you should start thinkin' about associatin' with a better class of people."

"I'm dyin', ain't I?"

"You ain't in the best shape I ever seen a man to be," Preacher acknowledged. "But I reckon if I was a mind to, I could fix up some poultices and such for your legs and set that shoulder and arm."

"For the love of God, man—"

"Don't you be talkin' 'bout God to me, you trashy bastard. Anybody that would ride with the Pardees don't need to be mentionin' God."

"You a mighty cold man, Preacher."

"No, I ain't. I just don't like the Pardees nor anyone who consorts with them." He picked up his rifle. "I best be movin' on."

"Wait! Are you just going to leave me here?"

"I could shoot you, I reckon. I'd do that for a horse," Preacher said straight-faced.

"My God, man, but you a devil!"

"Well . . . you could make it easier for yourself by talkin' to me," Preacher suggested.

"About what?"

"Malachi Pardee and his plans."

"I don't know nothin' about no plans," Ned said, a sly look creeping into his eyes.

Preacher started to walk away.

"Wait!" Ned called weakly. "Don't leave me like this. I don't know much but I'll tell you what I do know."

Preacher squatted down beside the man. Ned wasn't going to die — providing gangrene didn't set in — but he would never be one hundred percent again. His shoulder was crushed and his arm broken in several places. If his legs weren't treated fast, both of them would rot off. Preacher told him that.

"You're gonna hep me, aren't you?" Ned begged.

"Depends on what you tell me."

Ned laid his head on the ground. "All right," he whispered. "All right. I ain't never in my life seen a man as hard as you, Preacher. Never."

Preacher fixed poultices for the man's badly injured legs — but the plants really needed weren't growing this high up. Then he set Ned's arm and shoulder as best he could. Ned passed out from the pain and Preacher left him like that. There was nothing else he could do for him. Ned hadn't known much, but what he did know was a help.

Only a few of Red Hand's renegades had stayed with the Pardee gang. The renegade leader had taken most of his followers and left out. Ned seemed to think they had gone east, believing that would provide them with easier pickings. Ned had the impression that Malachi Pardee was even too gamy for Red Hand.

Preacher doubted that. Red Hand was as cruel a man as Preacher had ever seen. He probably just wanted to get shut of the crazy Pardee brothers. Preacher knew them all, and with the exception of Malachi and Kenrick, the rest of them were as nutty as a pecan tree. Ansel was by far the bloodthirstiest. He was killing crazy.

As for Ned, he would die if his friends in the gang didn't take care of him real soon. And Preacher doubted any of them would take the time or expel the effort to do so. More than likely, Malachi or one of his goofy brothers would give Ned a ball right between the eyes. As bad hurt as Ned was, that might be a blessing. Or they might just leave him to die. This was no country to be bad hurt in. There was a doctor back at the post, but that was days away, and riding would be agony for the hurt outlaw. Preacher didn't have any sympathy for the highwayman. Ned had voluntarily chosen his vocation. No one had held a gun to his head and forced him to become an outlaw. There were some—mostly back in the settled East—who were starting to say that outlaws and the like should be pitied. Preacher thought that was some of the biggest crap he'd ever heard of. He couldn't imagine why anyone would think that. But he knew there were people in the world who always placed the blame elsewhere, never looking square at the problem, always looking for an excuse for bad behavior. Preacher didn't have any use for people like that.

Preacher moved on, staying just below the timberline and leaving a clear trail for those behind him to follow. As long as they wanted to play Preacher's game, he'd lay down the rules. And they'd be mighty damn savage ones. At least this way he was keeping Malachi and his crummy bunch away from what few settlers there were and the wagon trains that were beginning to prod slowly westward.

Preacher would have scoffed at any suggestion that what he was doing was noble. He would have had a good laugh at that. That thought had never entered his mind. He did know that what he was doing would be considered no more than murder by some folks back East. But folks who stay settled and safe in populated areas like cities tend to lose sight of matters. Preacher knew that for a fact. He didn't understand it, but knew it to be true.

The truth was, Preacher just didn't like Malachi Pardee nor anyone else who thought and behaved as Malachi and his followers did. No man had the right to take from another. It was just as simple as that. A man had a right to take gun in hand to protect what was his. Whether it be wife and family, hearth and home, or a man's horse or dog. A body had a right to use force to keep what was his. Preacher had heard that a lot of folks back East, them particular in the cities, had stopped totin' pistols and was leaving all the duties to the police and the constables. As far as Preacher was concerned, that was plumb stupid. If something like that kept on, soon they'd be laws forbiddin' a man to tote a pistol and protect himself.

Preacher shook his head and dismissed that thought. That was too ridiculous to even consider. That would never happen in America.

SIXTEEN

Malachi Pardee sat before the fire, a cup of coffee in his dirty hands. His thoughts were just as dirty as his body, and that was filthy. Malachi was between a rock and a hard place, and he knew it only too well.

That wagon train with the good lookin' women and the prime young girls in it was getting further and further away, and there was no telling when another one would form up and pass through. It was getting late in the summer and few would chance the crossing this close to snowfall. But Malachi knew he could not take his gang and leave the mountains after the train. Not with Preacher up here. Preacher would just swing in behind them and pick them off one at a time. No, Preacher had to be dealt with here and now and left dead in the Big Empty. That was all there was to it. The goddamn worthless, shiftless mountain man had been a thorn in Malachi's side for too many years. Just the thought made him angry. Who in the hell did Preacher think he was, anyways?

Brother Henry looked at his big brother from across the fire where supper was cooking. "Is we gonna have Preacher a-doggin' us forever, Malachi?"

"Yes, if we don't come up with a good plan to get shut of him," Malachi replied sourly. "Cut me off a hunk of that there meat, Henry. Hit's got me salivatin' something fierce."

Henry whacked off a hunk of hot, half-raw meat, and Malachi fell to gnawing. Thank the Lord they all was blessed with good strong teeth, he was fond of saying.

With blood and juices running down his chin, Malachi said, "I just can't figure why Preacher hates us all so. Lord have mercy knows we ain't never done a harm to him. We's just tryin' to make a livin', that's all. If folks that have would just share with us, we wouldn't have to do what we's doin'. T'ain't right, for a fact. The government ought to provide for poor folks like us."

Preacher knew that he'd made Malachi and his greasy bunch very nervous and very cautious, so they would be watching the ground for trip ropes from here on in. So he changed his tactics. Knowing that lazy, shiftless people rarely looked up, Preacher concentrated his efforts on up instead of down.

Preacher occasionally chuckled as he worked swiftly but carefully removing and relocating rocks of various sizes, placing them on the lip of a gently sloping ledge. The ledge was above a long and deep grade of very loose rocks, a slide area, some of the rocks huge boulders. Just above the newly piled rocks were several boulders that Preacher had tested and found he could dislodge by bracing himself and shoving with his feet. When they hit the newly placed rocks, a monumental slide was going to occur. And anyone caught on the trail below was going to be in real serious trouble.

Preacher climbed down carefully and moved some rocks and logs, partly blocking the trail he had used to get up above the timberline. He disguised his work and then made his way back up. The Pardee gang would be forced to leave their horses and follow his false trail on foot.

His work done, Preacher then deliberately built a fire and cooked some deer meat and boiled some water

for coffee. He figured the Pardees would come rompin'
and stompin' in the morning, hell bent on killing him.
Well, they could damn well try it.

"Look, Malachi!" Valiant hollered, pointing to the
thin line of smoke in the distance. "That's got to be
Preacher."

"Goadin' us," Malachi said, after doing some pretty
fancy cussing. "That damn Preacher. He's a-funnin'
with us and a-woolin' us. Laughin' at us whilst he
makes fun of us. Makin' fools out of us. Well, I ain't a-
gonna stand still for no more of this. I've had all this I
can take, boys. Tomorrow we're gonna do the bastard
in for good."

Ansel Pardee did a little dance and slobbered down
his chin. Ansel wasn't good for much, but he was a real
good slobberer. "We gonna peel the hide offen him,
ain't we, Malachi? So's we can listen to him holler.
Cook his bare feet in a far and gouge out his eyes, ain't
we?" Ansel was really a swell fellow. Lots of fun to be
around.

"Wipe your mouth and chin, boy," his big brother
told him. "Yeah. We can do that, I reckon. If we take
him alive. That might be fun."

The Pardees could be quite inventive when it came
to torture and the general abuse of prisoners. Ansel
was so happy he did a little jig right there in the camp.
Ansel was at his best hurting people. Especially
women and kids. But someone like Preacher would be
just as much fun . . . almost, he reckoned. Ansel
danced around the camp, flapping his arms and hum-
ming.

"Mamma was too long in the tooth when she
whelped Ansel and Radborne," Kenrick remarked to
Malachi, both of them watching their baby brother
prance around.

"Well, hell," Malachi replied. "Henry ain't but two

170

year behind me and his bread ain't baked right neither."

"For a fact. But I always suspicioned that Uncle Dunbar slipped over the woodpile one night when Pa was gone and lifted up mamma's gown."

"There was that talk as I recollect. You know, Kenrick, to turn out as well and fine as we did, we shore did come from mighty poor stock."

"I will agree with both them things, brother."

"Shhhiiittt!" Valiant said, looking at the narrow and rocky trail that lay beyond the boulders blocking their way. "Don't tell me we got to *walk* again?"

Malachi did look up, suspecting a trap, but nothing seemed out of the ordinary. The birds and squirrels had grown accustomed to Preacher and were going about their business as usual. Still, he didn't like it.

High above them, Preacher was in place and braced. When the rocks started going, half of that grade of loose rocks would break free under the rolling and bouncing impact. Some of those below would have time to get clear, maybe. And some wouldn't. And every one that went down was one less Preacher had to worry about. Not that he was very worried about any of that damn trash down below him.

Malachi looked back at his men. "George," he called. "Go check it out. Go all the way across and see if his trail is over yonder on the other side and see how far it goes for a ways."

George didn't want to make himself a target, but he went, expecting to feel the rip of a bullet in his guts or in his back with every step he took. But he went. When he reached the other side, he paused to wipe the sweat from his face and from the inside of his hat, even though this high up it was cool. He found Preacher's false trail easily enough and shouted that news across the several hundred yards' distance that separated him from the bunch.

"He's headin' this way for a fact, Malachi. I can see where he rested ag'in' this here boulder for a time, catchin' his breath, I reckon."

Malachi had him a bad feeling about the passage that stretched out in front of him. A real bad feeling. But if they didn't make this crossing here, they would have to ride a dozen miles around the mountains and then be faced with a hard climb back up. As it stood now, he was going to have to send men the long way around with the horses.

Hell, Malachi, he told his mind. Give it up and leave. Look to another part of the country. Head for the Oregon Territory and be a road agent there. Preacher will never leave these mountains and you wouldn't have him to put up with.

But Malachi knew he wouldn't do that. Now it was down to a matter of pride.

But pride can get you killed, he reminded himself.

Got to be this way, another part of him said. Can't have the talk a-goin' around that Malachi Pardee backed down from the likes of Preacher.

"Start crossin'." Malachi gave the orders. "You, Coyote Man, take the lead. Harold, you and Slim follow after him. Cotter, you and Shockly go after them. Move out."

"I will go after that," Little Wolf said. "Kills the Enemy will follow me."

"I will go after that," Big Eagle announced. "I am not afraid of a rocky trail."

"All right," Malachi said.

Miles back, Ned lay unconscious and dying in the deserted camp of the Pardee gang. They had left him to go it alone with no more thought than they would have given a dying snake. Probably less, for one of them would have surely killed the snake.

From where he lay, braced and ready, hidden from the eyes of those below, Preacher could not make out individuals as they began their crossing. But he could count seven or eight of them all bunched up on the safe side. No one, it seemed, wanted to be the one to take that first step.

Not that Preacher blamed any of them for hesitating. But he knew *he* wouldn't have been dumb enough to fall for such an obvious trap.

Pride's got Malachi now, Preacher thought. Old Man Pride has done took control of his senses. He don't want to lose face by turnin' back. And that's liable to be the thing that gets you killed, Malachi.

"I do not like this," Crooked Arm whispered to a friend as they stood at the end of the line of outlaws. "Bloody Knife is playing games with us. Deadly games."

His friend, called Running Dog, nodded his head solemnly. "If we are smart at all, we will disappear from this band of fools."

"And go where?" Crooked Arm questioned. "To forever wander the land without family or company?"

"We will be alive," Running Dog said.

Crooked Arm thought about that for a moment. "That is surely something to be considered. Now?"

"Now."

The two renegades started walking backward and soon vanished around a bend in the narrow trail. They were the smart ones. They would be alive to tell others how the man called Bloody Knife tricked Malachi Pardee. The tales would spread and grow and so would the reputation of the mountain man called Preacher.

Eight men, nearly a third of the Pardee gang, committed themselves to the rocky trail. Preacher tensed his legs against the boulder. Just a few more seconds, a few more steps, and the outlaws would be caught with no place to run.

In the center of the narrow trail, Coyote Man stopped and carefully looked all around him. Something in his guts was telling him, silently screaming at him, that death was near. But he could see nothing.

"What is wrong with you?" Big Eagle called from the rear of the line. "We are standing out here as plain as a wart on the end of a nose. If you are afraid, then get out of the way and let me lead."

"Shut up, you fat cow," Coyote Man called. "You could not lead a horse to water." He started forward and the others crowded in close behind him.

Preacher shoved with all his might and the boulder went rolling.

All on the trail and at both ends of it felt the ground begin to tremble. Little Wolf looked all around him, not understanding what was happening. Kills the Enemy looked in but one direction—up. He opened his mouth and screamed in terror as tons of rock were gathering up more tons of rock and all the mass was hurtling downward.

There was no place for the men trapped on the rocky trail to run. They stood as if frozen in place and waited for death.

"Goddamn you!" Malachi screamed, his words unheard over the thundering roar of the avalanche. "I'll kill you, Preacher. I swear I'll kill you."

Then a cloud of dust the size of a mountain enveloped the area, shrouding everything, tearing the eyes of those left alive, and causing a fit of coughing. When the dust had settled and the area was deadly silent, what was left of the gang looked toward where the trail used to be. It was gone, swept clean and covered. There was no way across and there was not a trace left of the eight men. On the other side, George looked back in horror and terror. He was trapped and alone.

"Stay where you is, George!" Malachi hollered, not knowing that George was so scared he couldn't have moved even if the Lord had commanded it. Besides that, he had crapped his drawers. "Start workin' your way down and we'll meet you by the river with the horses. We'll wait for you."

Malachi and the others waited for some sort of taunting jeer from Preacher. But all that greeted them was silence and the low moaning wind.

"We ought to say something." A Pardee follower called Curtis finally broke the silence. "I mean, I ain't no church-goin' man, but they's all buried under them rocks."

Ansel giggled and slobbered and picked his nose.

"Preacher!" Malachi hollered, the word echoing back to him. "You dirty son, can you hear me? Answer me, damn your eyes."

Silence.

"I know you're up there, you ambushin' no-count. Come down here and fight me like a man, you bastard!" Malachi was so mad he had forgotten that Preacher had already twice stomped the crap out of him.

But Preacher was a long way off and running hard. He had left under the cover of the enormous dust cloud. He reached the outlaw's horses and quickly went to work. He jerked the picket pins and sent them stampeding. He cut up the cinch straps, slashed the fenders and stirrups, and then set about destroying and scattering the supplies. He dented their coffee pots with rocks and threw everything he could lay hands on, including their saddles and bedrolls, over the side and into a deep ravine. They could reach them, but they'd have to work doing it. He quickly added one final touch and then Preacher slipped back about five hundred yards, found himself a safe and comfortable spot, and waited for the outlaws to return.

It was not a long wait. Malachi Pardee and his gang, minus seven or eight dead and two that had slipped away and one that was stranded on the other side of the avalanche, straggled back into camp and stood for a moment, dumbfounded. With Ansel, it was no act.

Malachi didn't even cuss at the sight. He sat down

on a log and sighed. He was tired, his feet were sore, he was disgusted, and just about played out. "Some of you fellers see if you can locate the horses," he finally said, weariness in his voice. "Rest of you start gatherin' up what supplies we got left and somebody build a fire. Them ashes is dead. Get one of them beat-up coffee pots and get some water. If it don't leak," he added, then added, "Goddamn that Preacher." Makin' a joke outa this, he thought. That's what it is to him, just one big damn joke. He thinks this is funny. Funny! Well, if I get a chance, I'll make this joke on him. If.

But Preacher had left a surprise in the cold ashes — in the form of a black-powder bomb he'd made with spare powder he'd found in the supplies of the outlaws. Preacher lay in the rocks and watched, hardly able to contain anticipatory laughter over what was going to happen in a few minutes.

One outlaw began gathering up twigs and sticks and a few larger branches of dead wood. He got the twigs blazing, then laid on a few sticks. Malachi stood up and walked over to warm his hands, as did several others, for the day had turned off cold in the high country.

The men stood in silence, their expressions glum.

They'll soon be a lot glummer, Preacher thought. He had to stick his fist over his mouth to stifle his laughter.

"Far shore feels good," Kenrick said, rubbing his hands briskly.

"Shore do," an outlaw named Clifford said. "And some coffee would be right tasty too. I think Dillman done found a mite of it."

Dillman walked up just as the bomb blew. The fire pit contained most of the killing effects of the blast, but dirt and rocks and ashes were flung all over the place, and the force of the explosion knocked down those who were standing around the fire. The charge created a huge dust and ash cloud that completely engulfed the camp for a few seconds. Dillman's sack of coffee went one way and he went the other, tumbling ass over elbows. Malachi took a stone right between his eyes and it knocked him to the ground and out like a snuffed candle. Several horses had wandered back into camp and the explosion sent the already skittish animals off and racing away, galloping at full tilt. Ansel had dropped his trousers and hung his butt over a log just as the powder blew. He landed in what he had just deposited as a fist-sized rock impacted with the top of his head. If it was possible to be goofier than he already was, Ansel Pardee had reached the zenith. Kenrick had been completely lifted off his boots and thrown backward, slowly twisting in the air. He landed on his belly and the wind was knocked from him. Clifford had turned his back to the fire to warm his butt and the blast not only set his trousers on fire, but lifted him into the air and tossed him about fifteen feet from the fire pit. Clifford was now scooting around on the ground, bellering and cussing, trying to put out the fire that was scorching his butt.

Animals were snorting and rearing and running around in a wild-eyed panic. Men were hollering and cussing and in a state of utter confusion. Finally, the shattered camp began to calm down as the dust began to settle.

Preacher knew it was foolish to stay around any longer — he'd taken a terrible chance by staying around this long — so while a bit of confusion still held sway over the outlaw camp, he took off. The last thing he heard was Ansel's voice. The fool was shuffling around the camp, his pants down around his ankles, singing an old church song. However, it seemed that he could only remember one line.

"Hark, the glad sounds, the Savior comes . . ."

Preacher shook his head and hit the trail. As soon as he was far enough away, he'd sure sit down and have himself a real good laugh about this day.

"Hark, the glad sounds, the Savior comes . . ."

"Aw, shut up, Ansel!" one of his brothers said. "And pull your britches up, you fool."

Malachi sat up on the cold ground, one hand to his throbbing and aching head. He listened to the song. "I've done died and gone to Heaven," he mumbled. Then he opened his eyes and saw Ansel, standing bare-assed and bellering out song. "Or Hell," Malachi added.

BOOK TWO

There is no arguing with Johnson: for if his pistol misses fire, he knocks you down with the butt of it.

Oliver Goldsmith

ONE

"Preacher ain't fightin' fair," Valiant Pardee said.

Malachi looked at his brother and shook his still-aching head. He used to think there might be some hope left for Valiant. But no more. "How much did you boys salvage?"

"Not near 'bout enough," Henry Pardee grumbled. He wore a bloody bandage around his head where a panicked horse had run over him.

"We lost eight or ten horses," Kenrick told his brother. "But then, we lost eight or ten men, too, so that all evens out. We got enough supplies to go on . . . if you want to go on."

"Damn right I want to go on!" Malachi snapped. "Way I see it, we ain't got no choice in the matter. None a-tall. We can't let this story get out. We wouldn't have no respect from nobody if it do."

"Running Man picked up Preacher's trail," Clifford said, wearing a pair of pants he had taken from the supplies of the dead men. They were too short and made him look about as stupid as Ansel was. "He said Preacher was a-layin' over yonder in them rocks just a-watchin' us all the time." He pointed.

"That sounds about right," Malachi said sourly. "Preacher had him a good laugh, too, I reckon. On us. Well, from now on we don't fall for no more of

Preacher's tricks. We got to sit down and work us out a plan."

"I been thinkin' some on that, Malachi," Ansel said, wiping the slobber from his lips and chin.

"Lord help us all," Kenrick muttered.

"I can't hardly wait to hear this," Malachi replied in a whisper. "All right, Ansel, let's hear it."

"Let's make Preacher come to us 'stead of us al'ays a-goin' to him."

The gang members all exchanged glances. Malachi was silent for a moment, then said, "You be right, Ansel. That there is a good scheme. You done come up with a right good plan." He was forgetting that Preacher came to them in the first place, with disastrous results for the gang.

"How does we do that?" Clifford asked Ansel.

"Don't strain his brain too hard," Malachi said quickly. He glanced at Ansel. "You done good, Ansel. Real good. Now go somewheres and rest for a time."

"How *does* we do it?" Kenrick asked his big brother after Ansel had danced away. His performance posed absolutely no threat to any ballet dancer in the world.

"I don't know," Malachi admitted. "I got to ruminate on that for a spell. Go on and leave me be for a time." Truth was, Malachi desperately wanted to just give it up and get the hell gone from this part of the world. More and more he was getting the feeling he had just about played out his string and what little was left on the spool was being controlled by that damn Preacher.

He looked around the ruined camp and at what was left of his gang. He shook his head. At one time, Malachi Pardee ran the most powerful and feared gang of road agents and outlaws west of the Mississippi. And not that many months ago, either. Sure as hell didn't look like much now.

Malachi had the sinking feeling that the game was just about over for him. He tried to push that emotion from his mind, but could not. It was just too incredible for him to accept that one man could destroy an entire gang of some of the meanest cutthroats in all the West.

But he had only to look around him to see the truth in the matter.

"Damn!" Malachi whispered.

Miles away, Preacher rested and waited. For the time being, he didn't have a clue as to what he might do next to harass the Pardees, but then this came to him: if he were in their shoes, he'd do nothing and try to draw the enemy to him.

Preacher chewed on some jerky and thought about that. The more he thought about it, the more he became convinced that was what the Pardees might try.

If so, what was next for him?

Preacher didn't try to kid himself a bit. He'd been lucky so far. Real lucky. He wasn't dealing with amateurs, even though the Pardee gang had behaved as such since this personal little war began. Preacher realized that had to end and he'd better stop treating the conflict as a joke and tighten up. No more stunts like the one he'd pulled this day, hiding in the rocks and stifling laughter at the antics of the Pardee gang. That had been dangerous and plumb foolish on his part.

True, his actions had taken a fearful toll on the Pardee gang. But he'd been brash in the doing of it. He'd have to cut back on some of that.

He wondered how the wagon train was faring. He'd been so busy of late he hadn't had much time to ponder on those folks. Well, least he was keeping the Pardees busy and away from the train. And the train was of a size that it would take a goodly bunch of Indians to attack it. By now the train should be clear out of this part of the country.

In all the weeks that Preacher had been trailing and doing battle with the Pardees, the train had made good time. But sickness had overtaken the movers and brought the train to a halt. The sickness, a strange fever that weakened muscles and caused the joints to ache and brought on chills one minute and burning-up hotness the next, had even struck the mountain men, putting Carl and Caleb and Windy flat on their backs along with most of the others . . . except for the kids. Not a one of them had been touched by the odd sickness. Now it was the kids taking care of the adults and the seeing-to of the livestock and such.

As the days drifted by, the mountain men worried that none of them would have the strength to push on in time to beat the snows. And if they weren't over the mountains come snowfall, they would be stuck right where they was till spring.

What finally saved their bacon was the return of Rimrock. The huge mountain man had a change of heart and turned around, riding back and picking up the ruts of the train and following it. Rimrock took one look at the adults a-layin' flat of their backs, weak as sick cats, and the exhausted and drawn faces of the kids, who'd been doing all the work, and he pitched right in.

"I seen this 'fore," Rimrock told Weller. "I don't know the name of the sickness, but I seen it 'fore. You ain't gonna die from it, but it makes a body so sick and weak some folks might wish they was dead to get some relief."

"I certainly agree with that," Weller whispered. "Any news of Preacher?"

"Injuns say they's a big war goin' on in the high country. East of here. Two renegades that broke from the Pardee gang claim that Preacher brought a whole mountain down on some of the gang. Wiped 'em out without no trace left. I doubt if it was an en-tar mountain, but Preacher probably caught some in a slide. Preacher is something to be-hold when he gets his dander up."

"You'll stay and help us, Rimrock?"

184

"Shore. Wouldn't be fittin' for me to do nothin' else. You just lay back and take 'er easy. I'll see to the rest of it."

Squatting down beside Windy, Caleb, and Carl, he said, "I can't leave y'all for no time 'fore you get in trouble. I reckon I'm gonna have to nanny the three of you for the rest of your days."

"We've got to get these folks well fast, Rim," Caleb said. "We ain't got much time left 'fore the snows come. They'll die out here."

"Forget it," the big man said. "It's gonna take weeks 'fore ever'body gets their strength back. Like I told Weller, I seen this sickness 'fore. That winter you went to St. Louie, Windy. I told you about it."

"Then we're in bad trouble," Carl said.

"Maybe not. The Whitman Mission ain't far from here. 'Bout a hundred miles. Worst comes to worser, we'll winter there. They'll welcome us."

"They might," Windy said, his voice weak. "But them Cayuses might not."

"I know Chief Tamsuky," Rimrock said. "I've et with him and slep' in his lodge. He's all right. It's all them gospel shouters up yonder that he don't take to worth a damn. They gonna keep on stirrin' up them Cayuses and one day it's gonna backfire on them all. You boys rest now. Ol' Rim's here. So don't worry."

The first movers up were Miles Cason and George Martin, and tenderfeet they might be — in Miles case that was still more than true — but Rimrock welcomed their help. The big man had shouldered a terrible burden taking care of everything.

"I have never experienced anything like that debilitating malaise we just recovered from," Miles told Rimrock. "It rendered me quite impuissant."

Rimrock stared at him for a few seconds. "What the hell did you just say?"

"The sickness."

"Oh. Yeah. Ain't got no name yet, that I know of.

185

But it's tough. I ain't never had it and hope I never get it."

Betina and Coretine and a few of the other pioneer women were soon up and moving around, able to cook and wash a bit. But they couldn't do much for any length of time, having to rest every few minutes. But what little they could do was a godsend to those few who were handling the whole load.

"First decent meal I've et since I happened along here," Rimrock said, spooning another plateful of stew that Coretine had prepared. "I never was no hand at cookin' fancy things like this here. And anything Miles and George dishes up tastes like a boiled moccasin."

Windy staggered up, using his rifle for a crutch, and sank down to the ground with a sigh. "I reckon I'll live," the little mountain man declared. "But for a time there, I shore had some serious doubts."

"I's a hopin' when you recovered your looks might have improved," Rimrock said, eyeballing his friend. "But you just as ugly as ever."

"I'd talk was I you," Windy retorted. "Thank God it's nigh on to fall and your beard is bushy-out. Any of these kids see your face, they'd run off into the woods and hide." He thanked Coretine for a plate of food and said, "Rimrock's the onliest man I ever knowed who could frighten a grizzly bear just by lookin' at the poor beast. He shaved off his beard one spring and come face to face with a she-bear out eatin' berries. You never heard the like of bellerin' and snortin' and car-ryin' on. That bear was so scared she took off runnin' and didn't stop 'til she reached the Canadian line. Never did come back."

"I think, Mr. Windy," Coretine said, "I know how you got your nickname."

Windy grinned up at her and winked. "Mayhaps you do, missy. Mayhaps you do."

186

* * *

Preacher went back down his trail and erased all the sign he had deliberately left for the Pardees. Then he found him a nice snug spot and waited. The Pardees and those with the gang, he felt, would not be good at the waiting game. Preacher could, and had in the past, gone without food for days. He did not believe any member of the Pardee gang had such patience. He had access to water and plenty of jerky and pemmican. He would do all right. He had strong doubts about the Pardee gang sitting still for very long.

The spot Preacher had chosen was in timber, about a hundred yards from a spring, and protected by rocks. He had a clear view of all that might go on in front of him. To his rear was the face of a mountain, loose rocks on both sides would warn him if anyone tried that approach. Now all he had to do was wait. And Preacher was real good at that.

Miles away, the Pardees made ready for the anticipated visit from Preacher. They fortified their camp and turned it into a minifortress. Then they all smiled at one another and waited. And waited.

On the afternoon of the fourth day, Malachi said, "It ain't workin'. Preacher ain't gonna fall for this."

They were nearly out of everything. They had no coffee, no salt, no beans, and were living mostly on what they could slip out and hunt. And a body can only live so long on rabbit. Man needs fat. Fat's scarce on a rabbit.

"We got to do something almighty quick," a gang member said. "We can't go on like this."

All the gang sure agreed with that and all were very vocal about it.

"I'll think on it some," Malachi told them.

"Malachi," Kenrick said when they were alone. "Let's call it quits and get shut of here."

Malachi looked down at his filthy hands and ragged clothing. Everyone of them, including Malachi, stunk worse than buzzard puke. None of them were prone to taking many baths, but he couldn't remember being this dirty and ragged. He sighed and nodded his head. "All right, brother," he said softly. "But we got to ride far and fast to outrun the stories. We'll head for Californy. Get a fresh start out there. Change our names and Pardee will be no more. Pickin's ought to be good out there."

"I'll tell the boys," Kenrick said.

It did not take the outlaws long to pack up their meager possessions and saddle up. Malachi looked all around him at what he could see of the Big Empty. "You won this time, Preacher," he muttered. "But there will be another time. Bet on that." He grabbed hold of the saddle horn and stuck his boot into the stirrup. The patched cinch strap broke and dumped Malachi on his butt on the hard and rocky ground.

Flat on his back, Malachi said, "I hate you, Preacher. As God is my witness, I hate you!"

TWO

"Gone," Preacher said, standing in the middle of the deserted outlaw camp. He had tired of waiting and had sensed something important was happening in the high country. He had left his hiding place after five days and cautiously made his way to where he had last seen the outlaws.

"I never thought he'd do it," Preacher said to the winds and the emptiness. And to the cold. It had really turned cold. Preacher squatted down by the long dead ashes of the old campfire and tried to figure out what month it was. September, he thought it was. Where had the summer gone? Seemed like only yesterday he'd come up on that little settlement of people, and that had been back in the late spring or early summer. He disremembered exactly.

He began the long trek back to the little valley where he'd left his horses.

Hammer was glad to see him and told him so by the way he acted. Horses get used to human company and miss that when they're left alone. Even the Appaloosa he'd taken from that dead Indian seemed glad to see him. The 'paloosa was a big animal, weighing, Preacher figured, about a thousand pounds, near 'bouts as big as Hammer. He talked to them and petted them and got them calmed down and then saddled up. He wanted to get on the trail of the Pardees and see just where they were heading. Initially, they had headed west, the route they'd taken putting them well north of the new wagon-train trail. But with the Pardees, you just never knew.

It startled Preacher when the first snowflakes began falling. It was just too damn soon for that—unless he'd missed his calendar date by a month or six weeks, and he didn't think he had. No matter, he thought. By now Carl was probably nearing the last leg of the train's journey and weary pilgrims would be getting their first glimpse of the promised land. And judging from the gray and leaden skies, none too soon, neither. Preacher figured this was going to be a bad winter in the high country.

Several days later, Preacher reined up in some timber and watched as half a dozen riders cut in front of him, heading across a little meadow. He knew one of the men: that no-count Son. Now he'd picked him up three, four men and was headin' out to do some mischief. Preacher waited until they were long gone and then fell in behind them. Whatever Son and his friends were up to, it was no good. Preacher had never known Son to do anything for the general good of anything or anybody.

Several days later, Preacher ran into a hunting party from Weasel Tail's village and the men fixed venison and sat around the fire and talked.

"Much sickness among the wagon train," a brave named Bear Killer finally told him. "They have spent weeks without moving. Even those like you were sick."

"You have seen this with your own eyes?" Preacher asked.

Bear Killer shook his head. "Talked to some who have. They speak the truth. Too many saw it for it to be wrong. The wagons are moving now, but the snows have come to the high places. They will not be able to cross the mountains until spring."

Long after the Indians had left, Preacher sat before the fire and thought about what he'd been told. According to Bear Killer, the train had not even made fifty miles before the sickness struck them and stopped everybody cold.

Preacher did a little figuring. As soon as they were

able to travel, Carl would head them straight for the mission on the divide and hope to winter there. That would be the only logical thing to do, for the winter was coming early this year, and from all indications, it was going to be a hard one. The movers would be low on food, some of them probably out of food by now.

All in all, everybody was going to be in for a damn rough time of it 'fore spring poked her head up again. Preacher saddled up and pulled out.

Twice on his way toward the mission, he cut the trail of Son and his no-counts. Then, on the northwest side of the Little Popo Agie, he stopped and swung down at a deserted camp for a look-see. After carefully reading the sign, he concluded that Son and his bunch had linked up with the Pardees. And that damn sure meant trouble for someone — or a whole bunch of someones, for the tracks leading away from the camp were heading straight for the mission.

Preacher built a small fire in the old fire pit and broiled him a venison steak. He longed for a cup of coffee, but he was slap out of that. While he ate, he made up his mind. There was no way the movers would survive the winter without more supplies. So somebody was going to have to take mules over the mountains to a Hudson's Bay Company outpost and bring back supplies. Any of the mountain men with the train knew the horse trail and had been over it many times. It wasn't that far away from the mission. Getting there would be no problem without the wagons, if one discounted hostile Injuns, blizzards, outlaws, and such, but with winter looming so close, getting *back* might be somewhat difficult. But it had to be done if those in the train stood a chance of surviving. Dawn found Preacher on the trail and a day later he rode into the mission and there was the train.

The missionaries there had not hesitated in taking in the members of the wagon train, but existing supplies were not nearly ample enough to carry everybody through the winter.

Over a cup of coffee and a bowl of stew, Preacher laid his plan out for his friends.

"You're right about not enough supplies, Preacher," Windy said. "I'm game for the mules. How about you, Rim?"

The big man nodded his head. "Suits me. But them at the post sure ain't gonna give them supplies to us. What are we gonna use for money, our good looks?"

"Wagh!" Caleb said. "We're all dead from starvation if that's the case."

Rimrock looked at the rail-thin mountain man. "I shore better not tarry with them supplies. Strong breeze would carry you off now."

"I'll go talk to Betina and Coretine," Preacher said. "They'll know how these movers are fixed for money."

Preacher laid it out for the two women, not downplaying their plight one bit. "I can see the signs, ladies, and the winter is gonna be a bad one."

"The people have some money, Preacher," Betina said. "Enough, I believe, to purchase supplies."

Preacher nodded his head. "Place of the Rye Grass," he said.

"I beg your pardon?" Coretine asked.

"Actual the Cayuse call it The People of the Place of the Rye Grass. Waiilaptu. Why the hell Whitman ever chose this spot is beyond understandin' far as I'm concerned."*

*Marcus Whitman and his wife, Narcissa, built their mission in 1836 and maintained it until both were killed by rampaging Cayuse Indians in 1847. In addition, eleven other men, one woman, and three children were killed that night. The Cayuses took some forty-odd others captive and held them until Hudson's Bay Company officials ransomed them free.

More than two years later, after being pursued by a pioneer militia, five Cayuse warriors turned themselves in and were tried and hanged for the murders.

"To Christianize the savages, of course," Coretine said.

"Well, they ain't takin' hold of it much, girl. Injuns got their ways and we got ours. Bes' leave other folks' beliefs alone, I say."

"But they have to be baptized," a mover woman who was nearby said. "Or they'll not enter the Kingdom of Heaven."

Preacher smiled gently. "How 'bout them folks over to the Dark Continent of Afreeca? Or them heathens in India or all them yeller people? They don't believe like you do. Are you sayin' all them untold millions is a-goin' to burn in the hellfires?"

"Yes." The woman's reply was firm. "That is why we must carry the Word to all the savages of the world."

"Amen," Marcus Whitman said, strolling by.

Preacher shook his head. Marcus was a good man, and a fine doctor, but he didn't always get along with the mountain men. Marcus didn't like the language used by the mountain men or their penchant for strong drink. And some of the Cayuses didn't like him either.

Preacher looked up as snow began to fall. It was early for that. Too early. It was going to be one hell of a winter for sure. Within hours, the land was blanketed with white.

"She's gonna be a bad one, Preacher," Caleb said.

"Yeah," Preacher agreed. "I got to get these pilgrims settled . . . some way. Ain't no time for buildin' cabins, and not enough know-how. Goddamnest place I ever seen for folks to settle. They're gonna have to winter in their wagons and we're gonna lose some to sickness brought on by the elements." Preacher shook his head and sighed. "And to make things worser, Son and his scummy bunch has linked up with the Pardees, and I don't know where they are."

"You think they'll attack us here?"

"No. Too many Injuns close by. But they may try to take the supplies. I think we'll all cross over. Be safer that

193

way."

The mountain men began their journey across the Cascades the next morning. The men at the Hudson's Bay post were startled to see the five men and even more incredulous when Preacher told them why they had crossed the mountains.

"They'll never last the winter without proper shelter," one man bluntly stated. "This winter is shapin' up to the worst anyone can remember."

"Way I see it," Preacher said, handing the clerk the list of supplies, "they ain't got no hell of a lot of choice in the matter. You wanna try gettin' all them wagons 'crost the mountains axle-deep in snow? Them people is best right where they's at until spring comes. Then them that survive can cross the mountains to the valley of the promised land," he added grimly.

The man stared at Preacher for a moment, then shook his head and walked off muttering, "Fools. All of them. Wagons acrost the mountains. Can't be done."

Preacher just smiled at the man's remark. He knew it could be done. He'd done it.

Preacher's friends caught the smile and winked. Caleb said, "Let's be findin' us a jug, boys. That ride made me thirsty. And we'll get a couple of jugs to take back."

"Don't let them gospel-shouters back yonder discover no strong drink," Windy cautioned. "They do and they'll pour it all out on the ground."

"Now I love the Lord," Rimrock said. "But that would be pushin' my faith just a tad."

Back at the mission, Preacher knew damn well he wasn't going to stick around there the whole winter. First thing you know, Betina would be snuggled up with him in his buffalo robe and Preacher would have a permanent ring in his nose.

Caleb and Carl, Rimrock and Windy watched him pack up his gear and load up his animals. "You take care

194

of this spotted pony of mine, now, Caleb," Preacher said. "I'll be back for him 'fore you know it, and I want to find him in good shape."

"Will do, Preacher."

"I'll be checkin' back in time to time. I want to find them damn Pardees and Son and his bunch. Makes me uneasy knowin' they're out there close and plannin' no tellin' what kind of mischief."

"You just want a good fight, Preacher," Rimrock said. "I know you too well."

"Mayhaps you be right, Rim. This thing between me and Malachi is personal; been growin' toward a showdown for years. It's bad enough when one of our own kind turns outlaw, but to have trash like the Pardees a-ridin' the high country don't set well with me worth a damn."

"You know where they are, don't you, Preacher?" Carl asked.

"I got me a good idea. 'Sides, I got to get back to Weasel Tail's winter camp and see what his braves come up with. I'm long overdue. Then I'll come back here. During my absence, you get Weller and the others to take pen to hand and write out all they know about Sutherlin." He mounted up and Hammer pranced a bit, wanting to hit the trail. He was a horse who liked to see the country about much as his rider. "See you, boys." Preacher headed east at a lope.

Betina and Coretine stood by their wagons with a group of people and watched him ride out. One of the missionary women looked at the expression on Betina's face and said, "Never set your eyes for a mountain man. They're like the wind. You might never see him again."

"Even the wind rests every now and then," Betina replied, her eyes on the now dark dot in the distance.

"Not for long," the woman said, and turned away, walking toward her quarters.

"He'll be back, Betina," Coretine said gently, the words only for the other woman's ears.

Arm in arm, they walked around the mission complex. The first snow of the season was gone, and they stepped carefully to avoid the mud.

"I know she's right," Betina said. "But I can't help the way I feel."

"Do you love him?"

"No. But I could. And that's just as bad."

Coretine looked at her friend. "Maybe worse."

THREE

Preacher was aware of a trading post on the Columbia that catered to both legitimate trappers and to outlaws and renegade Indians. It was run by an Englishman who, so the stories go, had been forced to leave England just ahead of the hangman's noose. Because he dealt in guns and whiskey to the Indians, they left him alone. He would also buy stolen pelts from outlaw trappers . . . of which there was more than people liked to believe. As he rode, Preacher struggled for a time to think of the man's name. Finally it came to him. Dirk. That was what he was called. Dirk. Preacher had never been to Dirk's place, but he knew where it was. Odds were, that's where he'd find the Pardees and Son and his bunch. Or close by there.

Then something else came to him. He'd have to be doubly careful. Dirk, so the stories went, was a poisoner. Had disposed of several men and women in England 'fore he was caught. He was supposed to be some kind of expert with potions and such. Preacher made up his mind that he'd not drink nor eat at Dirk's place.

Then he smiled a hard curving of the lips. He just might put Dirk out of business, too, while he was up this way. Might as well do the good people of the world several favors while he was in a favorin' mood.

Hammer's ears pricked and Preacher felt the big horse tense under him. Stopping in a glade, Preacher

197

waited. He could now hear the prod of horses' hooves. He eased the hammer back on his Hawken, then slowly let the hammer back down as the rider came into view. The rider was a trapper named Quinn.

"Ho, Quinn," Preacher called out. "It's Preacher here."

"Wagh, Preacher!" Quinn yelled. "You 'bout skirred me out of my moccasins, boy. Blackfeet done monikered you right when they named you Killin' Ghost. You quiet, boy. Spooky so."

"Thank my good horse for that, Quinn. Hammer picked up on you long 'fore I did." Preacher kneed Hammer out of the glade and up to Quinn.

"You lookin' prosperous," Quinn remarked. "You been eatin' home cookin', maybe?"

"Movers been feedin' me from time to time. Whole passel of 'em down to that gospel shouter's mission."

"I'll fight shy of that place then. I know it ain't a polite question to ask, but I got reasons aplenty and I'll tell you. Where you bound?"

"Up to Dirk's place on the river."

Quinn shook his shaggy head. "You be in mortal danger up yonder, Preacher. The country is fairly aboundin' with scoundrels. I seen that damnable Son up there, and I also gleamed a couple of them crazy Pardee brothers. Talk is, they runnin' from you and has decided to flee no more. And you know well as me if you see one Pardee, the others ain't far away."

"For a fact, ol' hoss. For a fact. But they'll be a lot less Pardees when I'm done with them."

Quinn smiled. "I reckon they done tugged on your halter 'til they got you riled. Be a sight to see, I'm thinkin'. I'd go if my woman wasn't waiting for me at the lodge. Winter gonna be a hard one this season, Preacher, and my rummetism is a-hurtin' me something fierce. I'm lookin' forward to hot fires and warm robes this winter."

Rheumatism was the trappers' main complaint, for

during the trappers' two seasons, spring to midsummer, when the beaver molts, and again from autumn to waters' freeze, they stand in icy cold waters.

"I be headin' west come the spring," Quinn continued. "Me and my woman done talked it over an' she's agree to go west with me. We're bound for Callyforny where it's warm all the time. They's a dozen or more mountain men done pulled up stakes and headed there."

"What you gonna do when you get there?"

Quinn shrugged. "Beats me. But I'll find something to do. It's over for the likes of us, Preacher."

Preacher nodded his head. He had been one of the first to know that. "See you, Quinn. Good luck."

"The same to you, Preacher."

Quinn headed south, Preacher continued on to the north. As of one mind, the two mountain men looked back. Both lifted a hand in farewell and then they were gone. For one, a way of life was ending; for the other, a new era was just opening.

Preacher made his camp not far from the Crab, in the Saddle Mountains. This area was the home and the range of a half dozen Indian tribes, including the Walla Walla, the Spokane, and the Yakima. But Preacher got along well with those tribes, and while he rode cautiously, he was not particularly worried. The Indians knew Preacher and most accepted him as one of their own. Preacher would fight if he was pushed to it, but left alone, the mountain man could be a good friend and the Indians knew it. Twice on his way north, Preacher stopped in Indian villages to socialize and eat. Indians loved to talk and had a high sense of humor, although most did not let that side show around whites they did not know.

As he drew nearer the trading post of Dirk, Preacher began to ride with more caution, for the Indians he'd spoken with told him there were plenty bad men around the post and that they were up to no good. And that the trappers that were like Preacher did not come to that trading post any longer.

Preacher didn't tell them so, but if what he had in mind came true, there wouldn't nobody ever come to that trading post again — ever.

But he wasn't going to just ride in there big as brass. He'd have more holes in him than a tree full of woodpeckers if he done that. Preacher made his camp a few miles from the trading post and set about pondering just what he might do.

"Get it right," he told himself and the gathering shadows. " 'Cause it could be that you ain't gonna get but one chance."

Come the morning, he picketed Hammer and the packhorse on a few hidden acres of grass on the edge of the Cascades and pressed on on foot. Why that damn crazy Englishman ever wanted to build a trading post around here was a mystery to Preacher. Damn wind blew all the time, storms could whip up out of nowheres, and the place wouldn't grow diddly squat. But then, he figured, nobody ever come here, and it damn shore was off any known and well-traveled trail, so maybe that Brit wasn't so stupid after all, considerin' the ugly business he was in.

He made his way to within sight of the trading post, and it was a run-down, ramshackle place, looking more like a roofed and walled hog pen rather than a place where human beings frequented. But, Preacher reckoned, considering the caliber of men who visited this place of late, it was fitting.

Preacher's cover was adequate, but not the best by a long shot. He watched as several riders approached the building and dismounted. He didn't recognize any of them. Whatever their business was, it didn't take long. Within minutes, the three men exited the building, mounted up, and rode off.

Preacher knew that out here, three visitors a day was considered a heady business. There might not be anymore customers the rest of the week, for that matter.

Preacher made up his mind and carefully changed locations after taking a long, low look all around him. He worked his way around to the back of the building, taking the better part of an hour to complete his swing. Now came the hard part, for several acres around the building had been cleared and only stumps remained. He started to move forward, then checked the movement, every sense telling him that something was mighty wrong. He remained motionless behind a stump, his buckskins blending in with the early-winter terrain. Something was wrong, but what?

He scanned his surroundings, only his eyes moving. He could not check behind him without moving, and he wasn't about to do that. But he had inspected the flats behind him carefully before moving to his position, and was secure in his belief that no one was back there. At the time, he amended.

Preacher watched the rear of the cabin, keeping his eyes on the windows. The "windows" of most buildings were no more than a small sliding door without glass. One window moved slightly, cracking open a few inches, and Preacher tensed. How could they know he was here? Or did they only suspect? Either way, he was in a pickle and knew it.

He could hear the murmur of voices from inside the cabin, but could not make out any words. After several moments, one man said, "Oh, hell, Dirk! Preacher ain't nowheres near here. I'll show you." The back door opened and a burly man stepped out to the ground and stood there. "Hey, Preacher!" he shouted in a strong voice. "You no-good son of a bitch!" Then he proceeded to call Preacher every vile and foul name he could think of, which was a-plenty. He traced Preacher's ancestors back several thousand years, and just before running out of breath and names to call him, he compared the mountain man to a monkey in a cage, and worse.

Preacher lay behind the stump, on a slight backward sloping incline, and waited motionless. He would deal

201

with this loudmouth in due time — and deal with him he would, Preacher silently promised.

"See?" the loudmouth said proudly, as what had to be Dirk stepped out of the door and stood looking around.

"I guess you're right, Hubert" the second man said. "From all that I've heard about Preacher, he certainly wouldn't tolerate all that name-calling. But that red savage certainly said he'd seen Preacher."

"He lied," Hubert said. "Tryin' to get in your favor for a drink of whiskey or a blanket."

"I suppose you're right. Let's get in out of this cold. It's going to be a bitter winter, Hubert."

Preacher wondered if there were any more men inside the small post and decided not. The instant the window slide was closed shut to keep out the cold breeze, Preacher made his move, leaping to his feet and dashing to the rear of the building and flattening out against the logs. Preacher moved around to the side of the building and pushed up against the base of the chimney to catch some warmth from the heated rocks. From about head-high on up, the rocks changed to a stick chimney, the sticks held together with a mixture of mud and clay. It was a common-enough affair.

On Preacher's side of the stones was the woodpile, stacked high, so Preacher moved around to the other side in case the wood box got low and Dirk or Hubert came out for more firewood. Preacher saw an old dog-house someone had made, and looked in it. Cobwebs had taken over, the dog long gone. With a smile, Preacher crawled in the doghouse. It was a large dog-house and Preacher hoped the long-gone dog would not return to claim its house anytime soon. A dog that needed a house this size would be big enough to give a grizzly some problems. Since the rear of the doghouse was built up against the side of the stone chimney — the outside of the fireplace — the hut was surprisingly warm. Preacher made himself comfortable and waited.

One side of the doghouse was the wall of the cabin, so

with his knife, Preacher began digging out a hole between the logs, carefully working out the mud that was chinked between the logs and pulling it toward him until he had him a hole just big enough to see and hear through. The darkness of the interior of the doghouse would, he hoped, prevent those inside the post from noticing the tiny hole.

"Them others gonna get here?" he heard Hubert say.

"Today is all I know," Dirk replied. "Put us on some meat to cook, Hubert. This cold gives me an appetite."

Somebody is always cookin' when I'm in a position to do nothin' but smell it and salivate, Preacher thought. He stuck a piece of jerky in his mouth and chewed. Then he heard the sounds of horses.

"Son and his bunch," the voice of Hubert came to him. "I reckon the others will be along shortly. I hope they brought their own food."

Son and his bunch stomped in amid a lot of laughing and cussing and rough humor, on both sides, and after the jug was passed around, they got down to serious talking. Preacher had his ear pressed to the tiny hole.

"The way Malachi sees it," Son said, "is we hold off until spring and then hit the wagon train two, three days out of the mission. It'll be clear of the Hudson's Bay post by then and we can all take the wagons and possessions and sell them. I think it's a grand idea."

"And the people?" Dirk asked.

"All dead. And the dead can't hook us up with anything."

"I hear Preacher's tied in with them, as well as three, four other mountain men."

"Where'd you hear that?"

"From an Injun who passed through yesterday. He said he saw Preacher about twenty miles from here. He swore it was him."

"I don't believe it," Hubert said. "I just don't believe it."

"Neither do I," one of Son's bunch piped up. "He

thinks he's got the Pardees run clear out of the country and I believe he's 'way south with the train."

"It's a deal, then?" Son asked. "We take the train, and with your connections on the coast, we get rid of the stuff?"

"It's a deal," Dirk told him. "I've been wanting to leave this wretched country for some time."

"The both of you have to understand this," Son said. "Oncest we start, we can't have no soft hearts 'bout none on the train. They all got to die—men, women, and kids alike. We can hump the women and the girls, then they got to die."

"That's understood." Preacher recognized Dirk's voice. "I've done in all three in my time. I have no use for kids anyway."

And I understand it, too, Preacher thought. I understand that you all are the most black-hearted band of cutthroats I ever seen in all my borned days. And now that I heard with my own ears what you plan to do, I ain't got no sympathy for the lot of you.

In other words, Preacher added silently, you bastards are in for a world of woe—from *me!*

FOUR

Preacher figured there wasn't no time like the present to get into action. The fact that he was out-numbered about ten to one didn't bother him at all. It never had.

He crawled out of the doghouse and turned all but one of the horses loose . . . quietly. Then he began working swiftly in the gathering up of dry grass and twigs and then larger sticks from the woodpile. He crawled around the trading post/cabin on all fours and placed the material on all sides. Then he set all the bundles burning. He led the best horse around back, took out both pistols, and waited, figuring it wouldn't take long for those ninnies inside to start smelling smoke. Both pistols in his hands and the two more in his sash were double-shotted, so Preacher was expecting to inflict some serious wounds.

So intent were the men inside the trading post/cabin in their planning of murder and rape and robbery that not once had anyone opened the sliding windows to look outside . . . and that was something Preacher had been counting on. The men had not disappointed him.

Preacher sat down on a stump and waited, his hands filled with pistols.

"Hey!" someone within the building hollered. "I smell smoke."

"Do tell?" Preacher muttered. "I was beginnin' to think your blowers was stopped up."

"The damn cabin's on fire!" another yelled. "Lemme out of here!"

He ran out the back door and Preacher shot him, one ball taking the man in the chest, the second ball striking him in the face, making a great big mess. Blood and bit of bone struck the man right behind the mortally wounded outlaw and he screamed in panic.

Preacher ended his screaming when he fired his second pistol, the double-shotted charge taking the man in the chest and knocking him backward. He fell against another man and both of them went to the floor.

The air around the post was now thick with smoke. Men were staggering out, nearly blind from the smoke, tears streaming down their cheeks and all coughing badly. Preacher had pulled out his other two pistols and stood up, waiting for a clear shot.

Hubert ran out, stumbling and staggering. Preacher ended his outlaw life with a ball directly in the heart.

"The damn horses is gone!" a man screamed from around the front, then broke out in a coughing fit.

Preacher put a ball into a fourth man, jammed the empty pistols behind his sash, and jumped on the horse he'd borrowed. Staying low in the saddle, he headed for the brush. Just inside good cover, Preacher leaped from the saddle and began quickly reloading. When his pistols were charged, he looped the reins around a skinny bush and grabbed up his rifle. He made his way back to the edge of the clearing.

The men were working frantically to contain the blaze, but from where Preacher stood, it looked hopeless. The dry logs had turned the building into a blazing ball of fire. Neither Son or Dirk could be seen. Dropping to one knee, Preacher sighted in a man and pulled the trigger. The man stood up on his toes, stiffened, then threw his hands into the air and fell to the ground, landing on his face. The boom of the Hawken was lost in the roaring of the flames and the cracking and popping of burning logs. Preacher reloaded and waited, trying to peer through the dense smoke for a target.

"Give it up!" a man shouted, just then noticing the newly dead man sprawled on the cold ground. "We're targets out here. Head for cover."

The men vanished into the thick swirling smoke and Preacher gave it up and ran back to the stolen horse, jumping into the saddle and taking off. He rode for about a mile, then circled around, coming up into the woods about half a mile in front of the source of the black smoke arching into the skies.

Sitting his saddle, he listened for a moment and picked up the sounds of many hooves pounding in his direction. Preacher took the prudent course and got the hell out of there. He hadn't killed any of the principals, but he'd blooded the gang some, and given them something to think about.

He left the horse and took off on foot, in a distance-eating trot, heading north and staying close to the river on the timber side. They'd come after him, he was sure of that. The outlaws had no choice in the matter. They had to kill him. Preacher smiled grimly. And that was going to take some doing.

"Lost everything," Dirk said sourly. He sat on a log, his face grimy with soot and his clothing coated with dirt and ash. "Everything I owned went up in smoke. Goddamn that Preacher. Damn his eyes, I say!"

"I do know how you feel," Malachi said. "Believe that."

"I can't believe that no man would have the balls to just walk up and set fire to a building and then wait outside and shoot folks down as they run from the flames," an outlaw called Gil said, as he looked around him for the tenth time in that many minutes. Preacher made him nervous being this close. Real nervous. The man was new to the West, having broken jail in Maryland the past year. The first thing he'd been told when he hit the wilderness was to leave mountain men alone. Especially one called Preacher. Everybody had told him that Preacher was bad news.

He had scoffed at that.

No more.

"Settle down, Gil," Malachi told him. "We'll never kill the bastard if we all get spooked."

"I still think we should have gone on west," Kenrick said. "This is a bad mistake we're makin', I'm thinkin'."

"I wish we'd had some fresh meat," Ansel said. "Them coals of the cabin is right for cookin' now."

Dirk looked at the hulking stupid oaf and resisted an impulse to flatten him with the butt of his borrowed rifle. He decided it just wasn't worth the effort.

"Let me go a-huntin', brother," Ansel said. "I be's hongry around the mouth."

"Shut up, Ansel," Malachi told him. "Sit down and be quiet. Keep a lookout for us."

"You think Preacher will be back?" Dirk asked.

"I don't know. Maybe. With him, you never can tell."

"Probably lookin' at us right now," Kenrick said. "Let's get out of here, brother. Like right now."

"No!" Dirk said sharply. "No, by God. We go after the man. I will not spend the rest of my life looking over my shoulder. And there is a very good reason for us doing that: Preacher probably was listening to us make plans. He knows what we're going to do. He's got to die."

Malachi reluctantly nodded his head. Lord knows he didn't want to pursue Preacher; Malachi had him a gutful of the mountain man. But there was wisdom in Dirk's words. He picked up his rifle. "Let's do it, people. Preacher's got to die if we's goin' to survive. There just ain't no other way."

Back in Missouri, in a small town on the Osage River, on the edge of the unorganized territory known at the Great Plains, Edward Sutherlin tossed out the dregs of his coffee cup and looked at the six men who had accompanied him from Ohio. They were all tough, very capable men—men who would do anything for money. And had.

Edward Sutherlin rose to his boots and began rolling his blankets and groundsheet. He knew it was a bad time to be heading west. But it was something that had to be done. He'd received word that his operation was in jeopardy and that some stupid, illiterate, unwashed mountain man with the improbable name of Preacher was to blame.

Well, he'd soon settle Preacher's hash. He had too good a deal going to let one man louse it all up. With Malachi and his boys, and the six tough men he was bringing, that should be plenty. They'd leave this Preacher person's body for the scavengers and then get on with their business.

He just couldn't imagine why Malachi was so afeard of one man. It just didn't make any sense. Ridiculous is was it was. "Let's ride," Edward said. "We've got a thousand miles in front of us."

One of Son's men showed his head and Preacher's rifle boomed. The slug took the man right between the eyes and removed the entire back of the outlaw's head, flinging him backward, dead before he hit the cold ground.

The two dozen or so trash that made up the gang flattened out and hugged the rocky ground on the edge of the Cascades.

They tried not to look at the careless outlaw who now lay with his brains leaking out.

Ansel got to his knees to shift positions and Preacher's rifle boomed again, its ball smashing into a rock and sending bits of rock into the outlaw's face. Ansel whooped and hollered and fell to the ground, wiping the blood from his face.

Dirk and his boys didn't move. Dirk knew all about the mountain man called Preacher and knew what he was capable of. A man took no chances when dealing with Preacher. None. Dirk cut his eyes, looking around him. He was safe from Preacher's bullets as long as he stayed put, but he was pinned down tight.

Malachi looked back at Ansel. His brother wasn't hurt, just bloodied up some and scared. Malachi's own position was like that of Dirk. He was safe, but he couldn't move. Preacher had picked a dandy spot for an ambush. Something that Malachi should have known.

Son lay on the ground, looked at his fallen companion, and cussed Preacher. Ted had been a good man. One moment of carelessness had cost him his life. Now there was one less to fight Preacher.

"Malachi," Son called in a hoarse whisper. "We's just in good rifle range. We can't go forward, but we can damn shore go backerds. 'Nother fifty yards and we'll be plumb out of range. I say we roll backerds."

"You roll backerds," Malachi said. "I ain't movin' 'til I'm shore it's safe."

Flat on his back several hundred yards away, behind rocks on the incline, Preacher pulled his bow unto a U shape and let the arrow fly, not dreaming for a moment he could hit anything. With their heads down, the outlaws did not see the arrow arch high into the air and start down. A man named Fabor suddenly let out a mighty roar as the arrow point drove deep into the right cheek of his butt. He leaped to his feet, dancing and howling in pain. Radborne tackled him and brought him down before Preacher could shoot him dead.

"My ass is on fire!" Fabor squalled.

"The next time Preacher fires, make a run for it," Malachi called. "We'll be out of range time he can reload."

"Oh, Lord, Lord, my ass hurts!" Fabor hollered. "Somebody do something."

"I'll be durned," Preacher said, peering through the rocks. "I hit someone."

Preacher studied the situation for a moment, then picked up his Hawken and shifted a few yards. He sighted in on what appeared to be a boot sticking out from behind a log and squeezed off a round. Wild screaming came his way as one of Son's men had several toes blown off. Son grabbed the man and dragged him downhill, the others quickly following as Preacher reloaded.

Preacher lowered his rifle. The crap and crud were well out of range. Fabor was hollering about his butt and Son's man was screaming in pain from his blowed-off toes. Preacher gathered his gear and slipped back into the timber and began slowly working his way down the grade.

"Get that son of a bitch!" he heard Dirk the Englishman scream. "You men, circle around and trap him up there. You three to the right and you three to the left. We'll have him in a box. Move!"

Preacher smiled and continued moving downward, working his way toward where they had picketed their horses. He pulled up short in the timber. Malachi was wising up. He had left a guard with the horses. Preacher notched an arrow and let it fly. The point drove through the guard's neck and he fell to his knees, coughing and gagging with blood pouring out of his mouth. Preacher ran to him and smashed his head with the butt of his Hawken. He gathered up all the reins, tied them together with rope from one of the outlaws' saddles, mounted the best-looking horse, and took off at a gallop, screaming out Cheyenne war cries as he raced off down the slope and into the valley below.

Malachi jerked off his hat and threw it to the ground. "God*damn* that man!" he yelled.

Preacher stopped and wheeled around. "I am Man Who Kills Silently," he shouted, his words clear in the cold air. "I am White Wolf. I am Bloody Knife. I am called Killing Ghost. I am Preacher. I've lived with wolves and fought grizzlies. I've tamed pumas and talked with eagles. I'm surlier than a badger, got more pison in me than a den full of rattlers, and I'm tougher than any man you ever seen. You hear my words well. You will all die. All of you."

Several of the brigands shuddered as the words sent chills racing up and down their spines. All the outlaws stood on the hillside and watched the mountain man as he sat the horse about a thousand yards from them. They were powerless to do anything except watch and listen.

"Leave now and never return, or you'll all die in these here mountains!" Preacher shouted. "From now on I show you no pity nor mercy. Get gone east and don't never come 'crost the Missouri again. You best hear me well and heed the warnin', for them's my last words on the subject."

Preacher put the horses into a trot and soon disappeared over a rise. When he knew he was safe from view, he cut west and then, after a mile, turned north and rode steady until he figured he was a good six or eight miles from the now afoot outlaws.

He found him a fast-running creek and let the horses blow and water. He stripped the saddles from them, including the one he'd chosen to keep for a time, and dumped out their saddlebags, carefully picking through the supplies.

He kept the coffee and a small pot and a side of bacon. Somebody had fixed up some pan bread and carefully wrapped it. Preacher washed out a small skillet and set about frying up some bacon and boiling water for coffee. While that was sizzling and boiling, he carefully loaded up all the spare pistols he'd found in the saddlebags and in holsters on the horns. He'd have to take an extra horse just to tote around all the guns he was now in possession of. But he figured they'd come in handy, for he knew damn well those highwaymen weren't going to heed his words to leave and that sooner or later they'd come a showdown.

He now had a right smart amount of powder, more than he'd use in a year's time, so he set about making some bombs, using pieces of britches and shirts he'd found. He wouldn't even think of touching the longhandles he'd found. Filthiest things he'd ever seen. Preacher had handled them with a long stick and then burned them.

This was fir, hemlock, and pine country. Come the spring it would be some of the most beautiful country in all the Northwest, with tall yellow spikes of false hellebore, clusters of bleeding heart, white and yellow daisies, the umbrella-shaped cow parsnips, white bunchberry dogwood, blue lupine, lavender fireweed, and scarlet paintbrush. It was a scene that, once witnessed, would stay with a body for a lifetime. Peaceful and serene. But for now, Preacher was making bombs to kill people.

The Pardees and Son and Dirk and their gangs had to come after him. He had their horses. And in this country, a man without a horse was a dead man.

Preacher piled up the saddles and bridles and burned them, knowing the gang members would see the smoke. Indians would, too, of course, but Preacher was on good terms with most of the Indians who roamed this part of the country. He had a hunch the gang members were not. But by now the Indians would be in their winter camps and not all that anxious to make war.

Preacher piled all the supplies and clothing he couldn't use on the burning leather and destroyed it. Now all the gang members had was what they had with them when they came after him back down the trail. And that would be precious little. Now they had no blankets, no food, no nothing.

Preacher knew he was sentencing some of the outlaws to a hard death. That fact didn't bother him a twit. He had given them warning the game was about to turn rough. Besides, there wasn't a man back yonder who hadn't tortured and raped and killed innocent people. Whatever they got in the way of misery, they richly deserved.

Preacher drank the last of the coffee, ate the bacon, and sopped out the skillet with a hunk of bread. He washed the pot, the cup, and the frying pan in the creek and carefully packed them away.

He saddled up and cinched the pack frame, carefully balancing the load. He started the horses north, toward the Entiat. He knew a spot where he would make his stand and win and put an end to this war. Then he'd get on back to the mission and help see to the needs of the pilgrims, for the winter was going to be a harsh one.

He looked back once and muttered, "Follow me and die, boys. I warned you."

FIVE

"He's headin' for a spot of his choosin' for the showdown," Son opined. "And we ain't got no choice in the matter. We got to follow."

The others said nothing for the time being, just stood and stared at the hoofprints that headed north. They all knew that without horses, they stood a very good chance of dying in the Big Empty. They also knew that they stood a very good chance of dying if they went after their horses.

Dirk picked up his rifle and began walking the hoof trail. He did not look back to see if the others were following. One by one, the outlaws fell in behind him. They walked with a feeling of dread lying across their shoulders, but they simply had no choice in the matter.

They had no blankets or groundsheets, no robes or spare clothing, no supplies of any kind. They left the man with the blown off toes lying on the ground and walked away, ignoring his screams for help. He called after them until his voice was gone. No one looked back. The outlaw that Preacher had drilled through the noggin was left in the rocks where he had fallen. The varmits and carrion birds would feast on him. The man with the ruined foot tried crawling after his gang. He crawled until his hands were bloody and nearly useless and he could go no further. He lay on

215

the ground and cursed those whom he had called friends. When his panic had subsided, he gathered what wits he had left and fashioned a crutch of sorts and started back down the trail they'd blazed after Preacher. He hoped all those bastards who had so coldly left him to die would meet a horrible fate at the hands of Preacher. He could not know just how accurate his wishes were to be.

Preacher put the horses in a little valley that had good graze still and good water. He knew that as long as the food and water held out, they wouldn't wander far. He cached loaded pistols and shot and powder in spots, as well as packets of food and water and blankets. Preacher ranged about five miles in his hiding of weapons and supplies. Satisfied that he was ready, he found him a vantage spot and waited.

It was a sullen and silent group of outlaws that trudged on, following the clear trail that Preacher had left. The leaders had no illusions. They all knew that this was the final showdown. They would die, or Preacher would die. It was that cut and dried. They had to have horses. If they didn't find mounts, they would die. Already the nights were cold, and getting colder with each passing night. They had to get out of the high country.

"We're walkin' right into it, Malachi," Kenrick said. "Playin' right into Preacher's hands. This is his game all the way."

"I know it," Malachi panted the words. "You got any better plan?"

Kenrick was silent.

The outlaw who had taken the point suddenly threw up a hand, halting the column. "This is it, boys," he called. "Come take a look at this, will you?"

The outlaws crowded forward and everyone of them sucked in their gut at the sight. Huge peaks lay on both sides of the wide valley; no way over them. At the end of the long valley, four or five miles wide and about that deep, more mountains loomed, beginning with a gentle sloping and charging upward.

They all knew that at the end of the valley, hidden amid the rocks and brush and timber, was Preacher. Waiting. To a man they cussed.

"I suggest we break up into groups of two and three," Dirk said, squatting down and resting his tired legs. "I think we'd have a better chance that way."

"I agree," Son said.

"All right," Malachi said. "Kenrick, you take one group of our boys, I'll take one, and Radborne can take the other."

"Two groups of my boys," Son said.

"Three of mine," Dirk said, standing up. "No point in wasting time. We might as well do it."

The men got their positions and trails straight and began moving out. Alone, on the other side of the valley, Preacher looked through the spyglass he'd found in the saddlebags of the outlaws—it probably belonged to the Englishman, for it was said that Dirk had once been before the mast, probably as a pirate—and watched the men split up and come toward him.

Some were going to work both sides of the valley and try to get around him and box him, while others came straight in. "Ain't gonna work, people," Preacher said. "You'll be so busy lookin' for traps that ain't there, you ain't gonna be givin' your full attention to all the surroundin's. And that's when I'm gonna nail you."

Preacher chewed on jerky and waited. He was going to drop the first one that came into rifle range, just to give the others something to think about.

"Stop that damn gigglin', Ansel," Malachi told his goofiest brother. "This ain't no joke, you fool."

"Can I sing?"

"No. Just shut up and keep your eyes wide open for booby traps. You know that damn Preacher laid some out for us."

The man with the arrow point still embedded in one cheek of his ass hobbled along at the rear of one group. No one had wanted to dig the point out, so he just broke the shaft off and endured the pain . . . which was considerable. But it wouldn't be for long, as he was motioned up to take the point. His group was going straight up the valley.

"I really 'preciate you guys offerin' to dig out this damn arreyhead," he bitched. "Some friends you are."

"Aw, shut up and take the point, Fabor. No one wants to look at your smelly butt."

"When I get my horse back, I'm gone from this bunch. Jinked is what we is."

No one replied, but they all agreed with him.

Fabor limped along, his eyes trying to take in everything around him and, in doing that, missing much. The group made the center of the valley and stopped to rest by a creek. After a drink of water, they pressed on, each step taking them closer and closer to where Preacher lay in the rocks.

Preacher cocked his Hawken and waited.

The other groups of outlaws were moving out of the valley and onto the first gentle slopings of the mountain. No one had spotted Preacher's hideout.

"There ain't no traps," Malachi said. "That ain't like Preacher. Maybe he ain't here."

No one replied to that because all knew it was wistful thinking. Preacher was close. They all felt it.

218

Fabor stopped for a moment just at the edge of the slope. He stood still, his eyes inspecting the rocks and the brush and the timber ahead of him. He opened his mouth to speak just as Preacher fired. The big slug took him in the center of the chest and dropped him dead as a stone.

Preacher immediately shifted positions, reloading on the move.

"He's in them rocks up yonder!" a man called Curtis yelled from his belly-down position on the ground.

Preacher was in the rocks, but the rocks and boulders ran for hundreds of yards west to east, with twisting passageways weaving in and out. It was a death trap and the outlaws knew it.

Dirk motioned one of his men forward and the man reluctantly obeyed, moving very slowly and cautiously. He entered the rocks and the silence fell about him. The rocks blocked the cold winds, but the outlaw took no comfort from that. He'd much rather face the winds than Preacher. He paused for a moment, listening. But all he could hear was the low moaning of the winds.

He turned toward a narrow passageway and caught the butt of Preacher's Hawken square on his chin. The heavy rifle smashed his jaw and knocked out teeth. The outlaw was unconscious before he sprawled out on the ground.

Preacher picked up the man's rifle and checked it. He wasn't familiar with the rifle. It looked like a .69 caliber English rifle, which fired a very respectable ball. Preacher turned at a slight noise and fired. The ball struck the man in the belly, and the range was so close the wadding as well as the ball tore into the brigand's stomach. The force slammed the outlaw against a boulder and he sat down on his butt, screaming as waves of pain tore through him. He hollered and cussed Preacher as the blood leaked from his mouth, dripping onto his filthy shirt.

Preacher vanished into the maze of passageways he had thoroughly checked out that morning, marking the dead ends with small rock cairns.

"Roy!" someone called. "Peter! Answer me."

The wind moaning and sighing was the only reply, since Roy was gut-shot and dying and Peter's jaw was broken in so many places he was not capable of speaking . . . even if he was conscious. Which he was not.

Ansel suddenly left Malachi's side and went screaming into the maze of rocks. Preacher heard him coming and braced himself, not wanting to kill the fool. Preacher reversed the outlaw's rifle and waited. Ansel's screaming drew nearer. Behind him, Malachi was shouting for his brother to come back. Ansel rounded the curve of rocks, panting and cussing and hollering and slobbering. Preacher gave him the stock of the English rifle smack in the face. The stock broke off and Ansel went down in a sprawl of arms and legs, minus a dozen teeth and with his jaw smashed horribly. Preacher grabbed up the nitwit's rifle and took off, winding his way through the huge boulders.

"You hurt my baby brother and I'll tear your eyes out, Preacher!" Malachi screamed out his rage. "Ansel, honey, you all right?"

It would be a long time before Ansel even woke up, much less managed to speak. Roy lay dead, his back to a boulder. Peter had not moved. Fabor's body lay cooling on the slope.

Preacher checked Ansel's rifle and waited patiently in the rock maze.

"Goddamnit!" Dirk shouted. "He's just one man.

One man. Get him. Come on. Everybody into the rocks."

"Yeah!" Malachi shouted. "Surround him in there. We can starve him out if nothin' else."

Fools, Preacher thought. Nothin' but fools. I'm a-squattin' here in about ten acres of rocks and I know all the ways in and out. So come on, you sorry pack of worthless ne'er-do-wells. Let's settle this now.

"Baby brother!" Kenrick yelled. "Where are you, boy? Call out."

"Here's Peter," a man called. "His face is all tore up bad. His jaw's busted. Roy's dead."

Preacher picked up a fist-sized rock and chunked it over the boulders. It crashed against the side of a passageway and a dozen rifles roared. The sounds of ricochets screaming around the rocks was fearsome. Then a scream ripped the early afternoon's cold air as Preacher began working his way toward the unconscious Ansel.

"You bastards!" a man cried out. "You've shot me. Oh, God, help me."

"Hell with you," Radborne called. "Here's our baby brother, Malachi. Oh, Lordy, he's hurt bad."

Preacher stepped out onto the narrow path, leveled his Hawken, and dusted Radborne from side to side, the ball tearing through the man. Radborne screamed and fell across his brother, mortally wounded. He struggled to rise to his boots and failed. Preacher vanished back into the maze, reloading quickly.

"He's in the center of the rocks," Son called, frantically reloading his rifle. "Damnit, stay away from the center of these rocks."

"Radborne!" Kenrick yelled. "Where are you?"

That was a very good question, but money placed on Hell would probably be a sure bet.

Preacher mentally counted up the score in this deadly game. He figured six were out of it, dead, dying, or badly injured. Not a bad day's work, Preacher thought.

A cry of anguish went up out of the rocks as Henry Pardee found his brothers. "Radborne's dead, Malachi. And Ansel don't answer me. His face is all swole up. *Preacher!*" he screamed. "I'm a-comin' after you, Preacher."

Come on, Preacher thought.

Son had linked up with Dirk. Each man wore an expression of hopelessness. The two men exchanged glances.

"Let's get out of here," Son whispered. "We'll find the horses and leave."

"I'm for that," the Englishman returned the whisper. "We'll not do nothing except die in here. Preacher is a devil."

The men began backing out of the rocks.

Henry began stalking the silent stone passageways, his face grim and angry. He ignored the calls from Malachi and Kenrick to come back.

Preacher waited.

The remaining outlaws stayed put, afraid to move.

Valiant Pardee joined Malachi and Kenrick. His face was pale under the dirt and he was badly frightened. "Son and Dirk pulled out," he whispered. "I seen them leavin'. I'm afeard, Malachi. I truly am."

"Preacher!" Henry screamed. "Come out and fight."

Henry was very close as Preacher pulled out a pistol and placed one hand over the hammer to muffle the sound of the cocking. He could hear Henry's heavy breathing and the scrape of his clothing as he brushed up against the sides of the rock passageway. Henry stepped in front of the narrow, almost hidden passageway where Preacher stood, and paused for a second. Preacher fired, the ball striking the Pardee brother in the temple and blowing out the other side. Henry Pardee dropped soundlessly to the rocks; his life of crime and depravity was over.

"There's one less of your kin, Malachi," Preacher shouted above the echoing of the shot. "You want the body, come get it. I'd hate to see a buzzard get sick from eatin' on it."

Malachi cursed Preacher until he was breathless.

Son and Dirk had stripped the clothing from two dead men for extra warmth, leaving their naked bodies on the ground, and were now frantically searching for the hidden horses. They were not having much luck.

"They could be miles from here," Son said. "We got to chance walkin' out, Dirk. We stay here and Preacher will get us for sure and certain."

The Englishman thought about that for a moment. "All right. Let's go. We got ample powder and shot and we're sure to see Indians. We can shoot them and take their ponies."

"Grand idea. Let's get gone."

Preacher lit the makeshift fuse to one of the powder horns taken from the dead and chunked it in the direction of whispered voices. Sometimes black-powder bombs worked and sometimes they didn't. This time they didn't. It landed on an outlaw's head and knocked him to his knees and sent several outlaws screaming and racing away from the sputtering powder horn. Preacher stepped out and fired his double-shotted pistols. The four balls shrieked and howled off the rock walls of the passageways and took two of the outlaws down in a bloody sprawl, the flattened ricochets wounding them grievously. The wounded men lay on the rocky paths and screamed in pain.

"Don't be singin' no sad songs to me," Preacher muttered as he reloaded. "I didn't tell you to ride with this bunch."

"Bad," Malachi whispered to Kenrick. "We got to get Valiant and Ansel and get gone from here."

"What about the others?"

"Hell with them."

Valiant came crawling up, his eyes wild with fear. "Preacher just shot the legs from under Hosea and Campbell. It's a turrible sight to see."

"Go drag your brother back here, boy," Malachi told him. "We got to get shut of this place."

"Which brother?"

"The *live* one, you igit!"

"Oh. Right, Malachi. I'm gone."

"I been knowin' that for years," Kenrick muttered.

Six

Preacher Injuned his way up on top of a huge boulder, bellied down, and had him a look-see. He smiled at the sight. Two were running across the valley. He couldn't tell who they were. Dead and dying men were sprawled all around the narrow passageways. Then he saw a Pardee slipping up to his brothers, one dead and the goofy one still out of it.

Preacher leveled his Hawken and squeezed off a ball. The ball knocked Valiant sprawling, one arm dangling useless. But he still managed to grab ahold of Ansel and pull him from under Radborne. Preacher slid off the boulder and worked his way to the north end of the death maze. That put him higher up on the slope and gave him a clear field of fire. He reloaded both rifles and started picking targets.

One of the men he'd seen back at Dirk's place got careless and it cost him his life. Preacher shot him right between the eyes and watched him slide down the slope and come to rest against a boulder.

"I surrender!" another shouted.

"The hell you do," an outlaw said, and shot the man dead.

"Shore is a nice bunch of people down yonder," Preacher muttered, reloading his Hawken. He watched as Malachi, Kenrick, and Valiant dragged the still-unconscious Ansel out of rifle range. Out of the corner of his eye, he caught movement on the ridges about two miles or so away. Indians, and it was a big bunch of them. He couldn't tell what tribe, but he'd bet they were Shoshoni. Preacher slipped away, made the timber, and kept right on going to his little hidden valley.

All through the afternoon he heard the sounds of shots, and come the evening, faint screaming. The next morning, he turned the horses loose and mounted up. He rode down to just above the rocks, staying in the timber, and looked down at what the Indians had left. It was not a pretty sight. He saw where the Shoshoni had ridden off to the northeast, so Preacher headed south, leaving the bodies to the varmits and the carrion birds, which were already circling above. They were patient, knowing that death comes to all living things.

Preacher picked up sign almost immediately. Eight men, all scattered out and all on foot. And they would be runnin' scared as a rabbit with a coyote after him. Preacher chuckled without humor and fell in behind one group. Some would call what he had in mind evil. Preacher called it ridding the wilderness of undesirables.

Preacher could have struck at the outlaws within hours of picking up their tracks. But he wanted some distance between himself and that roaming band of scalp-hunting Shoshonis. Odds were they probably wouldn't bother Preacher, since he got along fairly well with most Indian tribes. But he decided to play it cautious this time.

He came up on the body of an outlaw and

chased off the buzzards. They didn't go far. The body had been stripped of all clothing and was naked, stiffening in the cold air. Looked like to Preacher the man's own buddies had knocked him in the head and taken his clothing for added warmth. Two of them walked away from the scene, if he was reading the sign right. Preacher left him where he lay and moved on. Somewhere Preacher had heard about honor among thieves, or something like that. Sure wasn't none of that to be found in this bunch.

He was following a creek when he suddenly reined up. Hammer's ears had pricked up and Preacher took note.

About three hundred yards ahead of him he saw three men, staggering along. Their clothing was in rags and they were clearly exhausted. But all were still armed.

Preacher sat his horse and watched them until they were out of sight. He felt no pity for the outlaws. Preacher was a hard man in a harsh land. As far as distance went, the men were not that far away from a trading post. But the Cascades lay between some vestiges of civilization and them. The Whitman Mission lay a couple of hundred miles to the south—they would never make that.

Preacher lifted the reins and cut east of the trio, following the Columbia south toward the mission.

Son, Dirk, and the Pardees had fared much better than their men . . . in a manner of speaking. They had come up on a band of friendly Yakima Indians, men and women who were moving to winter campsites, and brutally murdered them all, taking their horses and robes. The outlaws had their way with the women, and then strangled them. Preacher came upon the awful sight just as another

227

band of Yakima warriors reached the site.

It got real chancy there for a few moments.

"I'm trailin' the men who done this," Preacher told the war chief. "But if you find them 'fore I do, you're welcome to them."

The Yakima looked at Preacher through steely eyes. Preacher was known to his people as a fair man who loved the land and coveted no Indian territory for his own. The war chief slowly nodded his head. "You have names?"

"The Pardee brothers, a man called Son, and an Englishman named Dirk. Dirk ran a trading post north of here."

"I know the men. They are evil."

A young brave said something and the war chief shook his head. He looked at Preacher. "Leave now, Preacher. We must bury our own."

Preacher left without another word. The Yakimas were killing mad and some of the younger braves looked like they'd as soon kill him as anyone else. He resisted an urge to glance over his shoulder, knowing that would be considered a sign of weakness on his part. He began to breathe easier a couple of miles later.

He couldn't figure out where the gang was heading. It looked like they might be going into the Rattlesnake Range or the Horse Heaven Hills; but he had serious doubts about that. That was rough country, and as far as he knew, they wasn't a livin' soul down there. Then their trail cut due west and Preacher knew they were heading for Fort Vancouver, which some folks was already calling the New York of the Pacific. A regular little city it was, by western standards. Preacher figured they'd waylay some trappers or movers, steal their clothing to get duded up better, and then travel on to the fort.

Preacher swung down from the saddle and built a hat-sized fire for coffee while he ruminated some.

Snow had dusted the land again, thicker and heavier, and the nights were turning bitterly cold. His horses were rough looking in their winter coats and Preacher knew he was rough looking . . . and rough smelling, too. He hadn't shaved in several weeks and he'd been in his clothing for longer than that.

He drank his coffee and made up his mind. He'd head for the mission to see about the movers. He'd catch up with the Pardees and their ilk sooner or later. But for now, he'd be content with the knowledge that he'd pretty much pulled their stingers out. Come the spring, he'd start tracking again.

What was left of the gang had found several old abandoned Indian winter homes: semiunderground earth houses that many of the Northwest tribes used during the harsh winter season. Along the way, they had killed any trapper they found and seized the supplies, including precious powder and shot and coffee. Their existence this winter would be bleak, but they would make it. At least, they figured, they had succeeded in shaking Preacher off their trail.

Malachi had set Ansel's busted jaw and tied a rag around his head to immobilize it. But the jaw was healing crooked and the blow to the head had addled Ansel even more. Now he was just plain crazy as a bessy bug. He had trouble speaking and hardly anyone could understand a word he tried to say.

Dirk had fallen sullen and silent; he stayed alone and contented himself with cursing Preacher. He did not think he had ever despised a man as much as he did Preacher.

229

Son passed the long days and bitter nights by dreaming of torturing and killing Preacher in all sorts of ways.

Malachi would look at what remained of the family and shake his head in sorrow.

Edward Sutherlin and his party had made the fort on the Laramie River and settled in to winter there. Along the way he had picked up four more toughs and come the spring he would make his move to settle Preacher's hash.

On a bitterly cold early winter's day, Preacher rode onto the grounds of the Whitman Mission.

"Ol' hoss," Caleb told him, "you look as mangy as a bear come out of hibernation."

"Feel like it, too," Preacher said, climbing wearily out of the saddle and handing the reins to a mover boy. "I got fleas and ticks and spiders and mites all over me. Is there a place to take a bath?"

"We built us a cabin," Windy said. "Come on. It's snug."

"Get me over there 'fore Betina sees me," Preacher replied, looking all around him.

"She's with Miss Narcissa," Rimrock said. "They's ed-ecatin' the Injun children."

"Good. Maybe she'll leave me be then. Stoke up the fire and heat the water. I got things *crawlin'* on me!"

Preacher took two baths before he felt clean. Carl Lippett came over to say hello, took one look at what was going on, and hit the air, saying he was going out for game. He'd be back when all that damn hot water and soap was gone.

Preacher trimmed his beard but left the face hair on as some protection against the cold. He'd shave

230

come the spring. Then he walked over to the community building to see if he could bum something to eat. The movers had done themselves up right proud in the getting ready for winter. They'd built log floors under the beds of the wagons for more room and secured the sides with canvas and what lumber they could mill. When the Cayuses had learned the movers were not going to stay on permanently, they helped the movers get ready for winter. All in all, it was a fairly snug camp. But they would suffer come the long months of winter, Preacher had no illusions about that.

Betina was rather stiff and formal when she saw Preacher, which was fine with him. He didn't want to hurt her feelin's no more than he already had, but his life had no room in it for a female . . . especially an eastern female with settlin' down on the brain. Maybe she was finally gettin' that through her head. Preacher hoped so.

"Was your mission successful, Preacher?" Betina asked coolly, after introducing him to Narcissa Whitman.

"I reckon you'd call it that. I killed ten or twelve of them."

"Ten or twelve of what, Mr., ah, Preacher?" Narcissa asked.

"Men. You got anything to eat?"

"Men!" Narcissa cried, horrified.

"Sorry lot they was, too. World's better off without them. Is that stew over yonder?"

"I'll pray for you, sir," Narcissa said.

"Thanks. I probably need it." Preacher walked over to the fireplace and ladled out a heaping plate of stew from the big blackened iron pot. He grabbed up a fresh loaf of bread and fell to eating.

"Did they receive a proper burial?" one of the

231

mission's helpers asked.

"Buzzards seen to that," Preacher said.

"My word!" the missionary said.

"They was gonna hit the wagon train come this spring," Preacher explained. "Kill all the men, violate the women and girls, and sell the youngsters into slavery and bondage and whorin'. They wasn't very nice people."

"We must bring law and order to this land," the missionary said.

"In about fifty years, maybe," Preacher said, after swallowing a mouthful of stew. It needed salt but he wasn't going to complain.

Miles Cason and George Martin came in, and Miles went immediately to Betina's side. Preacher noticed that and hid a smile.

"Did you track down those miserable excuses for men, Preacher?" George asked.

"That I did. Two or three Pardees got clear of me, and I think Son and Dirk did too. But I left them terrible short of a gang. What I didn't get a band of Shoshonis did." He looked over at Miles. "You two sparkin', I see."

"Sir!" Miles protested, as Betina flushed and fanned herself vigorously with a little hankie.

"Ain't nothin' to get all worked up about. You two make a mighty handsome couple. Hee, hee, hee!" he chuckled at their red-faced expressions.

"We must get back to work, Betina," Narcissa said, smoothly getting her off the hook.

"Yes, quite," Betina said, and the two women left the room.

Preacher finished his stew, sopped out the plate with a hunk of bread, then refilled his coffee cup. "Place looks pretty good," he remarked. "Y'all done a bang-up job in gettin' ready for the winter."

"Thank you," Miles said. "Might I have a word with you, Preacher?"

"Have two or three. They're free."

George and the missionary left the room and Miles sat down at the long table. "Betina and I have been taking a more than casual interest in one another, Preacher."

"Thought so. Good. Y'all get married and have babies. I give you my blessin'."

"You're not upset?"

"Hell no!"

"Her feelings toward the young man back East have faded considerably."

"He's there and she's here. 'Sides, she showed more nerve than him in comin' out here. Pioneer stock needs to breed together. Is George sparkin' Coretine?"

"Yes."

"Then it 'pears to me that everything is gonna work out all right, ain't it?"

Miles fiddled with his coffee cup for a moment. "I was on a fool's mission in my quest for gold. Those ideas are gone. Betina and I have agreed that we shall push on come the spring and settle in the new land and farm."

"Regular city over 'crost the Cascades now. Y'all will do well."

"And your plans, Preacher?"

Preacher smiled at the younger man. "You don't want me around here, do you, Miles?"

"I . . . I don't know, Preacher. Part of me does. We all owe you our lives. I can't—won't—forget all that you and the other mountain men have done for us, and are continuing to do for us. We all feel somewhat sorry for you men."

Preacher looked at the man, amazement in his

233

expression. "You feel sorry for *us?* Lord God, man, why?"

"What will you do when this area is settled, Preacher? Any of you?"

"Boy, that's years down the trail. This land will be wild and woolly and full of fleas for another fifty years . . . maybe longer than that. Right now they's more outlaws and brigands and highwaymen in this country than pilgrims. Maybe ten to one. And the Injuns ain't even yet begun to fight you people for real. They can't understand that the white man is gonna pour into this country by the thousands. Right now, it's just a trickle. It'll soon turn into a ragin' river of people. That's when your troubles will really begin. Outlaws will pour in here, wantin' something for nothin' like outlaws always do, whole Injun tribes will go on the warpath, killin' and scalpin'. That's when people like you will start hollerin' for people like me to help pull your bacon out of the fire. So don't you be feelin' sorry for me. That makes me laugh."

"The Army will be in to protect us," Miles rebutted.

"Not for years, boy. This is disputed territory. You got British and French and Americans all squabblin' over this country. They'll get it settled someday. Until then, it's ever' man for himself 'cause there ain't no law west of the Missouri 'ceptin' the gun and the knife and the bow and the war axe. You best be mindful of that at all times."

"I am much more optimistic than you."

Preacher nodded his head and drained his coffee cup. He glanced out the window . . . a real window with glass and all. It was snowing again. Big, thick, wet flakes. He wondered briefly where the Pardees and Son and Dirk had holed up for the winter. He

234

wondered, should he stay here or hunt him up a cabin for the cold season? Or mayhaps ride over the mountains and hole up with some trappers over to the Hudson's Bay post? One thing for sure, Miles and Betina didn't want him around, and he didn't blame either of them for that. Betina knew she had made a fool of herself earlier and that stuck in her craw.

"You folks set up huntin' parties, Miles?"

"Yes," he said shortly.

"I seen where you been draggin' in wood and stackin' it around. That's good." When Miles did not respond, Preacher stood up and said, "I reckon I'll ride." He walked out of the community building without another word.

SEVEN

"They don't want me here, Rim," Preacher said, saddling up. "It don't sadden me none 'cause I understand it. You boys stick around and see these pilgrims through the winter if you're a mind to. Grub's pretty good, if a body can put up with all the gospel shoutin'. I'm gonna ride a ways and find me a good camp and then ponder for a time how come it is I keep gettin' myself in these situations."

Hammer was tired, but he was, as usual, ready for the trail. Preacher rode out within the hour and headed for the Blue Mountains. He knew he wouldn't near 'bouts make them, but he knew of a little place about ten miles from the mission that was out of the wind and near a creek. He made it before dark and picketed his horses in a protected area with some graze left and set about making his lonely camp. He rigged him a lean-to in front of a boulder so the stone would reflect the heat from the fire back into his open-front shelter. He gathered up wood to last several days and stacked it close. Then he fixed him something to eat and put water on for coffee.

People sure were funny, he thought. Hard to figure them out. When a body thinks he's doin' right, turns out he's doin' wrong. Strange. He give his blessin' to Betina and Miles, and still they got all swole up about him being in the mission proper.

Hell with them.

Preacher lay about the camp for two days and finally got restless and saddled up. Hammer was snortin' and pawin', ready for the trail. Preacher then began a lonely odyssey across the southern part of what would someday be called Wyoming. He camped very near the spot that would someday become Fort Bridger. Only a few years in the future, Bridger and Vasquez would build a trading post on almost the exact spot where Preacher now sat before his small fire, pondering the fates that had led him to this desolate spot. But Preacher wasn't going to ponder long, for action seemed to find the man. In this case, in the form of two Arapaho Indians who were wandering and saw the fire. Preacher knew they were there, but he made no move toward his Hawken. Just kept it very close.

"Shore is gettin' tiresome talkin' to myself," he said, raising his voice to be heard. "I'd be pleased to talk to someone. Even two mangy Arapaho called Kicking Bear and Runs Fast."

Both the braves laughed and rode into the camp. "We thought it was you, Preacher. But we couldn't be sure. We have fresh buffalo hump if you have coffee."

"Gather 'round, pull up a rock, and sit. We'll eat and talk."

"It is good to see you, Preacher," Kicking Bear said, pouring a cup of coffee. "In more ways than one. But we bring trouble to you."

"My middle name. What's the matter?"

"A band of war-painted Pawnee trails us." There was a definite twinkle of high humor in his eyes. "But since we know how Preacher loves the Pawnee, perhaps we should ride on. Preacher might not want to bring harm to his favorite people."

Preacher looked at the man and smiled. "Oh, yeah. Them's my favorite, all right. I been stuck with several arrows over the years, all of them Pawnee. How many and how far away?"

"Ten or twelve. Perhaps they will hit us at first light."

Preacher took note that both Arapaho were carrying new Hawken rifles in addition to bows and quivers of arrows. He did not ask where they got the guns, the powder horns, or the shot. "We'll eat and then move over yonder in them rocks. A trickle of water flows through there and they's some graze for the horses. Pawnees are a little out of their territory, ain't they?"

"They are mostly young men, hunting scalps to impress the girls," Runs Fast said, fitting hunks of meat on sticks. "They will be mostly dead when they find us, I am thinking," he added very dryly.

"They are also ugly," Kicking Bear added. "They paint themselves and make them even more ugly." He spat on the ground. "They look like something out of a nightmare. I hate the Pawnee."

The men ate their fill and more, belched loudly, then drank two pots of coffee. Preacher took out tobacco and they smoked and were content for a time. The fire was warm, the late afternoon still peaceful and safe, for the birds were singing and the little animals playing.

"White men from the East are wintering on the Laramie River," Kicking Bear said. "They have plans to come west in the spring." He smoked for a time and Preacher waited. "The leader of the group is the man who has an alliance with the renegade, Red Hand."

"Sutherlin," Preacher said.

"That is the name, I believe. But since the names of white men are so strange and one must twist his mouth all out of shape and almost swallow his tongue to speak them, I cannot be sure. But I believe that is the person."

"I kilt most of the Pardee gang and Son's bunch up north and west of here."

"So we heard. It is a good thing you did. They were bad people."

"How many men does Sutherlin have with him?"

"Ten or twelve, at least."

Preacher did not ask how Kicking Bear and Runs Fast knew all this. The Indians had a grapevine that was both astonishing and very fast and accurate. When around whites, Indians usually said little and listened intently. The language of the Plains Indians varied with each tribe, but most Indians were multilingual and all could communicate thousands of words and thoughts with a few hundred signals by hand. The Arapaho were friends of nearly everyone — when convenient — but most did not like the Pawnee. Their sign for the Pawnee was the first two fingers of either hand held up in a V. No one knew why, it just was.

Preacher cocked an ear and listened. The birds were gone and the woods animals had ceased their playing. "I think we best head for them rocks. I don't think the Pawnee are gonna wait for dawn to hit us."

In two minutes flat, Preacher and the Arapaho were in the rocks and taking up positions.

Then, from all around their stone fort, came hoots of derision and taunting catcalls. "Arapaho shit!" a Pawnee called out. "You will not die well, I am thinking."

"You are incapable of thinking," Kicking Bear

shouted. "Your mother was a buzzard and your father was a skunk."

The Arapaho warriors shouted insults for a time, and then fell silent.

"They got their courage worked up now," Preacher remarked. "They been slippin' all around us for a few minutes. They'll be comin' at us pretty quick now."

No sooner had the words left his mouth when the Pawnee braves rushed the rocks, screaming war cries. Preacher blew a hole in one's chest with his Hawken, picked up his other Hawken, and almost blew the head off another. He jerked out one brace of pistols just as the charge broke off. Preacher and the two Arapaho had done some fearsome damage to the young Pawnee warriors. Six of them lay dead or dying around the rocks.

"They will quit now," Runs Fast said as he reloaded. "We have wiped out half of their band. Their medicine is no good."

The sounds of ponies galloping away reached them and Kicking Bear snorted in disgust. "They leave their dead behind. Filthy cowards."

Kicking Bear and Runs Fast took out their knives and went to work. First they scalped the dead, then cut off their hands, took out their eyes, and cut off their genitals. Now, in the World That Came After, the dead would not be able to see their way, find their enemies, or breed young to carry on the fight. Preacher watched them dispassionately. Unlike the missionaries, he seldom tried to change the Indians way of thinking or questioned their customs. He figured it just wasn't none of his damn business.

Which was one of the reasons he got along so well with most tribes.

When Runs Fast and Kicking Bear had finished,

they held up their bloody trophies, grinned, and waved goodbye to Preacher. Preacher returned the smile, made the sign of thanks and farewell, and the two Arapaho rode off. Preacher packed up and got the hell gone from there.

Preacher found the trail of the Arapaho, followed it for a time to make sure they were not going to circle around back, and then cut north for a time. He wasn't in any hurry; had no place really to go and no timetable set for him. He wanted to meet up with this Sutherlin person, but didn't want to ride right into the post and start opening up. Also, one of the dead outlaws he'd left back on the trail had had him two pistols that Preacher had coveted something fierce almost immediately. Preacher had just now remembered that he'd picked up the broken guns and stashed them in his supplies. He wanted to find him a spot where he could work on the things.

The next afternoon, he made camp early and dug out the pistols. The pistols were complicated-looking things, each one of them having four barrels, over and under. He repaired the bullet-shattered butt of one with the brass butt plate from a spare of his own, then replaced the bent hammers on the second one with hammers taken from other spares he'd picked up from the dead and dying. They were the same caliber as his Hawken, so he loaded them up and taken them out to test-fire them. They were of a slightly shorter barrel than his other pistols, but gave him eight times the firepower. Once he got the hang of them, he was pleased, mighty pleased. Chuckling, he double-shotted two of the four barrels on each pistols and set about making holsters for them from a skin. Once that was done, he fashioned the holsters to his wide leather belt and went down to the creek to take a look at himself. He sure hadn't ever seen nothing like the image that reflected back up at him.

He looked like a . . . come to think of it, he didn't know what the hell he looked like. Then he taken rawhide thongs, punched a hole in the bottom of each holster, and tied the holsters to his legs so's they wouldn't flop around so much.

Then he decided he'd see how fast he could get them out of the holsters and cock and fire them. First time he tried it he damned near blowed his foot off. Then he decided he'd try it with the pistols empty. He spent a week in his camp, practicing several hours each day. Each hour he got faster and more accurate.

"By God," he said to the cold winds. "I just might have me somethin' here. I don't know perxactly what, but it's something mighty important, I believe."

Only problem was, when he mounted up to do a little scouting around the camp, the damn pistols fell out of the holsters. Preacher sat down on a log and done a little head ruminatin'. Then he taken some rawhide and fashioned some thongs at the top of each holster to loop over one hammer and that done the trick. To get in the habit, every time he dismounted, he slipped the thongs off the hammers to free his guns. Soon doing that became second nature to him.

Preacher would go down in history as being the first to do many things. Some had him as the first mountain man, but that was a lie. They was a lot of white men out in the wilderness long 'fore Preacher got there. What he didn't know, had no way of knowing, was that he would go down in history as being the first gunfighter to use the quick draw.

Preacher finally saddled up and packed up and pulled out, heading for the post on the Laramie in a roundabout way. Along the way, he met up with a disreputable-looking old reprobate of a mountain man called Natchez.

Natchez took one look at Preacher's rig slung around his lean waist and said, "What in the billy-hell has you got strapped around you, Preacher?"

"You know me, Natch. I'm always comin' up with something different."

"Looks plumb awkward to me. You be careful and don't get yourself kilt with them fool things."

"You been over yonder on the Laramie?"

"For a fact, I have. Man from back East is there, and a mighty quiet and secretive man he is, I say. He's got him ten or twelve brigands with him and they's tough enough, I reckon." The old man smiled. "Tough back East, that is. Out here, I 'spect they'll have to prove their mettle."

"This quiet man's name wouldn't be Sutherlin, would it now?"

"It would for a fact. You a friend of hisn?"

"No. Some Arapaho told me 'bout him back west of here a couple of weeks ago. I was also told he was up to no good."

"I don't take to him, for a fact. He's a tad on the sneaky side for me. Don't care for the look in his eyes. When he does bump his gums, you can tell he's a man with book larnin', but he talks down to people. I knowed if I stayed 'round there much longer I might have to shoot him."

"I do know the feelin'."

Natchez looked at the big four-barreled pistols slung in leather around Preacher's waist and shook his head. "Never seen nothin' like that in all my

243

borned days. See you around, Preacher."

Preacher lifted a hand in farewell and the two men rode their separate ways. In the Ferris Mountains, Preacher found a cabin that had been built years back by a friend of his—long dead—and since the weather had turned bad, he decided to hole up for a time.

He cleaned out the sooted-up chimney and laid in wood and mudded up the chinks between the logs, making the cabin snug. He killed two deer and skinned and dressed them out, hanging the meat high from a limb. In a few hours the meat was froze solid. Preacher started work on the skins, for he needed new high-top moccasins and a shirt.

For a month he saw no sign of a human being and he was content. He killed several more deer, and when he was ready to leave the snug cabin, he was dressed in new buckskins from neck to feet. He had cut his hair and trimmed his beard close. He had practiced at least one hour a day, and had become incredibly fast and deadly accurate with his awesome pistols with the complicated hammer systems and four barrels each. He had taken skins and hardened them, making better holsters for his guns.

He wondered occasionally how the folks were getting on back at the mission during this hard winter . . . but he didn't dwell on it long. He knew that Windy and Rimrock and Caleb would not leave them in the lurch. And even if the mountain men did leave the mission to go their own way—they certainly were under no obligation to stay—the movers would make it; if they didn't, then to Preacher's way of thinking, they should have stayed to home.

Preacher wanted to have done with Sutherlin by early spring, for that would give him several weeks to get back to the mission area to deal with what was left of the Pardees and their kind. Then he was through with movers and their damn wagon trains. He was going to head for the Southern Rockies; maybe go down on the Blue and get the hell away from wagon trains and movers and crazy women.

He got Hammer out of the little shelter and the big horse bucked and jumped and snorted and kicked and told Preacher in his own way that he was tired of being cooped up and let's get on the trail.

The day was pleasant, the sun warm and the snow melting—it would snow again, for winter was not over by a long shot—but the brief respite felt good. Preacher saddled up and pulled out.

"I'm gonna help these movers one more time, Sutherlin," he said to the warm winds as he headed east. "Then it's back to the mission, bury the Pardees, and I'm gone to the Big Lonesome down south."

Hammer shook his head and pranced in anticipation.

EIGHT

Preacher rode easy but in a distance-covering gait. He crossed the Shirley Mountains without incident and then got caught up in a blizzard near the southern curve of the North Laramie River. He forted up as best he could and he and Hammer and the packhorse sat it out. Finally the weather broke, the sun came out, the snows began to melt, and Preacher pushed on, reaching the post just as the first tentative touches of false spring were trying to shove winter aside.

He hadn't seen so damn many people all gathered together in years.

Indian tipis had been put up all around the post. Wagons were scattered here and there. A new corral had been built to handle the livestock and the post itself had been enlarged. Preacher sat his horse and stared in amazement.

"The push is on, Hammer," he said to his horse. "By May they'll be pilgrims all over the damn place. But if we have any luck a-tall, we'll be south of all this mess and bother. Let's go, Hammer, they's a whole feedbag of grain waitin' for you and my good packhorse."

Preacher wound his way through the tipis and movers' tents and wagons and what have you, and rode into the post. He stabled his horses and gave

246

the boy a coin to rub them down good and grain them. He saw no one he knew and no one called out his name. Which was just fine with Preacher. He found him something to eat and then went to the store, which had a room that served as a saloon of sorts. Preacher got him a cup of whiskey and found a seat at a table in a darkened corner of the room. He figured that sooner or later Sutherlin would show up . . . and Preacher was a patient man.

After a time several men—eastern men, by their appearance—strolled in and bought them a jug. They were rough looking and heavily armed. The three men tried to peer through the gloom to see who it was sitting alone at the corner table, but finally gave up and contented themselves with talking in low murmurs, occasionally glancing toward Preacher.

"You there!" one of them called sharply and in a tone that rankled Preacher. "I ain't seen you around here 'fore."

"I got caught up in a blizzard west of here and it blowed me and my horses all the way over here. That was some wind, let me tell you. But it set us down gentle like about a mile from the post. Does that satisfy you?"

The burly, unwashed, and stinking lout stared at Preacher for a moment. "Were you borned with a smart-aleck mouth or did you come into it as you got butt-uglier over the years?"

Preacher smiled at the man. "You callin' me ugly is like a frog callin' a buzzard ugly. I bet your mamma had to tie some fatback around your neck to get the dogs to play with you."

The lout narrowed his eyes and sat his cup of whiskey down and stood up.

"That's Preacher," a man spoke from the archway leading from the store into the bar.

The burly man smiled, exposing a mouthful of bad teeth. "The famous Preacher, hey? I heared an awful lot about you, Preacher. Some folks has you meaner than a bear and quick as a panther and all man. But lookin' at you, I can see they was all lies. I think I'll just break you in two."

"It's been tried," Preacher said, then took a sip of his whiskey. He set the cup down on the table. "More'n oncest." He cut his eyes to the archway. A mountain man name of John Morris stood there. "John. You know this loudmouth?"

"I seen him around. He's a trouble hunter."

"He's found it," Preacher said quietly.

"Not in here, Preacher," the sutler said, stepping up to the archway.

"I come in here for a quiet drink," Preacher told him. "You know me, Hector. I ain't never started no trouble in your place. But I ain't takin' water from this ugly bastard."

"Sit down, Talbot," one of his friends urged him.

But Talbot wasn't having any of that. "You callin' me a bastard, Preacher?"

"Yeah."

"I'll break you in half."

"You ain't done nothin' yet 'ceptin' run your mouth."

"Your employer will certainly pay for the damages," Hector stated. "Or you all shall be barred from the post, and from any other post from here to the Oregon coast."

"I'll pay." Another voice was added.

Preacher looked over at the man. A cruel-faced man with little piggy eyes. But a massive brute of a man nonetheless. He stood well over six feet and weighed probably two hundred and thirty pounds. He had the look of a man who had fought some for money. Big hamlike hands and huge wrists. One ear was slightly cauliflowered and his nose had been busted a time or two. Scar tissue over his eyes. Had to be Sutherlin. His clothing was either hand sewn or store-bought and tailored and very neat for the frontier.

Preacher had not risen from his chair. He drained his cup of whiskey and carefully placed the cup on the rough boards of the table.

"Fancy-pants," he said to Sutherlin, "you bes' tell your pet dog here to sit down and stop his barkin'. I just might decide to kill him."

"My name is Sutherlin. *Mister* Sutherlin, to you."

John Morris laughed at that and Sutherlin flushed under his clean-shaven face.

"Your name might be Sutherlin," Preacher said. "But it'll be a cold day in hell 'fore I call the likes of you mister."

Sutherlin's flush deepened and Talbot took a step toward Preacher, his hands balled into fists.

"I'll keep the others off of you, Preacher," John said, and pulled out two pistols.

"How do you want this, Talbot?" Preacher asked him. "Knives, fists, or guns?"

"Guns, Talbot. Let's be rid of him now."

Preacher stood up and all stared in confusion at the rig that hung around his waist.

"Guns it'll be," Preacher said. "Pull when you've a mind to, Talbot."

"We'll have a proper duel with seconds," Sutherlin said.

Preacher laughed at him. "This ain't New York, Sutherlin. You can forget all them e-laborate goin's-on. We like things simple out here. Now shut your flap and stand aside." He cut his eyes to Talbot. "Jerk and fire, you son of a bitch."

Talbot's hand flew to the butt of his pistol and that was as far as he got. Preacher pulled, cocked, and fired. One ball struck Talbot in the chest and the second ball tore a great, gaping hole in his throat. The thug was flung backward and died with his butt on the floor and his back to a wall. His pistol was still behind his belt.

Preacher holstered the awesome pistol and sat down in his chair.

"Damnest thing I ever seen," John Morris said. "I do believe you on to something, Preacher."

Sutherlin was visibly shaken by what had happened. His broad face was pale and his mouth was hanging open. While dueling was outlawed in most areas of the country, it was still practiced in secrecy in many areas. But no one had ever perfected the art of quick drawing, until now.

"Foul, I say." Sutherlin had found his voice. "That was not at all fair play."

"Gimme another drink of whiskey," Preacher said, tapping his cup on the table. "Shootin' makes me thirsty."

The men with Talbot had not moved, so shocked were they at the sudden events.

Hector brought a jug to Preacher's table and quickly backed away. Behind the plank bar, he pointed to the dead man. "Get him out of here and do it right now."

Sutherlin waved a hand at his men and they dragged the lifeless body of Talbot out of the room. He looked at Preacher. "We shall meet again."

"I'm countin' on it, fancy-pants," Preacher said, pouring a cup of whiskey.

Edward Sutherlin stared hard at Preacher, the

knowledge hitting him sudden that this rugged-looking and shaggy mountain man knew all about him. But *how?* No matter. He did. Sutherlin was sure of that. So this much was certain: Preacher had to die, and die quickly. Sutherlin had too much to lose for Preacher to stay alive and talk . . . and talk he would, Sutherlin was certain of that.

Sutherlin stepped from the room and went quickly to his quarters. His men would see to the burying of Talbot. The chief factor came to the saloon to briefly question Preacher and the matter was resolved and forgotten. Life was cheap in the wilderness. Staying alive was a day-to-day struggle that each man met in his own way.

In his quarters, Sutherlin sat down in a hide chair and pondered the situation. There had been no fear in Preacher — none; he had seen that. The man was totally unimpressed by either Sutherlin or his men. So in Sutherlin's mind, that made Preacher a fool.

Sutherlin would have liked to meet with Malachi Pardee and Son, but how? Communications were practically impossible out here in the wilderness, and for some reason as yet unknown to the man, his network of runners and riders had vanished. He did not know that Weasel Tail's braves had killed some of them and the others had fled for their lives, heading back across the Missouri into the safety of civilization . . . such as it was.

But no action could be taken against Preacher here at the fort. He was too well known and by now everyone would know that Sutherlin and Preacher had bad feelings between them. So Preacher must be watched at all times and Sutherlin and his men must be ready to leave at a moment's notice. He rose from the chair and walked outside to talk briefly with Lester, his second in command. Lester nodded his head and left to alert his men.

Preacher lounged in front of the store and watched the goings-on with a smile. He resupplied and toted the packages to the stable. There, he paid a man he knew very handsomely to sleep in the stall next to Hammer and report if anyone tried to tamper with his horses, supplies, or equipment. That taken care of, Preacher went outside the stockade walls and found him a Crow among the many Indians camped there. All Indians except Blackfeet were welcome at the post. He gave the Crow two of the pistols he'd taken from the dead, and a supply of shot and powder, to spy on Sutherlin and report back to him the man's every move. The Crow was known to Preacher and was a good man, friendly to the whites. Preacher had befriended the man several times, and the Crow was loyal to him.

Many at the fort eyeballed Preacher's guns and the way he wore them. Most shook their heads and dismissed the rig as being too cumbersome.

Before the dawning of the third day, Preacher was saddled up and ready to go. The Crow slipped into the stable.

"Piggy-face and his men are going to follow you, Preacher," the Crow told him.

"I'm countin' on it," Preacher replied. "You done good. I'll see you around."

The Crow nodded and slipped silently away into the predawn.

"What's with this Sutherlin feller?" the man Preacher had hired to stay with his gear asked, rising from the hay and brushing himself off.

"He's no-count. He's a murderer and worser. I aim to put out his lights."

"Power to you," the man said. "You want me to

bring you some coffee?"

"Had my fill. You take care, Jeff. I'll see you next time around."

Preacher rode out of the main gate and headed west, conscious of being watched by Sutherlin's thugs.

"Come on, people," he muttered. "Follow ol' Preacher. I got some surprises for you."

Before leaving, Preacher gave Sutherlin's men the slip and had talked long with the factor of the post, telling him all he knew about Sutherlin and all that the people in the wagon trains knew about him. The man's frown had deepened the more Preacher talked.

"He has been under suspicion, Preacher," the man said. "I don't believe he is aware of it as yet, but if he leaves unorganized territory and heads back to the States, there are warrants for his arrest waiting for him." He handed Preacher a letter from the United States Federal Marshal's office.

Preacher read the letter and grunted. "He won't never go back. I'll see to that."

"And I'll pretend I didn't hear you say that."

Preacher headed for the Laramie Mountains and set a grueling pace. He wanted those behind him tuckered when he made his move. He crossed the Laramie River and plunged into the deep wilderness. Wilderness for them struggling along behind him; home territory for Preacher. As he rode, Preacher allowed himself to recall the tortured and mutilated and raped and murdered bodies that he'd seen over the last couple of years . . . all of them due to the cold-hearted treachery of Edward Sutherlin.

"Sutherlin," Preacher spoke to the cold winds of late winter in the Big Empty. "You'll not be responsible for another death if I can help it. And I can help it."

At his camp that evening, in front of a small fire, Preacher again inspected his strange and deadly pistols. Whoever had made them had done so lovingly and with patient skill; they were the work of someone who possessed a great knowledge of firearms. Preacher had heard that firearms were in a state of advancement, and that some were even experimenting with some sort of revolving cylinder. He didn't see how anything like that would ever work, so he didn't dwell on it. But these pistols, now, these pistols were a work of art. And they gave him awesome firepower. Close in, he could damn near wage a full-scale war with these beauties.

Something he certainly intended to do.

Sutherlin and his men sat close to the fire, for the nights were still brutally cold. None of them had the foggiest idea where they were, only that they were staying on the trail of Preacher and they were heading west, in a roundabout manner. Sutherlin had heard back at the post that Malachi's gang had been savaged by Preacher, the mountain man nearly destroying the gang. Sutherlin found that hard to believe and felt the report was greatly exaggerated. No one man was capable of doing that.

Sutherlin knew little about the caliber of person called mountain man.

In their stinking, filthy lairs, Malachi and Dirk

254

and Son and what was left of their gangs brooded over their fires and waited for the arrival of spring. They had spent the entire winter nurturing the flames of hatred and now they could hardly contain themselves. To a man—even so far as Ansel, with all his goofiness—all they could think of was the killing of Preacher. And Ansel, at least in the minds of those near him, had gone completely around the bend. He mumbled and slobbered and grunted and had seemingly lost the ability to speak even semicoherently. Even Malachi had lost patience with him and now tried his best to ignore his brother. Couldn't nobody get any sense out of the fool. But they knew this: come the spring, they would hunt down and kill Preacher. They all agreed on that. Even Ansel, as far as anyone could tell. When asked, he would grunt and slobber and bob his head up and down.

"We kill Preacher come the spring," Kenrick said. "Even if we all die doin' it."

"Damn right," Son said.

Malachi nodded his head in agreement.

The men let their wild hatred fully consume them. They waited.

Preacher lay snug in his robes and slept. He didn't hate, he just knew what had to be done and he was going to do it.

At the mission, George Martin and Coretine, and Miles Cason and Betina were married by the missionaries.

NINE

Preacher had led the men deep into the wilderness. Now it was time to start the war. He struck the first blow between the Laramie and Medicine Bow mountains. Preacher was waiting on the west side of Muddy Creek when Sutherlin and his men stopped to rest and water their horses. He had Sutherlin all lined up in his sights, and just as he squeezed the trigger, a new man picked up back at the post made a very bad move by stepping in front of Sutherlin and took the ball directly in the center of his back. The big ball busted the man's spine, angled up and ripped out of his throat, and splattered Sutherlin with blood. Edward Sutherlin let out a scream of fright and shock, hit the rocky ground, and hugged it close as his men scattered out, seeking whatever cover they could find. The dead man fell directly on top of Sutherlin.

"Damn," Preacher said. He slipped back to his horses and pressed on westward, looking for another good ambush site. He consoled himself with the knowledge that at least there was one less to deal with.

Back at the creek, the outlaws dug a shallow grave and dumped the dead man in it. They didn't even take the time to cover the mound with rocks. The dead man was known only as Peter. The outlaws rifled his saddlebags and pockets, took his boots, and rode off without a word of prayer. From this time on, Edward Sutherlin would ride in the center of the column and always have someone close beside him after dismounting.

"A thousand dollars to the man who kills Preacher," he told his men.

A thousand dollars was several years' wages. The men needed no further incentive.

"You got the money on you?" a man named Mueller asked, his voice heavily accented, a sly look in his eyes.

"Don't be foolish," Sutherlin told him. "So you'd better keep me alive."

"Accordin' to this map," Lester said, "which ain't worth a shit as far as I'm concerned, they's another creek about five miles ahead of us. Then they's a river of some sorts and then we hit more mountains."

"Is there any way around them?" Big Max asked.

"Yeah," Lester said sarcastically. "About five hundred miles south or five hundred miles north."

Just inside the Medicine Bow range, Preacher was waiting, his bow ready for a silent kill.

Sutherlin swung into the saddle. "Take the point, Meeker. Let's go."

Meeker, wanted for rape and murder in several states back East. He nodded his head and took the lead.

Ward fell in behind him. Ward, wanted for killing his wife and children back in Vermont.

The third man in the rogues' column was Mueller, also a murderer and rapist . . . and those where his good points.

Next was Clubb, wanted for robbery, rape, murder, and numerous other infractions.

Doc Judd was a real doctor; unfortunately, he

also got a great deal of joy out of poisoning patients. Twelve of them before the law got wise back East and put him on the run.

Moffett was a con man, thief, and rapist.

Lester had done it all and was wanted in nearly every state in the Union for one thing or another. He was as ruthless as Sutherlin.

Big Max liked to beat people to death with his fist. And had, several times. Men, women, and children.

Beans Speer was a back shooter and would kill anyone for the right price.

Isaac was a knife man who liked to kill . . . slowly.

The other men Sutherlin had picked up along the way were Sharp and Bankston. Both murderers.

Thirteen brigands riding into the wilderness after one man. Each of them supremely confident he would be the one to kill Preacher and be a thousand dollars richer.

Had they had just one opportunity to take a look at what remained of the gangs of Malachi, Dirk, and Son, they might have changed their minds and ridden back East.

Bankston brought up the rear of the column, and Preacher waited until the others were around the bend in the trail and out of sight before he struck. From a distance of about twenty feet, he put an arrow all the way through the murderer. The arrow cut the spine and Bankston fell soundlessly from his saddle. Preacher jumped down from the rocks, grabbed the horse's reins, and calmed the jumpy animal, and then slung Bankston across the saddle. He led the horse into the rocks and waited, both hands filled with those deadly pistols.

But Sutherlin smelled something queer and refused to take the bait. Preacher could hear them talking and could pick out most of the conversation.

"Preacher got him," Lester said. "Listen to the boss and don't go 'round that bend. Let's get the hell gone from here 'fore he picks off another one of us."

"I got an idea."

"What is it, Isaac?"

"We know he's here, so let's settle it now. Fan out and take him. We got him twelve to one. Some of us will get kilt, for sure, but we can take him out here and now."

Yes sirree, Preacher thought. You folks just come right on and do that little thing. I didn't figure on none of you bein' that damn ignorant.

Sutherlin thought about that for a moment, being careful to stand with his men all around him as human shields. Finally he nodded his head in agreement. "Lester, you and Beans and Clubb stay here with me. We'll get in those rocks over there. The rest of you men fan out and hunt this bastard down. Let's get it over and done with."

Preacher slipped back and into the brush, kneeling down and waiting. That he would soon be surrounded didn't bother him one whit. He'd been surrounded before, by men much more skilled in combat than this bunch of white trash.

Preacher had holstered his pistols and once more taken up his bow, notching an arrow. He was in good cover and blended in. He had noted days before that these men were not skilled in brush warfare. They might be experts in dark alleyways and the streets of towns, but they were careless in the wilderness. And that was gonna get them killed.

One of Sutherlin's bunch passed so close to Preacher that he could smell the body odor of the thug. Moving only his eyes, Preacher watched as the man vanished behind rocks. Ward slipped through the rocks and brush, trying to be quiet about it. He was no woodsman.

Preacher put a arrow into the man's chest. The instant the arrow flew, Preacher was moving, changing locations. Ward was kicking his legs as he lay on the ground, his mouth working with no sound coming out. But he was making quite a racket with his boots.

"Ward!" a man called. "Hush up all that damn noise. What the hell's the matter with you?"

Ward let out a fearful shriek, drummed his boot heels on the ground, and died.

"He's in amongst us!" Sharp cried out. "Be careful. Ward's down and dead."

Preacher let fly another arrow and Doc Judd turned just as it was loosed. The arrow missed and careened off a boulder, sending Doc belly down on the ground. "Over here!" Doc yelled. "Be careful. The man's a damn ghost."

Preacher stayed where he was, knowing movement attracted more attention than noise. Why none of the men hadn't found his horses was a mystery to him.

"This is no good!" Sutherlin shouted out. "Gather around and let's get out of here. Come on, men."

Preacher let them go. He had pressed his luck to the maximum this day and knew it. He remained motionless and listened to them ride off. The body of Ward lay where he had kicked out his last. Sutherlin and company had made no attempts to tend to the dead.

"Sorry bunch of bastards," Preacher muttered, standing up and walking over to the dead man. He looked down at him. It wasn't sympathy; he was trying to figure out how to best retrieve his arrow.

It was a good arrow. Rolling the man over on one side, Preacher saw that when he fell, he had broken the arrow. Preacher dragged the man to a depression and kicked some dirt and rocks over him.

"You want him, Lord," Preacher briefly eulogized, "You got him. Here he is. Amen."

Now the chase was on and Preacher was at his best. He had them all running scared and knew it. He let them run for a full twenty-four hours before he made his next move. That night, he circled their camp, howling like a wolf, grunting like a bear, and coughing like a great panther. He was so convincing that a bear actually did come to investigate and Preacher damn near ruined his brand new longhandles when he turned around and the bear reared up not ten feet from him in the darkness.

Preacher hit the air and vacated the area. "Work, feet," he mumbled in a dead run, dodging trees and boulders and leaving the bear far behind. The bear had decided that Preacher was not worth the effort of pursuit—the camp held much more interesting smells.

"Holy shit!" Doc Judd screamed, catching sight of the great bear, a huge male grizzly. Doc lifted his rifle and the weapon misfired, momentarily blinding the man with powder burns. Doc threw the rifle at the bear and took off as the entire encampment went running in all directions. It scared the bear about as bad as the men and the griz took off in a lope, getting the hell away from that screaming wall of noise.

Sutherlin ran into a tree and knocked himself out. Lester ran right off the edge of an embankment and went rolling ass over elbows to the rocky ground below. Moffett climbed a tree. Mueller tried

261

to climb the same tree and Moffett thought it was the bear and kicked the man in the head. Mueller hit the ground, unconscious.

A good mile away, Preacher stopped to catch his breath. The faint screaming of the badly frightened men drifted to him and he smiled. He made his way back to his horses and rode for a couple of miles before bedding down for the night.

Preacher trailed along behind the men for several miles, then popped up alongside them further along, but stayed well out of rifle range. He waved and shouted and made terribly obscene gestures toward the men, trying to get one of them to lose his temper and come after him. But no one would take the bait.

"Steady, men," Sutherlin cautioned his band of cutthroats and thugs. "Just ignore him. We'll have our chance."

Just before leaving the Medicine Bow range, Preacher pulled ahead of the men and cut north, taking them—if they chose to follow his trail—into the high country. Dutifully, they tagged along behind him, with Preacher thinking this just had to be some of the dumbest men he had ever encountered. And he had met some real dumbos in his time. He decided to find out just what the hell was going on.

That night he Injuned up to their camp and lay for a time, his eyes picking out the guards. The bunch had wised up right smart, and had taken to choosing their campsites with a lot more care. Preacher moved only several inches at a time. At the end of two hours, he was within hearing distance of the men. They were all gathered around a fire, which was definitely not smart at all. Look into the flames and it destroys a man's night vision. They were just real lucky there were no hostiles about. Or that no Indians had located their camp, Preacher corrected, for hostiles were always about.

"This is no good," Lester said, pouring himself another cup of coffee. "The man is just leading us wherever he wishes. He's making fools of us, boss."

"I don't like this country out here," Clubb said, a blanket wrapped around his shoulders against the chill of the night. "It's almost as if we have dropped off the edge of the world. It's so damn *empty!*"

"You would rather go back and face a hangman's noose, perhaps?" Mueller asked.

Clubb shook his head and had nothing else to say on the matter.

"Lester is right, of course," Sutherlin said. "But I am sure that this Preacher person knows all about us and our operation. If he lives, we will not be safe anywhere. I wish I knew where Malachi and his bunch were hiding out. Or if they're still alive. I fear that many are not. And I also think that there are new warrants out on all of us back in the States. So you see, gentlemen, Preacher has to die. For if he doesn't, we have no place left to run."

"I long to see California," Meeker said, "where it's warm all the time, and have soft-eyed Spanish women. I like to force myself on Spanish women. I love to hear them scream when I take them. I hate this damn country here. I would certainly not relish the thought of being buried here in this cold and inhospitable clime."

Worthless, no-count son of a bitch, Preacher thought. Then he lifted a pistol and put a ball right through the rapist's belly.

Meeker fell backward without a sound, screaming as his back touched the cold ground that he hated.

Preacher cocked the second hammer and blew a hole into Sharp's belly. Then, while the camp was in turmoil, Preacher slipped away into the darkness.

The outlaws were firing at shadows, blasting away into the dead of night in their frightened panic. But Preacher had dropped into a natural depression in the earth and no bullets touched him as he ran back in the direction of his horses. He'd given the brigands quite enough to think on this evening.

When Preacher reached the camp the next morning, about an hour after dawn, the outlaws were gone and the ashes of their fires were cold.

Meeker lay on his back where he had fallen, and the gut-shot outlaw was not long for this world. His comrades had not even taken the time to dress his hideous wound. But they had taken the time to take his heavy coat and his boots. He watched Preacher through pain-filled eyes as the mountain man set about making a fire.

"Nice bunch of folks you took up with," Preacher remarked. "They sure cared a lot for you, didn't they?"

"Water seeks its own level," the wounded man said weakly.

"I reckon." Preacher tossed the man a rag of a blanket someone had left behind.

"Thank you."

"I'd do more for a wounded animal," Preacher said shortly. "You got a hole in your belly, but I 'spect a little coffee ain't gonna keep the dark angel waitin' too long for you to pass."

"I would appreciate that."

"You talk like you got some education."

"I have. I just took a wrong turn a long time ago and couldn't find the path."

"You *wouldn't* find the path," Preacher corrected. "Don't give me none of this 'couldn't' crap."

Meeker smiled faintly. "You also possess a fair amount of education, mountain man."

"I went to the fifth or sixth grades, I think. Mostly Ma taught me to home."

"That fire feels good."

"It do, for a fact, don't it? Where'd Sutherlin go this time?"

"I owe them nothing, so I'll tell you. They went hard to the ground. They're going to try to sit out the rest of the cold weather and then surface, heading west to the Oregon country to find Malachi and the others."

"They finally got smart, did they? Well, I doubt they'll lose me in this country, but it's been done afore, I have to allow." Preacher filled the coffee pot and put it on to boil, although he had doubts the man would live long enough to have him a taste of the brew.

"I have chicory root in my saddlebags over there," Meeker said. "If you like the added flavor."

"I do for a fact. It don't grow worth a damn out here, not this high up."

Preacher dumped the coffee into the boiling water, added some shaved chicory, and removed the pot from the fire to let the grounds settle.

"Does Sutherlin know they's federal warrants out for him?" Preacher asked the dying man.

"He suspects."

"The men ridin' with him?"

"They're all trash. Including me. They're riding away from a past that is filled with darkness and evil. You're doing the right thing."

Preacher glanced over at him. "Odd thing for a man like you to say."

"When one is dying, the truth is best, wouldn't you agree with that?"

Preacher nodded his head. "I 'spect."

"It's good to have someone near as the final moments grow closer."

Preacher looked at him. "What'd you do to turn bad?"

"I killed a man. Then another, then another. It reached the point where it simply did not matter."

Preacher noted that the man's voice was growing weaker. Now it was no more than a whisper. "I'll bury you proper."

"Thank you."

"Although I don't know why I should take the time," Preacher added.

Meeker smiled. "Because you are a man."

"Whatever that means." Preacher looked over at the outlaw. Meeker closed his eyes and died.

TEN

Preacher wrapped the man in the ragged blanket and buried him, piling rocks over the mound. He also buried Sharp, although not as deep or as well. He spoke no words over the graves. Preacher had his coffee and put out the fire, then swung into the saddle and began tracking the outlaws. They were heading for the high country, to the northwest, and they were doing their best to shake Preacher off their trail. The first creek they came to, they entered. They stayed with creeks until the water either played out or the creeks changed direction of flow. On the fourth day after Preacher buried Sharp and Meeker, it began snowing, and Preacher completely lost their trail.

"They holed up," he said to his horses. "They ain't far from here, but we lost 'em."

He knew to continue would be to no avail. He might wander for weeks and never cut their sign. He turned his horses west. Come the spring, and it was not far off, west was the only way open to the outlaws. That's the way they had to go, that's where Malachi and his pack of scum were hiding out, and if they still planned on striking the wagon train when it left the mission come true spring, that's where Preacher would be.

Or at least close by.

But winter was not yet ready to loosen its grasp

267

on the high country. The snows continued to fall and the cold winds blew. It was still bitterly cold when Preacher came to within a couple days ride from the mission and rode into the camp of Windy and Rimrock. They'd been out hunting and had no luck at it. They looked up at him, nodded, and Windy pointed to the coffee pot.

"We done hunted this area out," Rimrock told Preacher, handing him a cup of coffee. "Been a lot of mouths to feed this winter. How you been, Preacher?"

"Tolerable. Seems like to me I done crisscrossed this country so many times over the past two years I begun namin' the trees and the rocks. Got some chicory root in my saddlebags."

"Where'd you come by that?" Windy asked.

"A dyin' outlaw give it to me."

"Dyin' on account of you?" Rimrock asked.

"I 'magine. Right nice feller there towards the end."

Preacher told them all that had transpired since he'd left the mission.

Windy and Rimrock exchanged glances and Preacher caught the quick looks. "Say it," he told them.

"Betina and Miles got married. So did George and Coretine," Rimrock said it quick.

"Good," Preacher replied. "That's a load off my mind. I 'spect I better not hang around the mission much, then. It might make them newlyweds nervous havin' me around. You say food is gettin' scarce?"

"They're just about out," Windy said. "And game has took to cover in all this snow and ice."

"Caleb and Carl is huntin' to the west," Rimrock added.

The men rested and talked and made another pot of coffee. When they were talked out and the coffee was gone, Preacher stood up. "We best start foragin', then. I can't abide no thought of kids goin' hungry." He looked up at the sky. "I figure spring's a good three, four weeks off. We got our work ahead of us. I'll hunt towards the north and see you boys back at the mission when I get there."

Rimrock finally commented on the pistols belted around Preacher's waist. "That's the goddamnest rig I ever did see, Preacher. Where'd you come acrost them cumbersome-lookin' guns anyway?"

Preacher slowly removed the pistols from leather and handed one to each man. Windy whistled softly and Rimrock hefted the four-barrel and grinned.

"Fine, ain't they?" Preacher said.

"I'll say. Whoever made these had a love for firearms and knew what they was doin', for a fact," Windy said.

Preacher returned the guns to his holsters. "Let's go find some food for those hungry folks, boys."

Preacher hunted for two days and shot two deer, and mighty scrawny ones they was, for the winter had been hard. He skinned and dressed them out and headed for the mission, only a few hours ride away, for he had been working his way back with the first deer when he spotted the second one.

The three mountain men arrived at the mission within minutes of each other. Rimrock had killed a deer and so had Windy. But four deer wasn't going to last long with all these mouths to feed. Preacher swapped horses to give Hammer a much-needed rest and made ready to take out again when Miles approached him.

Preacher smiled and stuck out his hand for Miles

to take, which he did, with a surprised look on his face. "Congratulations, boy," Preacher told him. "You lucked up and got yourself a fine woman, you did."

"I think so, Preacher. And I'm glad you approve. Aren't you going to rest before taking off again?"

"Rest when you're dead, Miles. Lots of hungry folks here whose bellies think their throat's been cut. I'm takin' a pack-horse to tote back the meat."

"If you can find any game to kill."

"I'll find it, Miles. I ain't got no choice in the matter. A body needs fat in the cold to survive. See you." He swung into the saddle and rode off, leading a packhorse.

A missionary walked up to stand for a moment beside Miles, both of them watching Preacher as he rode off. "They are hard-drinking, hard-living, and profane men, Miles. But most of them are good men. They have their scallywags among them, of course, but just think what might have happened to all these people here at the mission had not those men chosen to stay and help."

"And did you notice that Preacher is taking only a few supplies for his personal needs in order to bring back more meat?" Miles added.

"Their day is almost gone in the mountains," the missionary said, a genuine note of sadness in his voice. "Some are glad to see it gone, but I'm not. Tell you the truth, I'll really miss them. But don't tell Marcus that," he was quick to add with a smile. "Although he is much more fond of the men than he likes to admit."

Preacher didn't kid himself. This area had been hunted out for miles around, driving the animals further and further away. Now that false spring had come and gone, with mother nature coming in right

270

behind it and dumping more snow and laying the heavy hand of cold all over the land, it was going to be difficult to find game.

But find it he and the others must.

At the end of his first full day out, Preacher hadn't even killed enough to feed himself. His supper was a skinny rabbit that he had almost had to fight a coyote over. But the next day he killed two big bucks that dressed out nicely and he returned to the mission with the meat. Rimrock had killed a bear who had wandered out of hibernation, Windy brought in two nice deer, and Caleb and Carl each brought in a deer.

But there was no time to relax, for with so many people to feed, that meat wouldn't last two days.

Late and unexpected winter locked up the land cold and tight, and the mountain men where forced to spend every waking hour in the search for food. And the men of the wagon train did their part and more. They had become trail-tough and resourceful. They set snares for rabbits and other small game — anything to add to their meager diet.

By the time the first bits of greenery began poking out of the soil, Preacher and the other mountain men were just about wore down to a frazzle.

By the time game had once more begun coming out of shelter and moving around, and the men from the mission and the wagon train could take over the job of providing food, Preacher and his friends flopped on their beds in a crude cabin and relaxed for the first time in weeks.

"This past month has been enough to make a body swear off the human race," Caleb said. "First warm winds that blow, I'm headin' for the Rockies."

"Me too," Windy and Rimrock said together.

Carl was taking the train on to the coast.

271

Nobody had to ask what Preacher was going to do. They looked at him, sitting on a bunk and carefully cleaning and oiling his guns. He had spent several days molding bullets.

"Snow's gone for this season," Preacher said. "Malachi and his bunch and Sutherlin and his pack of filth will be movin'. I'm thinkin' it would be best if you men stayed with the train to Oregon Territory. We got these movers this far. Be a shame to desert 'em for the human varmits this clost to where they want to settle."

"Mayhaps you be right, Preacher," Windy said. "The Rockies will be there for us."

Rimrock and Caleb nodded their heads in agreement. Caleb said, "When you takin' out, Preacher?"

"In about fifteen minutes. Malachi and his bunch are clost. I can smell 'em. And since trash seems to gather together, I 'spect Sutherlin and his gang will find them. If they ain't already done it." He stood up. "I'll see you boys at Fort Vancouver." He smiled. "I got me a pretty lady 'crost the mountains that I ain't seen in over a year. If she ain't done married up to some gospel shouter, I might do me some sparkin' of my own." He slung his pistols around his waist and picked up his Hawken. "See you."

Preacher had been resting Hammer and the big horse was rarin' to hit the trail. Preacher got him settled down and saddled and was no more than a dot in the distance by the time the others at the mission realized he was gone.

Preacher began working in an ever-widening circle, scouring the still-cold ground for tracks. On his fifth day out, he found a hoofprint that looked familiar to him. He dismounted and more closely studied the depression in the dirt. He recognized the print as a horse belonging to one of Sutherlin's bunch. He walked the tracks for a time, memorizing the prints, and then swung into the saddle. The gang was heading as straight west as they could ride.

"Now we end it, Sutherlin," Preacher said. "You have run your race and you're about to lose."

Hammer snorted his agreement.

Preacher had him a hunch that once Malachi and Sutherlin linked up, they would ride due west and not attempt to strike the wagon train until it was about midway between the mission and The Dalles, smack in the middle of the Blue Mountains. It was a hard and backbreaking two hundred and fifty miles over the Cascades to the Willamette Valley. Sutherlin and the others would probably have plans to hit the train when the movers were exhausted.

If Preacher allowed them to do that.

Which he most certainly would not.

Preacher figured Sutherlin had maybe ten men counting himself, and Malachi had about that many, maybe a few more. Say, twenty-five men all told. If Preacher could just figure out where Malachi and his pack of no-goods were hiding.

He linked up with a Yakima hunting party and ate and smoked and talked with them, slowly edging the conversation around to where he wanted it. Many Indians were notorious about not responding to direct questions, so a body had to work his way to that point little by little.

Preacher finally belched and wiped his hands on his buckskins and smiled at the subchief who was leading this hunting party. "Many bad white men live around here, so I was told."

The Yakima returned the smile. "Preacher walks all around what he has on his mind. Preacher is like us, one with the land and all things living on it. We are free people. Say what you wish, Preacher."

"Any white men livin' clost-by that you know of?"

The subchief opened and closed one hand three times. "That many live in old lodges that were abandoned. They are unclean people. Smell very bad. One of them is a child of the gods." That would be Ansel—crazy. "None of them wash properly. My people will not go near them for fear of catching some horrible disease." He pointed west. "Two days ride."

"You seen any other white men?"

The subchief nodded, his face grim. "Ten men ride one day ahead of you. Are more wagons coming, Preacher?" he asked abruptly changing the subject.

"Yes. And they will come always, each time bringing more people." Preacher was totally honest with Indians—just another reason he got along well with most of them. "Don't even think of stopping them. It would be impossible and the punishment would be harsh for your people."

"Little Hawk knows this. But he does not have to like the knowledge."

"I don't like it either," Preacher said.

"The whites come in and steal our land and we are supposed to behave as the Sanpoils?"

The Sanpoils were a small tribe who lived along about a one hundred miles stretch of the Columbia River. They were totally peaceful, and did not believe in warfare of any kind. They would not even revenge loss of life. Preacher doubted that any of the tribe would survive when the wagon trains really started moving through.

Preacher chose his words carefully before speaking. "I can't answer that, Little Hawk. Not an' give you no answer that would please everybody concerned."

"Whites are that many?"

"Oh, yes. More than ten of you could ever count in a lifetime. A hundred times over the number of buffalo that used to roam the land. A thousand times over. Makes my head hurt just thinkin' about it."

Little Hawk shook his head, his expression sad. "We are doomed, then."

"You will be if you fight them," Preacher said solemnly, thinking: And you damn sure will be if you don't fight them. Preacher knew that massive changes in everybody's lives was just around the corner. And he didn't like it any more than the Indians did. "You can't win by fighting them."

The Yakimas moved on, hunting game to feed their hungry camps, and Preacher moved on toward the west. He, too, was hunting game, so to speak.

Preacher was closing in on the gang fast, while still riding with caution. But even with all that going for him, he nearly got his head blowed off.

ELEVEN

Preacher had just turned his head at movement off the faint trail when the rifle boomed. The slug tore a narrow furrow in Preacher's scalp and blew his hat off his head. Preacher hit the ground and lay still, his Hawken in hand. Slowly, he cocked the rifle and waited, motionless. His head throbbed with pain and he had no idea how bad hurt he was, but he suspected not too bad, for his vision was still good and he knew who he was.

He waited.

"I got him!" a man shouted. "By the Lord, Moffett. I kilt the bastard, I did."

"You watch yourself around him, Beans. He's tricky."

"Naw. He's *dead*, Moffett. I shot him right 'tween the eyes, I did. Blood all over the place."

Any fool knows that head wounds bleed like crazy for a few seconds, you igit! Preacher thought. Now come on to me and let's settle this matter.

"I reckon you right, Beans," Moffett said. "His head shore looks a mess to me."

Boot steps drew closer. Preacher's eyes were slitted and he could see the man stop, laugh, and then twist to turn around. "He's shore deader than hell, Moffett." He laughed in a nasty way. "Why, I can practically feel that money in my hand. I'm agonna—"

"Die," Preacher said, coming to his knees and blowing a hole in Beans Speer. He lunged to the other side of the trail before Beans had hit the ground.

"Goddamn you!" Moffett screamed, and put a ball not half a foot from where Preacher lay.

Both men were then frantically trying to reload faster than the other, for the range was far too great for accurate pistol shooting. Like a fool, Moffett was standing in plain sight, in a clearing by the old trail.

Preacher swung the Hawken to his shoulder just as Moffett threw his rod to the ground. Preacher's Hawken roared and Moffett dropped his rifle and doubled over, the ball taking him in the belly. He screamed in pain and fell to his knees, both hands holding his burning belly.

Preacher took his time reloading and then jerked the powder horn from Beans. By its weight he could tell it was full. Even though Beans's rifle was of a different caliber than Preacher's rifle, he took the man's shot pouch, for the lead could be melted down and made into balls that would fit his Hawken.

He looked down at Beans. His ball had taken the man in the side at very nearly point-blank range and had torn through lungs and probably nicked the heart before exiting out the other side. Preacher walked up to where Moffett was kneeling on the ground. The man's face was pale and there was a ghastly look in his frightened eyes.

"You're a devil," Moffett said, looking at Preacher's bloody face. The dust from the trail had helped to stop the bleeding. Just as soon as Moffett passed, Preacher would clean the wound proper and make him a poultice from plants.

"I been called worse. Where's your buddies?"

"You go to hell, I say!"

Turned to leave. "Wait!" Moffett called, panic in his voice. Preacher turned around. "You're not going to leave me here to die alone, are you?"

"Why not? You ain't inclined to talk to me none."

"They're miles up the trail, man. I wouldn't lie to you moments from death."

"Maybe. Maybe not."

"I told you where they was," Moffett gasped out the words. "Don't leave me here to die alone. Please."

Preacher fetched his horses and picketed them on graze. Then he cleaned out the wound on his head, which started it bleeding again. He held a piece of cloth against the wound until the bleeding stopped. Moffett watched him in silence.

"I ain't no bad person," Moffett finally spoke.

Preacher looked at the man.

"I ain't," Moffett insisted, after fighting unsuccessfully to hold back a groan of pain. "I ain't. I was forced into this life."

"If you want me to stick around, you better pick another subject to bump your gums about. 'Cause I sure don't want to listen to this."

"I went to church as a boy."

"You should have paid more attention to what the minister had to say."

"We was poor."

"One more word and I'm gone." Preacher rose from the rock he was sitting on.

"Wait! Talk to me."

"I'm gonna drag your friend into the woods."

"You ain't gonna give him no Christian burial?"

"No. Shut up."

Preacher returned in a few minutes and looked at Moffett. "I was hopin' you'd passed by now."

"I ain't never seen no man as cold as you. You

just ain't got no sympathy for them that's less fortunate."

Preacher laughed aloud. "You wastin' your time tryin' to convince me. You got your work cut out for you when you meet your Maker. And I wish you'd hurry up." Preacher looked at the man. It wouldn't be long now. For all his tough talk, he did not take death lightly. Preacher was just a very hard man in a land and a time that allowed few mistakes. He softened his tone when he again spoke. "You got airy kin you want me to try to contact?"

"None that would give a damn."

"That is sad. Tell me about Sutherlin."

"I don't know much. He's cold, though, mighty cold. Nearabouts as cold as you."

"How many men do this leave him?"

"Seven, countin' himself." The man's voice was very weak.

"Where is Malachi Pardee hidin' out?"

"Just west of here. Some Red Indians told us. Sutherlin knows exactly. I don't." He closed his eyes and began to weep.

Preacher tried to work up some sympathy for the man. He could not. It's hard to feel sorry for a man who just tried to kill you. "I'll bury you," Preacher finally said. "I can do that much, I reckon."

"Thank you. I'm sorry for the hard things I said about you. I'm sorry for the hurt I've caused other people. I'm . . ."

Whatever else he had to say stayed unsaid. Preacher found the men's horses, took their bedrolls, and wrapped both of them up in dirty blankets. He dug a shallow grave and planted both the dead outlaws, then stripped bridle and saddle from the horses and set them free.

Preacher stood by the grave for a moment, thinking that wherever good people go, bad people always follow. He reckoned it was the same all over the world. Preacher tried to think of some words to say. He couldn't think of a thing.

He stayed where he was for a time, letting his horses graze and water and roll. He built a small fire and had himself some coffee he'd taken from the outlaws' supplies. He didn't know where they'd gotten it, and didn't want to dwell on that for long.

Preacher was suddenly tired. Very, very tired. He figured a part of that came from his slight head wound, but most of it come from the fact that it had been a hard winter, and bein' constantly on the lookout for people tryin' to kill you was wearin' on a body. He carefully put out the fire and moved on for a couple of miles, until he found himself a good spot to camp. He was rolled up in his blankets before good dark and didn't wake up until near dawn. He figured he'd slept a good ten or eleven hours and he felt refreshed.

He chewed on jerky while the coffee water boiled and then he was in the saddle again, putting the careful miles behind him. He was grimly amused by the thought that when Moffett and Beans didn't show back up, Sutherlin would know that his gunmen had failed to kill him and that Preacher was on their trail. By this time, Sutherlin had probably linked up with the Pardee gang and they were planning their evil deeds.

Preacher looked up at the sun. Near noon. He would be getting close now. He couldn't make a plan 'cause he had no idea of the layout. Preacher reined up and stripped his horses of their burdens and picketed them, then he took his bow and quiver, and plenty of shot and powder for rifle and pistols. He started out on foot, staying off the trail and in the brush as much as possible, stopping often to listen and look and smell for smoke. Finally he caught a faint odor of smoke. Slipping through the brush, he pulled up short at the sight. An Indian family on the move had stopped to rest and eat. A man, his woman, and two kids about four and six, Preacher reckoned. Yakimas. Preacher called out in their language and stepped into the small clearing.

They eyed him suspiciously, noticing how heavily he was armed, but still waved him to the fire and pointed to the venison steaks that were cooking.

"I am sad that I have nothing to offer you," Preacher said, squatting down.

"That you come in peace is enough," the man said. "I thought for a moment that you were part of the bad white men who stayed the winter not far from here."

"I hunt them to kill them. I am called Preacher."

"Ahh!" the woman spoke. "White Wolf."

"Yes."

"Eat, eat," the man said. "We will talk."

"Has more white men joined the group?"

"Yes. Yesterday. We hid until they had all gone."

"They rode west?"

"Yes. A large band of them." He opened and closed one hand five times. "They are all very much afraid of White Wolf."

Preacher ate and thanked the Yakima man and wife and returned to his horses, quickly saddling up and pulling out. The Yakima had said he had slipped in close to the men and overheard the man who appeared to be in charge say something about The Dalles. He said the men all smelled very bad and he wondered why they did not wash themselves. Preacher did not ask why the man and his woman and kids were out alone from their tribe. It wasn't any of his business and wouldn't have been a polite thing to ask. They might have been traveling to visit relatives on one side of the family or another. That the wife had spoken Preacher's name before her husband did told him that she was probably the daughter of a tribal leader with some power.

Preacher rode on to where the brave had told him the Pardees had wintered and found the dugouts. Lord, did they stink. A buzzard would have a hard time staying in these things. Preacher quickly backed out, feeling like he was in desperate need of a bath.

The Yakima told him the gang was heading for The Dalles, or close to it. Fine. Preacher would be waiting for them.

Malachi and his gang, freshly reenforced by Sutherlin and what was left of his party, and now numbering nearly twenty-five rather odious men, rode west with confidence. For the first time this year Malachi felt like they just might beat Preacher and be rid of the man once and for all. And then things could get back to normal.

So he had lost a couple of men back down the trail. That wasn't the end of the world. Sutherlin still wasn't sure whether they had been killed or had just given up and fled from Preacher. He tended to believe the latter. But Sutherlin, like Malachi, did believe their luck was about to change for the better and Preacher's luck had run out.

What none of the men could know, and wouldn't have believed it had they been told, was that Preacher had rafted down the river, arrived several days before them, and was waiting for the outlaw gang to show up.

TWELVE

"They's a place just up ahead that'll be perfect," Malachi said to Sutherlin and Son. "The wagons got to stop there 'fore they tackle the hills. They'll be all tuckered out and will rest for a time; maybe spend the night. That's where we'll hit them."

"Lookie yonder," a thug named Ed Murphy said, pointing to the river. "A raft, and a big one, too."

"It's old," Clubb said. "Somebody used it and then abandoned it. See where some of the ropes has rotted and then somebody else come along and used thick vines to patch it up."

"I'll check it out," Mueller said.

"Why?" Clubb said.

"Because I want to," Mueller replied, as he walked down the slope to the river's edge.

"I'll go with you," Ed said.

Both men inspected the big raft, which was almost too big for one man to handle, and looked at each other.

"Vines is fresh," Mueller called back up to the trail.

"So what?" Lester returned the shout. "Some movers used it and then left it."

"I don't think so," Mueller muttered to Ed as both men stood up from their squat and started back up the slope.

"You think—?" Ed broke it off.

"Yeah. I think so."

A Hawken boomed and Ed went down, a huge hole in the center of his forehead. Mueller hit the ground, scrambling for cover as the gang scattered.

Preacher shifted positions and reloaded swiftly. He held the high ground in brush and rocks and was approachable only from the front. He was under no illusions that the fight would end here, but he could do some fearful damage to the gang before he pulled out.

Both Sutherlin and Malachi Pardee lay on the ground and cursed Preacher. They knew it wasn't Indians or another gang of outlaws. It was Preacher. Their constant and unforgiving adversary. For near 'bout a year now, the man had been on Malachi's back, very nearly destroying what had, at one time, been the most feared outlaw gang in all the West.

Now look at them. Malachi's thoughts were savage and tinged with bitterness.

Ansel jumped up and began shouting and grunting and waving his arms. Preacher held his fire. He did not want to shoot the fool, and he wouldn't shoot him except as a last resort.

Valiant jerked his brother down to the ground and pulled him back to the safety of cover.

Dirk lay on the ground and cussed Preacher until he was breathless. His eyes were wild and he was trembling with rage. The bastard had burned him out and hunted him like some sort of wild animal. No more, Dirk made up his mind. No more. He had taken all of this he was going to take. He rolled from cover and dashed to the timber, running in a zigzag movement.

Preacher held his fire and let him come on.

With Dirk running up one side of the hill, Lester decided to try the other side. Preacher ended those thoughts by putting a ball through Lester's brisket that doubled him over and sent him rolling back down the slope.

Damn! Sutherlin thought, just as Preacher started a huge rock rolling and crashing down the hill. The horses went into a panic and bolted, running in all directions. A man jumped up and tried to grab the reins of his horse. What he got was a hole in his side, the ball busting out the other side. The man dropped to the ground, dead.

Dirk chanced another short run and made it, closing the distance.

"Everybody stay down," Sutherlin called. "I do believe Dirk is going to make it."

Dirk didn't.

He got about fifty yards from Preacher and his boot hung on a loose rock and the man went rolling and tumbling down the grade, breaking bones on his trip down to the trail by the river. Dirk bounced once and then lay still on the rutted trail, unconscious, one arm and one leg broken badly. His scalp was torn open in several places and bleeding.

Malachi looked up at the sky and shook his head. Hell, it wasn't even midmorning. It was going to be a long day.

Preacher pulled out just about noon. But he left behind him a terrible scene. Five dead and Dirk out of commission. Preacher found several of the outlaws' horses and removed bridle and saddle, tossing them into the river. He found a full powder horn and kept that. Then he found him a good spot about a mile from the original ambush spot and waited.

"Let's pull out of here, Malachi," Valiant suggested. "You know Preacher is waitin' for us up the trail. And look over yonder." He pointed. "They's Injuns all up and down the ridges. They been watchin', enjoyin' the show. Preacher done whupped

285

us, brother. We gotta admit that."

The Indians, from several tribes, hooted and laughed at the outlaws, but stayed well out of rifle range. They had heard that the outlaw gang was coming and that Preacher, the White Wolf, was going to kill them all. Indians enjoyed a good fight, for courage was what they respected the most. And this was going to be something fun to watch.

"Dirty, stinking savages," Sutherlin muttered darkly. "Up there ridiculing us."

"Why don't they attack?" Doc Judd asked.

What the outlaws couldn't know is that Preacher had recruited the Indians. He'd had plenty of time to do that, arriving several days before the outlaw gang.

Clubb had scouted back east of the ambush site and walked back to the main group, a grim look on his dirty, pale and frightened face. "Injuns has blocked the trail," he told the men, after pouring a cup of coffee. "One shouted out to me that we got to go on. They ain't gonna let us go back . . . even if we was of a mind to do that."

Kenrick Pardee sat down wearily on a log and sighed long. "That's it, then." His tone was deadlike. "Preacher's done gone and set up firm with the savages. Hell, he ain't no better than a savage hisself. We should have guessed he'd eventual do something like this. We ain't got no choice in the matter. We got to push on."

"What did the Injuns say they'd do if we was to try to head back?" Big Max asked.

Clubb looked at the man. "They said they believed that we would not die well."

Preacher made his coffee and chewed on a piece of jerky and waited. He knew the end was very near for the gang of cutthroats. He had them in a box they could not get out of. The Indians he'd talked with had said they would not attack the white outlaws. But they would certainly make them think they would. And Indians could be very convincing without saying a word.

Preacher put out his fire and took Hawken to hand. He walked up the trail a ways, threw back his head, and howled like a great gray timber wolf. The wild and savage call drifted down the banks of the river, faintly touching the band of outlaws. They looked at one another, fear in their eyes. Above them, on both sides of the river, Indians stood silently, watching them.

Malachi stood up and gripped his rifle. "I never took water from no man in my life. I'll die 'fore I do." He started walking up the trail. "Let's go, brothers," he called over his shoulder. "We got to accept the challenge and maintain the dignity of our good name. Never let it be said that no Pardee wasn't an honorable man."

Sutherlin looked at the man in amazement. He didn't believe he had ever before in his life heard such drivel. But picked up his rifle and waved what was left of his men forward.

"What happens if we kill Preacher?" Isaac asked. "I mean, with the savages?"

"They let us go," Clubb said. "So we better fight like we ain't never fit before. Or start makin' our peace with God."

A man called George was stumbling along with tears streaming and streaking his dirty face. "I jist don't wanna die. I don't wanna die."

"You should have thought of that 'fore you crossed the line from good to bad," Curtis told him.

"I didn't have no choice in the matter," George sobbed.

"Shit!" Curtis replied.

"We all have a choice," Sutherlin said in a firm

voice. "It's pure balderdash that anyone thinks we don't. To a very large degree, we all control our destinies."

The men had left Dirk where he lay on the trail. His head busted open, limbs broken, and bleeding from internal injuries. They had left him without a second thought. Although a man called Jeff had taken the time to rip Dirk's watch from his dirty vest and stick it in his pocket. No point in leaving a good timepiece with a dying man.

"Why the hell did we even come out to this god-forsaken land?" Delbert asked, tossing the question out to anyone who might have an answer.

"I don't believe God forsake this land," Kenrick told him. "I think He don't even know it's *here!*"

Delbert opened his mouth to speak and a ball took him square in the chest and knocked him flat on the ground. The men left the trail and hunted for cover.

Preacher was pulling out all the stops now. He had loaded up three rifles and laid them out. He reloaded and waited, his eyes watching the suddenly deserted trail just below him.

"Did anybody see the smoke?" Kenrick called out hoarsely.

"Delbert damn shore didn't," Jeff replied, eyeballing the body of the outlaw. "I'd like to have them boots of hisn. Mine's plumb wore out."

"They ain't worth dyin' for," Valiant told him.

Sutherlin cut his eyes to the Pardee brother. We're all going to die right here, he thought. And I'm going to die with this trash if I don't start using my wits and think about getting out of here.

Sutherlin looked around him. He had chosen very good cover, on the river's side. He cut his eyes to Doc Judd, who had jumped into cover with him. "When the rest of them move out, we stay put," he whispered. "If we don't, we're going to be picked off one by one."

"What about the Indians?" Doc said, returning the whisper.

Sutherlin thought about that for a moment. "We'll just have to take our chances. Who would you rather face, them or Preacher?"

"That's easy. I'm with you."

Malachi and his followers began slipping up the trail, staying with the cover, now lush and green in full spring, vegetation blossoming everywhere. Sutherlin and Doc Judd stayed still and quiet. A silent tribute to the awesome fighting power of the mountain man called Preacher.

Something in Ansel's warped brain straightened out and a voice in his head told him not to follow his brothers and to hunker down in some bushes and be quiet. Ansel slipped off the trail and slid down the riverbank. He crouched in brush and closed his eyes.

The Indians watching the men knew that Ansel was touched by the gods and they were wary of him. The actions of Sutherlin and Doc Judd had not escaped their eyes, either. Let the white men be afraid of them. Fear was sometimes a good thing.

Preacher lay in cover and watched the men slowly advance toward his position.

"You're a murderin' no-count, Preacher!" Malachi shouted. "I challenge you to step out here and fight me fair and square, man to man. How 'bout that, Preacher? You got the belly to face me eyeball to eyeball?"

Sure, Preacher thought. And as soon as I show myself I'll be shot full of holes.

"He's afeard of us, brother!" Valiant shouted. "We got him on the run." Valiant threw caution and good sense — the latter something he was woefully short of — to the wind and stepped out onto the trail.

Preacher sighted him in and the Hawken boomed, the ball dropping Valiant where he stood.

Kenrick looked at his brother, sprawled in death, and felt like puking. A wild rage seized the outlaw. He cursed Preacher, shouting out the black oaths from his cover.

Preacher waited.

"How come you doin' this to us, Preacher?" Malachi shouted. "We ain't done you no harm."

Preacher could no longer contain his tongue. "How many innocent people have you killed, Malachi?" he shouted. "How many children have you raped and sold into bondage? Answer me, you son of a bitch!"

"That ain't none of your affair, Preacher!" Malachi screamed. "Nobody made you the law out here. Git on out and leave us be. Ain't you done enough harm to my good family?"

"Not until I kill you all," Preacher told him.

Clubb left his cover and made a run for the rocks to the left of Preacher's position. Preacher knocked a leg out from under the man, the ball of lead shattering the man's knee. Clubb screamed and went rolling down the grade, losing his rifle along the way. He rolled across the trail and down the bank, landing in the river. The last anybody saw of him, he was caught up in the current and drifting downstream, screaming and flailing his arms.

"I can't swim!" he called out weakly. "Halp!" The current took him on and around a bend, then he was out of sight.

Ansel thought it was very funny and had to stifle his urge to giggle.

Sutherlin and Doc Judd looked at each other, both sharing the same thought: If they could somehow make the river, they'd swim for their lives.

Indians were sitting, squatting, and standing on both sides of the river, watching the show. This fight would provide them with many hours of talk around the fires. The one man who was called by many names, including Bloody Knife, fighting alone against many, was surely the bravest of the brave.

Mueller called out in a foreign tongue and leaped from cover, dashing to rocks below Preacher's position. Preacher fired too late and missed the man. Now his smoke was seen and the outlaws blasted at him, the lead howling and shrieking all around him. Preacher shifted locations, moving away from the river. Mueller panted up to the rocks and cursed when he saw that Preacher was gone.

The big man turned and felt a heavy blow strike his chest. The pain hit him a split second later. He looked down in amazement at the shaft of the arrow sticking out of his chest. Mueller fell backward, all sprawled out on top of the rocks. He stretched out his arms, sighed once, and the murderer and rapist died, his face to the sky.

"Damn," Big Max whispered. Then he made up his mind. "Preacher!" he called. "Big Max Delvin here. I'm gone if you'll let me. I'll leave this country and you'll not see my face here no more. How about it?"

Malachi turned around and shot the man through the chest with a pistol. "It just don't pay to associate with trash," he told Kenrick. "Cain't trust 'em to have no honor."

Thirteen

This is not happening, Son thought, looking back up the bloody and body-littered trail. One man could not have caused all this havoc. But he knew that one man had done it. He silently cursed Preacher. Son looked around for any of his men. He could not find a one left.

Then the thought came to him: Where was Sutherlin and Doc Judd? He had not seen either man in a hour or so. He could see Malachi and Kenrick. There was Isaac. Jeff. Dill was over there. Good God, was this all that was left? Impossible. He looked all around. The Indians were gone. He blinked and looked again. They had vanished.

Sutherlin and Doc Judd had noticed that several minutes before Son. The two men had begun working their way back down the trail. They made their way slowly and cautiously, always keeping in the brush. Once they were out of rifle range of Preacher, they began to breathe easier. They found two saddled horses, swung into the saddle, and lit out down the trail.

Then they received yet another shock for that day.

Armed Indians blocked the trail. A lot of armed Indians. Doc and Sutherlin reined up and stared. There was no way around the Indians.

One Indian rode his pony away from the others and pointed his rifle back up the trail. Doc and Sutherlin didn't need an interpreter. They got the message loud and clear.

"Can't we talk about this?" Sutherlin asked.

"No," the Yakima said.

"I have money."

"Don't want money."

"There are guns and powder and shot up ahead."

"From the dead. We will have those anyway." He smiled. "Yours, too. Ver' soon."

The two men cursed under their breath and slowly turned their horses around and rode back up the trail.

"Where's Ansel?" Malachi asked Kenrick.

"I ain't seen him. Maybe he broke and run and got clear, you reckon?"

"I hope. He's a good boy, that one is."

"Malachi?"

"Yeah, boy?"

"I guess we 'bout run our string out, ain't we?"

"Looks that way. But we've had us a time, ain't we?"

"We shore have. How many squallin' and kickin' and bitin' and scratchin' women and girls you reckon we've helt down and humped, brother?"

"White women?"

"All of 'em."

"Oh . . . that'd be hard to say. I recollect the time over on the—"

His words were cut short by the crash of Preacher's Hawken. About fifty yards ahead of them, in a bend of the trail, Jeff slowly rolled out onto the trail, a large hole right between his eyes.

Malachi looked at the last of Sutherlin's men and shook his head. "Ansel," he called softly. "If you can hear me, listen to me. I want you to stay hid. Stay hid and don't move no matter what happens. Stay hid 'til come the dawnin' in the mornin'. Then you slip down to that raft we seen and get the hell gone from here. Good luck, boy."

"I'll be damned if he will!" Sutherlin spoke from the saddle, only a few yards behind the brothers. "I'll kill the goofy son of a bitch myself. Come out, you stupid oaf. Come out here and face me."

"Damn your eyes, you black-hearted bastard!" Malachi screamed at the man. He stood up, leveled his rifle, and blew Sutherlin out of the saddle before the man could protest.

Doc Judd's rifle crashed and Malachi went down to his knees, belly-shot.

Kenrick screamed curses and cocked a pistol and shot Doc Judd in the throat, almost tearing the man's head from his shoulders. Doc toppled backward from the saddle and Kenrick stood up from his crouch just as Sutherlin leveled a pistol and blew a large hole in Kenrick's head. Ansel roared and grunted and slobbered out of the brush, a pistol in each hand just as Son was running around the bend in the narrow road to see what in the hell was going on. He froze at the sight.

Ansel cocked and leveled his pistol at the dying Sutherlin and grunted and slobbered all down the front of his filthy shirt.

"You ignorant bastard," Sutherlin told him.

"No, Ansel!" Son shouted, waving his arms frantically. "No, boy. Don't do it. Don't shoot that man."

Ansel grinned at the man for a moment. Slowly he nodded his shaggy head. He grunted a time or two. "Aw rat," he said, and shot Son in the chest.

Son sat down hard in the rutted and bumpy trail. "Why, boy," he said. "I think you've killed me."

Ansel bobbed his head up and down and grinned.

"Git out of here, Ansel," Malachi groaned. "Run, boy."

"Go on, Ansel," Kenrick said. "Them Injuns around here nor no other place ain't gonna bother you 'cause you're titched in the head. Run, boy. Git gone from this killin' place."

"Squirrelly bastard shot me," Son groaned. "Shot me. And I was always kinda partial to him, too."

"He liked you, Son," Malachi said. "He really did."

"Well . . . how come the son of a bitch *shot* me?"

"He ain't neither no son of a bitch!" Malachi said, then pondered on that for a few seconds. "Well . . . maybe."

Sutherlin cursed the addled Ansel and lifted another pistol to shoot Ansel and Ansel put his feet to work. He whooped and hollered once and then hopped over the side of the bank and disappeared.

Kenrick lifted a pistol and blew the top of Sutherlin's head slap off.

Preacher had left his cover and was squatting above the men, watching it all, his hands filled with pistols, shaking his head at the wild scene.

Ansel ran down the bank and to the raft. He untied the rope and jumped on, grabbing the pole and shoving off. He went floating merrily down the river, singing church songs at the top of his lungs.

The Indians watched him leave and all made the sign of a crazy person. Ansel would not be bothered by any Indian.

"There was two more of your gang got clear for a minute or two," Preacher spoke from above the dead and dying. "They jumped in the river and tried to swim clear. I don't think they made it."

"What happens to us?" Kenrick asked.

"I reckon you'll just lay there and ex-pire," Preacher told him.

"I wish I'd never laid eyes on you, Preacher," Malachi said, his voice very weak.

"That's probably true."

"I hate you, Preacher," Son said.

"Man shouldn't ride off to his judgment day with no hate in his heart," Preacher admonished the man. "That wouldn't set well with the Lord, I'm thinkin'."

"Who gives damn what you think?" Kenrick said.

Preacher tried his best to look deeply hurt and extremely offended. He couldn't quite pull it off. "My dear sainted mommy did."

"You didn't have no mommy," Malachi said. "You was thrown up here on the earth from the hellfires."

"My daddy would have broke off a limb and wore your ass out if he heard you say that, Malachi. My daddy was strong on them thumb-sized branches, he was."

Several Indians had gathered around, picking up rifles and pistols and shot pouches and powder horns.

"Y'all can have their scalps if you've a mind to," Preacher told them. "But I'd appreciate it if you'd wait until they's all dead 'fore you jerked 'em off."

"Jesus Christ!" Son yelled.

"He make prayer to white man's God?" a Yakima questioned.

"Well . . . sort of," Preacher replied.

Kenrick laid his head down and rattled and died.

"My brother's daid!" Malachi wailed. "Oh, Lord!"

"He make prayer to God?" the Yakima asked.

"In a way," Preacher told him.

"White man pray funny."

"Some do. But if you think this is something, you should have seem them all-day singin's and shoutin's we used to have back in the hills. I got me enough religion in one day to last a whole lifetime. That gospel shouter damn near drown-ed me in that cold-ass creek that day I turned to the Lord."

"You?" Malachi sneered.

"Yeah, me. I been baptized."

"In what? A keg of gunpowder."

"You 'bout to make me mad, Malachi."

"Help me, goddamnit!" Son squalled.

"Help you do what?" Preacher asked. "You doin' a right good job of passin' without no help from me."

"Well, I was washed in the blood of the lamb my-self!" Malachi said.

"You was washed in blood, all right," Preacher said. "But not of no lamb."

"I hate you," Malachi said.

"I'll see you in hell, Preacher!" Son yelled. Then he screamed. "Oh, God, it hurts, it hurts." He jerked a couple of times and bought the farm.

Preacher stood up and holstered his pistols.

"Don't leave me for the savages, Preacher!" Malachi whispered.

"You can't give me no good reason why I shouldn't."

"I'm a Christian."

Preacher spat on the ground. "Well, I'll just consider them Yakimas Romans then." He turned and walked away.

FOURTEEN

Ansel came up on a very waterlogged Clubb clinging to a log and dragged him on board the raft. A few miles further down, Isaac waved frantically from the north shore of the river at the men in the raft and Ansel somehow managed to get the raft over to the outlaw and get him on board.

"Just get us away from here," Isaac panted. "Get me away from that mountain man from Hell. I ain't never gonna go past the Mississippi again. I swear on the Good Book I ain't never gonna do it."

"What are you gonna do once we're safe?" Clubb asked with a groan, his shattered knee swollen and throbbing with pain.

"Farm," Isaac said. "Go to church and become a Christian. Find me a good woman and settle down. Never again will I raise a hand against a fellow man. Or woman," he added.

Ansel giggled.

Preacher pointed his horse's nose east, heading back to intercept the wagon train. He stopped briefly to look at Dirk. The Englishman lay dead by the trail. "You should have stayed in England," Preacher said, then lifted the reins and rode on.

A hundred yards further on, he came up on a gut-shot and dying man. "Who the hell are you?"

"Curt Morgan," the man gasped. "No, you didn't shoot me. Sutherlin stabbed while I was tryin' to get away from you. Him and that damn Doc Judd both stuck me."

Preacher stepped down and squatted by the man. Curt had been stabbed twice, once in the chest and once in the belly. There was nothing Preacher could do for him and told him so.

"I know it. I'm done for. I hooked up with this bunch about three weeks ago. Knew I was makin' a mistake when I done it. They all dead?"

"Near 'bouts."

Curt nodded his head. "A sorry lot they was, too. I tried to get shut of them, but them crazy damn Pardees said they'd shoot me if I tried. Stay with me. I ain't got long."

"I'll stay with you."

"I ain't never seen nobody like you in all my life, Preacher. Nobody in their right mind tackles twenty-odd men alone."

"Somebody had to," Preacher said simply. "What was left turned on each other. Damnest thing I ever seen."

"Don't let the savages get me, Preacher."

Preacher smiled. "These Yakimas are friendly. They was just runnin' a bluff like I asked them to. They wouldn't have hurt none of you had you tried to leave."

Morgan shook his head. "We was suckered."

"Right down the line."

"Well, I'll be damned." Morgan smiled for a second, then closed his eyes and died.

"Probably," Preacher said.

Days later, Preacher hooked up with the wagon train just as they were making camp for the night. He accepted a cup of coffee from Rimrock and sank wearily to the ground, stretching out with a sigh.

"Y'all ain't got nothin' to fight but the elements from here on out," Preacher told them, as movers began gathering around. "The gang of brigands is gone. Three or four got clear, but I 'magine they're headin' east just as fast as they can."

He did not elaborate and nobody asked him to. The mountain men knew they would hear the story later from Indians. Preacher was already a legend in the Big Lonesome, and whatever he did was usually remembered by one tribe or another and talked and sung about.

"Where you bound for, Preacher?" Rimrock asked.

"The Rockies. I got me a cravin' to be alone for a time. I think I'll head 'way down deep in the mountains and just do nothin' for a while. I was goin' on to the Coast to see a little filly, but I changed my mind. I might get myself into a trap I couldn't get out of."

He drank his coffee and relaxed for the first time in days. He stayed by the fire as the wagon train pulled out early the next morning. The pioneers waved at him as they rode and walked past, and Preacher returned the farewells. A few moments later, the silence wrapped itself around Preacher.

While he had the safety of others around him, Preacher had taken a bath the past afternoon and washed his longhandles. He reckoned he'd gotten most of the fleas off him and discouraged what remained.

He lay back against his saddle and relaxed by the fire, a fresh pot of coffee on the rocks by the fire. His horses grazed nearby and it was a comforting sound. A pleasurable sound. What else does a man need? Preacher pondered. The Indians are right in a lot of way, he thought. The white man worries about things that are not important. The Injun don't have no watches or clocks so he don't know whether it's nine o'clock in the mornin' or two o'clock in the afternoon and don't give a damn. Time takes care of itself.

A wolf pack loped up to scavenge amid what the movers had left behind in the garbage pile. They lowered their heads and looked at Preacher, sprawled by the fire.

"Go ahead," he told them. "I ain't gonna bother you."

Preacher had never been afraid of wolves and they had never bothered him. Unlike most men, Preacher had taken the time as a boy to understand their ways and pay heed to what he had learned, and to keep on learning about their ways. That was all it took—that and a bit of caution. Don't make no sudden moves around them, don't get between a male and his mate, and don't never try to make a pet out of one, for that was impossible. A wolf is a wild animal and you can't tame no wild animal. It wasn't fair to the animal to even try.

He'd known of men breeding dogs with wolves. He didn't approve of that. A dog is a dog and a wolf is a wolf. Problem was, when you done something like that, a body never knew which side was gonna be the dominant one. If it was the wolf, the animal might turn on you. If it was the dog, what the hell had you accomplished? It went a'gin' the order of things. Nature knew what it was doin', and Preacher didn't believe in jackin' around with nature.

The wolves snarled and mock-fought and tussled over this and that and Preacher watched them and was content. They had some pups with them and the mother and father was teachin' them things they would need to survive.

The big male, and he was a big one, walked over to where Preacher lay, staying about twenty-five feet from the man. Preacher didn't look the wolf in the eyes, for that was a sign of challenge and he damn sure didn't want to challenge no one-hundred-and-fifty-pound timber wolf to nothin'. When the wolf understood that Preacher was subservient to him, and meant him no harm, he shook his big head and rejoined the pack. Occasionally he would glance over to where Preacher lay by the fire.

"Don't never trust no human, brother wolf," Preacher spoke to him. "That would be a big mistake. Stay clear of humans, for they're afraid of you, and whatever a human person is afeard of, they tend to kill instead of understandin'. You run wild and free and wonderful like God intended you to do, and stay shut of humans."

After a time, the pack moved on and Preacher began packing up his gear. The wilderness lay all about him, clean and fresh, except for the pile of garbage the movers had left behind. And that irritated the mountain man. Why the hell can't people clean up after themselves and leave things as they found 'em? Why the hell do people think they have the right to come in and mess up whatever they touch? 'Fore long they'll be a goddamn garbage pile stretchin' from the Mississippi clear to the Pacific Ocean, Preacher thought sourly.

Why the hell can't we have a place that's left wild and free and untouched just like nature intended it to be?

He threw back his head and howled. In the distance, in the timber, a wolf answered his call, then another one joined in, and soon the pack was talking to him. Preacher grinned.

Felt good to be one with the wilderness.

FIFTEEN

Preacher headed southeast. He planned on taking his time and just enjoy being alone with no place in particular to go. Eventually he planned on lighting down around Bent's Fort, on the Arkansas in southeastern Colorado.

But that was subject to change, of course.

Preacher stopped often just to be doing nothing; but really he was doing something: he was *seeing* this land, all pure and untouched, for what could possibly be the last time. For once the movers started westward, there would be no stopping them. And it had started, and Preacher knew it.

Preacher rode across mountains, and sweated across desert country. But he knew where the water holes and the creeks were. He talked with friendly Indians and avoided those painted for war. In Nevada, one bunch did give him a run for it, but when three caught up with him and Preacher uncorked those fearsome pistols of his and left three braves shot all to hell and gone on the ground, the others wisely decided to let him be.

And there were cabins being built in the damnest places. Men were bringing their families out into the wilderness to live. Why, in one two-hundred-mile stretch, Preacher saw three brand-new cabins. He never heard of such a fool thing.

He just had to stop at the third one. Two kids and a woman run off into a cellar thing and slammed the door closed at the sight of him, whilst the man leveled a musket at him.

"Put that damn fool thing down, pilgrim," Preacher told him. "I didn't ride up here to do you no harm."

"What are you?" the man asked, not lowering the musket one inch.

"I'm a monkey from the Dark Continent. Hell's bells, what do you think I am?"

"I don't know. I ain't talked to no one 'ceptin' my wife and younguns for pert near a year." He lowered the musket. "I reckon you're human, for a fact."

"Thank you," Preacher said dryly. "Now can I get down and water my good horses and myself?"

"Oh, sure. You can see why we might be skittish about strangers, though, can't you?"

"Out here, it pays to be. You're in Ute country, mister. And them ain't the friendliest folks that ever lived." He lifted a gourd dipper from the bucket and looked at the man. "How in the hell did you *get* here?"

"Wagon most of the way. Then the wagon broke apart and we rode the mules."

A ungodly shriek came from the back of the cabin and Preacher damn near swallowed the gourd. "What the hell . . . ?"

"That's her brother, Simpson. He caught the fever on the way here and went out of his head. I'm afraid he'll never get any better."

"We have to keep him chained out back," the woman said, walking up with two kids, a boy and a girl, holding onto her skirts. "It's a shame, but what else can we do?"

"That's why the Utes ain't bothered you none. In-juns are fearful of crazy folks. Keep him alive and

305

they'll never come near this place exceptin' to maybe leave some trinkets for the gods."

"I'm Otis and this is my wife, Shirley, and our two kids, Otis Tom and Mary."

"Pleased. They call me Preacher."

"*The* Preacher?" the man asked.

"I reckon. I'm the only one that I know of."

"We heard of you all the way back in Illinois," the woman said.

"What are y'all *doin'* out here?"

A sly look came into the man's eyes and he and his woman exchanged glances. Preacher knew then the answer to his question without having to ask again. Gold. Well, he was in the right country for it. "Forget I asked. I know. Luck to you in your diggin' and pannin'."

The man and woman and kids stood and stared at him, no hospitality in their gazes. There came no invite to stay for food and that didn't surprise Preacher. Preacher guessed the man had found him a little pocket of gold or silver and he might be thinking that Preacher was out to steal it. Preacher stepped into the saddle and lifted a hand in farewell.

"You folks take it easy," he said. "You get the hungries for someone to talk with, you got a neighbor about thirty miles to the northwest and another one 'bout thirty miles past that. I seen the cabins but didn't stop to visit none."

Neither man nor woman had anything to say about that. Preacher shook his head and rode away without looking back.

"Friendly folks," he said to Hammer. "Gold does strange things to people. He'd have fainted if I'd a told him there was a pocket not two miles from his cabin. Just for meanness I ought to go over there and dig it out."

306

But he rode on. He had him a little sack of nuggets tucked back for any emergencies that might arrive and knew where more was if need be. When he was a good eight or ten miles from the cabin, he got him a rabbit and then found him a nice spot to make camp and settled in. He was carefully rationing his coffee now, for he was just about out and Bent's Fort was still a long ways off.

Preacher was in the high-up country now, in the land that he loved. All about him loomed the mountains, silent, snow-capped guardians of the wilderness. Preacher's hand closed on the butt of a pistol as his horses stopped their grazing and lifted their heads, ears pricked. He heard the sound of horses' hooves. Two of them, he guessed.

"Hallo, the camp," the voice called. "It's Elmo Pike and I be friendly."

"Come on in, Elmo. Be nice to talk with someone friendly."

"Preacher," the burly mountain man said, seeing to his horses first off. "Ain't seen you in near 'bouts three years, I reckon. You ain't got no handsomer."

"I'd talk was I you, Elmo. You got any coffee?"

"A-plenty, and I'll share. I put Bent's place behind me some days ago and stocked up right whilst I was there. Place got too damn crowded to suit me."

"Still sells whiskey, don't he?"

"That they do." Elmo sat down and poured a cup of coffee. "Got a drink there now called a hailstorm. Right tasty, it is. Whiskey and wild mint and ice."

"Ice?"

"Yes sirree. Bent built him an icehouse, he did. How long's it been since you seen the place?"

"Several year."

"It's changed considerable. You'll see." He peered at Preacher from under the brim of his battered old hat. "You becomin' a famous man, Preacher. They's talk that a big-city man who makes books wants to do a story 'bout you."

Preacher grunted.

"Bent's got lodgin' for up to two hundred men now. It's a regular city when it's full. And got him a cook that'll fair make you hurt yourself come eatin' time. Name's Charlotte. She's a lady of color, she is, and can shore make a table groan with vittles."

Preacher refilled his cup and leaned back. "I spent time with Rimrock and Windy and Caleb and ol' Carl Lippett. They all done give up furrin'."

"Carl still afeard of bathwater?"

"Worse than ever."

Elmo shook his head. "He's a good boy to have around when they's trouble, but he can get powerful odious at times. They give up furrin'? What they doin'?"

"Helpin' a bunch of pilgrims move to the Coast."

"Like you done last year, I think it was."

"Yeah."

"Sad times."

"For a fact."

The two mountain men talked until well after dark and then turned in. They spoke of men whom they had known, men who prowled the high country and the great plains. Men such as Beckwourth and Bill Williams. Fitzpatrick and Carson, and others less well known but just as brave and knowledgeable of the country they helped blaze. And they spoke of men who had gone into the Big Lonesome and never come out. They lamented the fact that settlers were moving in and cussed progress and so-called civilization.

Elmo was gone at first light, but not before leaving a packet of coffee for Preacher.

Preacher wondered if he'd ever see the man again, for with the coming of pioneers, the Indians were getting all riled up and putting war paint on, and he really couldn't blame them for it.

Preacher pulled out, riding cautiously and always alert, for he was in the heart of Ute country, and the Utes were fierce fighters and did not particularly like the white man. Preacher took to making a fire only in the mornings for coffee, and it was a very small one. At night, his was a cold camp. This high up it was cold in more ways than one.

Just south of Cross Creek, he teamed up with a trapper called Batiste who was heading for Bent's Fort . . . mainly for the lack of anything better to do. Batiste was a French Canadian who had just recently been up in the Northwest.

"You played hell, ma friend," he told Preacher. "Three men looking like something out of a nightmare stumbled into a camp on the Columbia telling wild stories about a devil they had fought near The Dalles. They said the devil was called Preacher."

Preacher smiled and Batiste's eyes twinkled.

"Oui, mon ami. It seems that these men had been part of a notorious gang. Now only the three of them are left. The Shoshoni camp I was in last week, I tink, they were singing songs about the man called Killing Ghost . . . among other names he has. What this gang do to make you so angry, Preacher?"

Preacher told him about the Pardees and Sutherlin.

Batiste shook his head. "You did right. But you beware, Preacher. Way I hear it, the Pardees have much cousins and such east of the Missouri, and they might come looking for you."

"I ain't hard to find. What happened to the three who rafted down the river?"

"The foolish one, way I hear it, he lef the camp and wander around in the woods. The trappers trew the utters out and tol' them to get gone quickly. I have a thought that they were kill' in the woods by Indians."

"Good riddance."

Batiste laughed and the men rode on.

Bent's Fort, a huge place with adobe walls fourteen feet high and four feet thick, with two musketry towers — which housed small cannon — and massive iron-sheathed front gates, was unsurpassed in size or importance anywhere west of the Mississippi. The fort was built in '33, by Mexican laborers, and could garrison more than two hundred men and about three hundred animals. The fort had a main dining hall, and blacksmith, tailor, and carpenter shops. The lodgings were built around a huge courtyard. From out of the fort, scouts and mountain men led the freight caravan wagons of the Bent brothers, which were loaded with everything from trinkets to axes. They would be traded to the Indians for buffalo hides. Inside the fort, Indians from a dozen tribes came to meet and trade in the main council room or on the grounds outside or in the courtyard. Hostilities were left outside the walls. The Indians came to swap for trinkets, knives, axes, and guns, powder, and shot — usually obtaining them for buffalo hides, for by 1839, the beaver trade just about finished.

A huge American flag flew atop the lookout post just above the front gates.

There was also a saloon and billiard room, which is where Preacher and Batiste went immediately upon seeing to their horses and gear.

"Easy you go, Preacher," a scout called Watson whispered to him just outside the room. "They's a man in yonder making war talk about you. He's big and ugly and mean lookin'."

"He got a name?"

"Kelly."

Preacher shrugged his shoulders. I don't know any Kelly right off . . ." He trailed that into silence. "Yeah, I do. Or did. Bum Kelly. I helped hang the no-count a year or so back. Him and three others."

"You done the world a favor. Mayhaps it's his brother. Man ain't old enough to be his daddy."

"Any in there with him?"

"Three others. Just as big and ugly and mean lookin'."

"Thanks. But I do want me a jug and I don't care if they' s fifty in there makin' war talk, I'm gonna have me one of them new whiskey hailstorms Batiste has told me about."

Watson grinned. "They some good. I think I'll join you."

"Both of you just stay out of the way when trouble starts. I stomp on my own snakes."

Both men eyeballed the guns Preacher was wearing about his waist and smiled. Watson said, "This ought to be fun."

Preacher opened the door and stepped inside. The men walked to the bar.

The big room was filled with pipe and cigar smoke. A few men were smoking tobacco rolled up tight in paper, a custom begun in Seville in the sixteenth century, when beggars shredded discarded cigar butts and rolled them in paper to smoke them. Roll-your-owns had not yet taken much of a hold in America and the unorganized territories.

"Give us all one of them hailstorms," Preacher told the man behind the bar. "And put lots of mint in mine. I do like the taste of mint."

"Watch your back in here, Preacher," the man replied in a whisper. 'The four men at the last billiard table are gunnin' for you."

"Thankee."

The trio drank their hailstorms and smacked their lips. "Another round," Batiste said. "You got anything to eat?"

"Bread and cheese and a roast over yonder," the man replied, pointing. "The beef roast is good. I guarantee it. Charlotte cooked it."

"You want some, Preacher?" the French Canadian asked, not speaking his name loud enough for it to carry.

"No. I'll wait 'til this dance is over. I fight better on an empty stomach. Makes me meaner. You and Watson go on over there and fill your bellies. This spot here might turn plumb unhealthy in a few minutes."

Preacher sipped his hailstorm and waited. He had turned as if watching his friends, but he was really looking over the four men at the billiard table. They were everything that Watson had said they were. Big and mean looking and as ugly a quartet as Preacher had ever laid eyes on. And he had seen some uglies in his day.

One of the men turned slightly and stared at Preacher. He said something in a low voice and the other three straightened up and all looked at Preacher.

"Here it comes," the man behind the bar whispered.

"I reckon," Preacher replied, holding his drink in his left hand. "You best get out of the way."

"My name's Kelly. You kilt my brother, Preacher!" one of the four man hollered, laying his cue stick on the felt.

"Son of a bitch needed killin'," Preacher calmly replied.

"Damn your eyes and your black heart," Kelly said, and jerked out a pistol.

312

Sixteen

Preacher stepped to one side and the ball smashed into an empty keg. Preacher drew and cocked his pistol and fired, the double-shotted barrel flinging out fire and smoke and lead. Both balls struck the man in the chest and knocked him off his feet, slamming him against the wall. He slid down to rest on his butt, his eyes wide and staring and dead.

The room was filled with smoke and shouts as Kelly's friends all drew their pistols and opened up. But Preacher had hit the floor and had both big hands filled with pistols. The shots from his would-be assassins hit the bar and the wall behind it while Preacher calmly pulled himself up to one knee, took aim, and placed his shots well.

Kelly was joined in death by two more. The fourth man, his pistols empty, dropped his pistols on the billiard table, threw his hands into the air and shouted, "I yield! Don't shoot no more."

Several trappers grabbed the man roughly and tossed him onto the floor, tying his hands behind his back with rawhide strips. Preacher calmly began reloading the empty pistols as other men gathered around, looking at the strange and deadly pistols.

"Look at them hammers," a trapper remarked. "The bottom pair's set forward of the top pair.

Damnest thing I ever did see."

"Looks awkward to me," another said.

"Wasn't awkward to Preacher," a third man said, quieting the debate.

Preacher looked at the remaining member of the quartet. He had been jerked to his feet and was staring defiantly at Preacher. "What's your quarrel with me?" he asked.

"Bum was my cousin and you kilt him."

"I helped hang him for a fact," Preacher said, holstering his guns. "And no man ever deserved it more."

"Here, now," a man said, bursting into the smoky room. "Cease and desist immediately. This type of behavior is simply not allowed inside the fort."

"Tell them over yonder on the floor all that," Preacher told the man, obviously some sort of official with the Bent brothers. "Well, tell *him* that. It'd be kinda hard to get through to the others, I reckon."

"Preacher didn't start it," Watson stated.

Preacher's name brought the official up short. He stared at the mountain man for a moment. "There will have to be an inquiry, sir."

"Have at it. I ain't goin' nowheres no time soon."

The inquiry was held within the hour and Preacher was absolved of all blame. The lone survivor of Kelly's party was shown to the front gates of the fort and told not to come back. He was last seen heading east.

Preacher lounged around the fort for several days, until the restlies got flung on him. Early one morning he saddled up and rode out, alone, heading northwest into the Rockies. There was a lot of summer left, and Preacher had him a craving to see some country that perhaps he hadn't seen before. He thought he might ride clear up into Canada

. . . but he wasn't sure. Two weeks later, a rider hailed his lonely camp.

"You be Preacher?" the man said.

"I be. Light and set. The coffee's hot and strong."

"There's a wagon train gonna form up next spring in Missouri," the man said, sitting down on the ground.

"Good for them. Now that you told me that, I know I'm goin' to Canada and I might not come back."

"Fifty wagons."

"Why are you tellin' me this? I ain't interested not nary a bit."

"I missed you at the fort by only a couple of days. Batiste told me which direction you took."

"That Frenchy should have buttoned his lip."

"They'll be a minimum of two people to a wagon come the spring."

"I told you, I ain't interested. Mighty pretty afternoon, ain't it?"

"This is an American-government-sanctioned wagon train, Preacher."

"Then let the *Army* lead it. I love this time of year in the high-up country, don't you?"

"That is disputed territory out there, Preacher. Other governments might look with disfavor at the American Army leading a wagon train. There are a lot of lonesome men settling along the Coast and in the interior."

"Tell 'em to marry a squaw. They's lot of fine-lookin' Injun women. And they make good wives. Work hard." He looked at the government man. "What are you tryin' to tell me, mister?"

"This wagon train will be comprised of approximately one hundred and twenty-five women, Preacher."

"*Women!* Are you out of your goddamn mind?

315

Women! Who's gonna be drivin' the wagons?"

"The women."

"You're crazy! Or somebody's crazy. Them women, for sure."

The man shrugged his shoulders. "The men out here want women, these women want husbands. They have elected to brave the trip. You know the way and you've taken wagons across."

Preacher sat speechless.

"You come highly recommended, Preacher."

"I'm a-fixin' to leave highly recommended, too. And if you try to follow me, I swear I'll shoot you."

"What I'm about to tell you must never be repeated, Preacher. The President of the United States is backing this plan. He wants you to take the wagons across. This land must be settled and it must be settled by Americans."

"It's already settled. Ask the Injuns."

"Sir . . ."

"Who is President?"

"Mr. Martin Van Buren."

"Who the hell is he?"

"Of course, you would have to come to Missouri."

"I ain't goin' to Missouri. I ain't leadin' no damn wagon train of petticoats, neither."

"Can you read, sir?"

"Of course I can read. I ain't ignorant."

The man handed Preacher a wax-sealed envelope. Preacher broke the seal and stared at the words. He blinked and rubbed his eyes and read again.

The messenger smiled.

"Twenty-five hundred dollars!" Preacher shouted.

"Then may I take it that you are interested?"

"Twenty-five hundred dollars?"

"May I tell the President that you will be in Missouri no later than April the first of next year?"

"Twenty-five hundred dollars!" Preacher shook his

head and stared at the man for a moment. "I probably am about to make the biggest mistake of my life."

"Oh, I think not, sir. You might even find you a good woman to marry."

Preacher glared at the man and shuddered at the thought. "How many women?"

"No less than one hundred and twenty-five, sir. Perhaps as many as a hundred and fifty. All the equipment will be brand new and you can hire some men to assist you."

Preacher shook his head at the awesomeness of it all. He didn't even know if something like this could be done. "I ain't never even *seen* that many fillies in one spot."

"I am thinking it will be a grand adventure, sir."

"I've heard that before." Preacher was thoughtful for a moment. Back in the States, twenty-five hundred dollars was near 'bout ten years' wages. But a hundred and twenty-five women all in one bunch?

Preacher looked at the man and made up his mind. "Where is it you want me to be come next spring?"

The messenger smiled. "You'll not regret this decision, Preacher."

Somehow, Preacher doubted that.

THE FIRST MOUNTAIN MAN SERIES BY
WILLIAM W. JOHNSTONE

__**The First Mountain Man**
0-8217-5510-2 $4.99US/$6.50CAN

__**Blood on the Divide**
0-8217-5511-0 $4.99US/$6.50CAN

__**Absaroka Ambush**
0-8217-5538-2 $4.99US/$6.50CAN

__**Forty Guns West**
0-7860-1534-9 $5.99US/$7.99CAN

__**Cheyenne Challenge**
0-8217-5607-9 $4.99US/$6.50CAN

__**Preacher and the Mountain Caesar**
0-8217-6585-X $5.99US/$7.99CAN

__**Blackfoot Messiah**
0-8217-6611-2 $5.99US/$7.99CAN

__**Preacher**
0-7860-1441-5 $5.99US/$7.99CAN

__**Preacher's Peace**
0-7860-1442-3 $5.99US/$7.99CAN

Available Wherever Books Are Sold!

Visit our website at **www.kensingtonbooks.com**

THE LAST GUNFIGHTER SERIES BY
WILLIAM W. JOHNSTONE

__The Drifter
0-8217-6476-4 $4.99US/$6.99CAN

__Reprisal
0-7860-1295-1 $5.99US/$7.99CAN

__Ghost Valley
0-7860-1324-9 $5.99US/$7.99CAN

__The Forbidden
0-7860-1325-7 $5.99US/$7.99CAN

__Showdown
0-7860-1326-5 $5.99US/$7.99CAN

__Imposter
0-7860-1443-1 $5.99US/$7.99CAN

__Rescue
0-7860-1444-X $5.99US/$7.99CAN

__The Burning
0-7860-1445-8 $5.99US/$7.99CAN

Available Wherever Books Are Sold!

Visit our website at **www.kensingtonbooks.com**

GREAT BOOKS, GREAT SAVINGS!

When You Visit Our Website:

www.kensingtonbooks.com

You Can Save 30% Off The Retail Price
Of Any Book You Purchase

- All Your Favorite Kensington Authors
- New Releases & Timeless Classics
- Overnight Shipping Available
- All Major Credit Cards Accepted

Visit Us Today To Start Saving!

www.kensingtonbooks.com

All Orders Are Subject To Availability.
Shipping and Handling Charges Apply.